Till I
Kissed You

ALSO BY LAURA TRENTHAM

Then He Kissed Me

Kiss Me That Way

Melting Into You

Caught Up in the Touch

Slow and Steady Rush

Till I Kissed You

LAURA TRENTHAM

St. Martin's Paperbacks

TILL I KISSED YOU

For information address St. Martin's Press, 175 Fifth Avenue, New York, NY 10010.

ISBN: 978-1-250-07762-2

Our books may be purchased in bulk for promotional, educational, or business use. Please contact your local bookseller or the Macmillan Corporate and Premium Sales Department at 1-800-221-7945, ext. 5442, or by e-mail at MacmillanSpecialMarkets@macmillan.com.

Printed in the United States of America

St. Martin's Paperbacks edition / August 2016

St. Martin's Paperbacks are published by St. Martin's Press, 175 Fifth Avenue, New York, NY 10010.

10 9 8 7 6 5 4 3 2 1

For my kids—
not that they will ever
be allowed to read this book!

Acknowledgments

Although the towns I write about are entirely of my own imagination, both Falcon, Alabama, and Cottonbloom are shaded by my own experiences growing up in a small Tennessee town. The older I get, the more nostalgic I grow when I remember the simplicity of my youth. But, like any town, everything was not all rainbows and hugs. When I write about these towns, I don't want to ignore the racial and economic divides that I recognized even as a child. I strive for the towns I create to feel real to the reader. If you're from a small town, I hope you recognize the town of Cottonbloom. And, if you're not from a small town, my wish is for you to vicariously live in one for the time it takes you to read my books. Enjoy!

Chapter One

Regan Lovell ran her hands up the shifting muscles of her lover's back, lost in a state of wonder. The rhythm of his thrusts progressed from slow and steady to wild and erratic. It didn't take long. He moaned softly in her ear, his hot breath sending shivers through her body.

It was done. She'd lost her virginity to Sawyer Fournette.

While it hadn't been the out-of-body experience the romance novels she'd read in preparation would have her believe, it had been magical in its own way. She clasped her knees around his hips and wrapped him tight in her arms, his body sagging over hers, his breathing ragged.

Her mother would be horrified she'd given up her virginity at all, much less at eighteen, before she could use it to barter for a doctor or a lawyer at Ole Miss. She expected Regan to get an MRS degree, just as she had done thirty-odd years before.

But what would send her mother into an early grave was who she'd lost her virginity to. Her mother deemed Sawyer a Louisiana swamp rat and considered Regan's fascination with him a phase. A means to rebel against her parents and their expectations, and that's all.

What her parents didn't know, or couldn't accept, was that Regan had dreams and ambitions and a heart of her own. It wasn't a phase or a rebellion; it was love.

He stirred against her, his sparse chest hair tickling her breasts. She crossed her ankles around his backside, holding him inside of her. "I love you, Sawyer."

He pushed up on his elbows. "I love you too, Regan."

"Forever?"

"And ever." The humor and love in his voice were honestly more satisfying than the sex had been.

"Even after I eat too much barbeque and get fat and my hair turns gray and I lose my marbles like Nana Rosemary?"

"Even so." He kissed the tip of her nose, and she smiled at their game.

Other more immediate questions clawed at her chest. *Will you love me after we go our separate ways for college? Will you love me even though prettier girls will try to lure you away? Will you wait for me?*

He wiggled his hips free and dropped to her side in the bed of his brother's old pickup truck. She looked down her body, but everything was the same, not that she really expected this final crossover into womanhood to leave a visible mark. She was irrevocably changed but not in a way her mother or her friends could pinpoint.

Now that the sexual haze was clearing, she became acutely aware of her nakedness. Subtle rustling while he disposed of the condom had her biting her lip and reaching for the edge of the threadbare quilt as cover. Was there a bloodstain like she'd read about in books?

Cooling air wafted over her. Through the arms of the pines, twilight cast shadows that shifted with the breeze. The river was close enough to serenade them with bullfrog croaks but far enough to avoid the worst of the bugs.

Citronella candles burned on the tailgate, keeping the

mosquitoes away. She closed her eyes. The scent of the candles mixed with the pines and Sawyer to form an intoxicating blend she'd never forget.

Sawyer stripped the corner of the quilt away and blanketed her with his body. His expression was a mystery. He alternated between a too-mature seriousness and a boyish playfulness, leaving her unbalanced.

His everyday life was far removed from the plush elegance of hers across the river in Mississippi. But that's one reason he drew her. He was different, exciting, and had more depth than all the boys in her school combined.

There was more to him than sports and parties. With him, she wasn't afraid to talk about things that interested her—not cheerleading and beauty pageants, but world events and politics. He didn't laugh when she laid out her dreams even though she wasn't yet out of high school.

He believed in her.

"Did I hurt you?" He brushed her hair back from her forehead.

"A little. You were bigger than I expected."

His laughter made her smile. It always did. "That was the perfect compliment."

"Was it? Well, it's the truth. Not that I have any basis for comparison, but I'm sure yours is the best." His chest rumbled against hers, the vibrations electrifying her toes and fingertips. "Was I . . . okay?"

"Ah, baby, you are everything I've dreamed about and more." His lips tickled her ear, but she needed to see his eyes. See the truth or lie. She cupped his cheeks and forced his face up.

Nothing but love shone from his face. The kiss he gave her was sweet and retained a hint of the innocence they'd entrusted to each other that night. She squeezed her eyes to shut off the spigot of tears that threatened. His weight pressed her down into the ridges of the truck bed, not that she planned to complain. She would stay all night under him if she could.

She would love Sawyer Fournette forever.

Chapter Two

She hated Sawyer Fournette.

Regan tried to concentrate on the droning voice of the city accountant as he highlighted sections of the Cottonbloom, Mississippi, budget. They needed to vote this evening on the amendments since their fiscal year ran from July to July and it was already the first of August. She needed funds released to finish her plans for the Cottonbloom Tomato Festival.

Numbers garbled in her head as she wondered what the hell Sawyer, the parish commissioner of Cottonbloom, Louisiana, was doing at *her* meeting. Was he here to watch her squirm like a worm on a hook as people lobbed potshots at her town improvement plan or the festival?

It was standing room only tonight, and he had snuck in through one of the side entrances of the town hall after the meeting had been called to order. Ever since he'd quit his corporate job managing the auto parts factory, he'd let his dirty blond hair grow out a bit and kept a sexy stubble. He'd also traded his preppy button-downs and khakis for jeans and T-shirts.

Tonight a black T-shirt with a gray emblem on the front was tucked messily into a pair of jeans. He crossed one black boot over the other and leaned against the wall with his arms tucked over his chest. It made him look big and tough and not sexy in the least.

Her lady parts protested the white lie. Why couldn't the man have gotten fat and bald over the years? Was that too much to ask of the universe? Apparently it was, because Sawyer had matured like fine whiskey instead of skunking like cheap beer.

"I believe there are questions from the gallery, Mayor Lovell."

She peeled her gaze off Sawyer and took a steadying breath. "Of course. The floor is open for discussion." Rustling and whispers erupted from the packed room. She pounded her gavel, feeling ridiculous even as it quieted the crowd. "One at a time to the podium, please."

She nodded at Police Chief Thomason. He would keep things orderly and moving along. Ms. Martha, the owner of the Quilting Bee, was up first, and Regan winced behind her smile. She liked Ms. Martha and didn't want to offend her. Some of the older business owners were up in arms at the increased property taxes, but the improvements Regan was spearheading, the festival included, would benefit every citizen in the long term.

Ms. Martha cleared her throat when her voice cracked on her first try. The paper she held in her hands fluttered. "Mayor Lovell, I—not only me, but several of us—want to understand better where the money is coming from for this festival. Is it coming from my taxes? Because I don't want my taxes paying for some silly festival that will just drive up costs even more. I can barely keep up as it is."

The more she said, the stronger and more strident her voice grew. A smattering of applause acted as a punctuation mark. Ms. Martha wouldn't want to hear the hard truth. A quilting business in this day and age was a dying proposition.

"Yes, a small percentage of your taxes is funding the festival." A series of unintelligible shouts came from the back of the room, and she pounded the gavel once more. "The publicity Cottonbloom will receive from *Heart of Dixie* magazine will give our town a boost. And if we're named the Best Small-Town Festival in the South and win the grant money, then we can move forward with improvements that would take us years otherwise. We can turn downtown Cottonbloom into something special."

"We like Cottonbloom fine the way it is," Ms. Martha said. This time the vocal agreement was limited and most of the buzz was about the magazine competition.

Flipping through *Heart of Dixie* while waiting for her hair appointment, she'd skimmed over the call for entries into their competition. Then, read it again and again, her imagination going wild. The magazine was already a month old and the competition closed for entries in less than a week. She'd walked out before getting her monthly trim and blow-out, lists already forming in her head.

Even though it would be the first of what she hoped would be an annual Cottonbloom Tomato Festival, she had full confidence in her ability to pull off something spectacular. Something that would win the grant money and get them a full spread in the popular magazine. At the time, she'd honestly had no clue that Sawyer Fournette had read the same article two weeks earlier and already entered. Not that anyone believed her. Not even Sawyer. *Especially* not Sawyer.

Labor Day weekend had been the obvious choice, but because Sawyer had already claimed it, she had been willing to grit her teeth and pick a different weekend—the Fourth of July perhaps, even though it would make planning tight. But once the editor of *Heart of Dixie* got wind of their two festivals, they had insisted the two sides of Cottonbloom hold them the same weekend. The magazine wanted to play up the decades-old rivalry. Regan hoped they didn't come off as backward as the Hatfields and the McCoys. The grant money had been too important for either side to back down.

"This festival is not a major draw on your tax dollars. A copy of the budget has been available for review for several weeks. The vast majority of your taxes are going to infrastructure improvements and beautification projects. The trees downtown are beautiful, but we can't ignore the fact their roots are affecting our streets, our sidewalks, and our plumbing. You're all here because you care about our town, and no one in this room wants downtown Cottonbloom to follow so many American towns into disrepair. Don't forget, I am a downtown business owner as well."

"But not on the riverfront. Why was I assessed higher than a business not twenty feet away?" Ms. Martha asked.

"You understand, I didn't perform the assessments. We had an outside real estate firm examine all the properties."

"Well, they didn't look close enough at mine. I have plumbing backups that fall under city jurisdiction and there are"—she glanced down at the sheet in her hand—"structural integrity issues with the back alleyway brick wall that affects the value. I ask for a reassessment to be done taking all of this into account."

Regan massaged her temple. Someone must have fed Ms. Martha those lines. Someone out to sabotage her. Her gaze swung toward Sawyer. His expression hadn't changed from the mysterious, serious mask that had fascinated her as a teenager. Now though, she knew what was behind it. A two-faced jerk.

Her face heated. Damn her fair skin. She could almost feel the flushed splotches break out. Everyone would assume she was embarrassed or frustrated, when in truth she wanted to march over and punch Sawyer Fournette in the face.

Never let them see you sweat. The old line from a commercial from her childhood popped into her head.

"Is that acceptable, Mayor?"

She swiveled toward the town accountant. "I'm sorry, what was that?"

"Councilman Crane motioned to postpone the budget vote until Ms. Martha's concerns are addressed." She opened her mouth to protest until he added, "And I seconded it."

Unless she wanted to seem like a power-hungry steamroller, she couldn't see a path to push the budget vote through tonight. The smile she pasted on had been perfected on the pageant circuit. "Of course, I agree. I motion we reconvene one week from today. Same time and place to discuss any changes and vote."

One of the councilwomen down the line seconded her, and the meeting broke up. She stood up and turned toward the side door, but Sawyer's black shirt and fine backside were halfway out the door, leaving her killing glare impotent.

She scooted out of the meeting hall by the same door Sawyer had left through. A more patient mayor would have fought the gauntlet of people to the door, offering platitudes and reassurances. She wasn't in the mood for the kind of butt kissing politics demanded.

She wanted to stand up and tell them they either needed to accept the changes she was pushing through or accept that their town was dying. She wanted to ask why people couldn't see beyond their small patch of breathing space to embrace changes that would benefit future generations.

But she wouldn't. She would keep her mouth shut and smile while she worked behind the scenes to steer policies, compromising only when she was backed into a corner. Like tonight. No doubt, she'd be receiving emails and phone calls all week. A glass of wine and headache medicine were next on her agenda.

Her heels clacked on the marble floors, the air refreshingly cool after the body-jammed meeting room. Sawyer was probably laughing his butt off at her plight. Movement down one of the dim hallways leading to the county clerk office drew her attention, and she whipped her head around in time to see Sawyer slip around the corner and out of sight.

A banked fury that only he inspired filled her belly, and she didn't bother to muffle her steps. "Sawyer Fournette, what are you doing skulking around my building?"

He stepped out and propped a shoulder against the wall, resuming the position he'd held inside the meeting. This time she was close enough to see his ridiculous biceps pop. If anything, he'd gotten in even better shape working in the garage with his brother Cade. She couldn't contain a huff at the injustice.

"I'm not skulking." His gaze darted to the side.

"Well, the front door is back thataway." She kept her tone mocking and thumbed over her shoulder. "Are you planning to break into the tax assessments or something?"

This time he met her gaze with a huffy sigh of his own. "Of course not."

"Then why are you here?"

"Heard you were voting on the budget tonight. Checking out the competition."

Not buying what he was selling, she studied him, stepped closer, and hiked her purse up on her shoulder. "It was you, wasn't it?"

"What are you talking about, woman?"

"That you would stoop so low to give Ms. Martha a script to read from. Seriously, that is pathetic. Did you blackmail Crane into motioning for the delay too?"

He ran a hand through his hair and rubbed his nape.

"Let me get this straight. You think I masterminded the delay in your budget vote by secretly meeting with Ms. Martha and Councilman Crane?"

The way he said it made her feel like a fool, which only drove her ire higher. "Maybe. And it's your fault I was all distracted and didn't get a chance to respond."

"How was that my fault?" He leaned in. His scent muffled the institutional smell of the courthouse. Another black mark against him. Why couldn't he smell like BO or garlic instead of a woodsy, pine-scented cologne that cast her back a decade to the bed of his truck?

"I don't know, but it is," she said weakly. The truth was too embarrassing to speak aloud.

They stood too close. Neither of them pulled back or spoke. The moment veered from confrontational to uncomfortable to downright awkward, yet the way his hazel eyes warmed and narrowed on hers hypnotized her as if seeking all her secrets.

She didn't like him, not one bit. That fact didn't stop the call of her body whenever he was within ten feet. Okay, maybe closer to twenty-five feet. The physical attraction was an inconvenient echo from their past lives together.

Her brain clamped down on her body, and she spun around and stalked out of the hallway toward the front doors. The crowd had thinned out, leaving only a few die-hard citizens. One called her over. Even though she desperately wanted to be home, she smiled and changed directions.

From the corner of her eye, she saw Sawyer push the front double doors open. Her shoulders relaxed. She preferred arguing about the property tax increases to dealing with Sawyer. He left her feeling off-balance and unsure of herself. Unusual and unwelcome conditions.

It was another twenty minutes before she extricated herself from the next man who wanted to discuss zoning regulations of all things. The parking lot was almost deserted. Almost. A shiny black pickup sat two rows over from her red VW Bug. Sawyer was propped against a column in what she was now referring to as his Sawyer-stance. He must have practiced in the mirror and decided it emphasized all his good parts. Not that she'd noticed any bad parts, dangit.

"The custodian is fixing to lock up, so you won't be able to sneak back inside." She stomped down the stone stairs, and he fell into step beside her.

"Just getting some air before I head out. It's a pretty night, isn't it?" He sounded friendly, jovial even.

She shot him a suspicious side-eye. What was he up to? Deciding to play along, she looked up. Even with the town's light pollution, the sky was unusually full of stars. A cool front had moved in and cut the humidity, making the night pleasant.

When they reached the parking lot and he should have headed left toward his truck, he kept pace with her. She pivoted toward him with her hands on her hips. "Okay, what's going on?"

"It's dark. There's no one around. I'm making sure you get to your car is all."

A warmth unfurled in her stomach as a good portion of her vitriol faded. "I'm a grown-up. I can handle myself."

"I would do this for any woman, so don't go thinking you're special or something. 'Cause you're not."

His words snuck past her defenses. She swallowed against a sudden well of tears. What was wrong with her? The question had too many meanings. Why was she crying over some petty insult? Why had he cheated on her so many years ago? Why did he still have the power to wound her so brutally? Why couldn't she let the past go and move on?

She sucked her top lip between her teeth and bit down

hard. She spun away and strode to her car. Her heel stuck in a crack, and she stumbled. Cursing under her breath, she slipped her foot out, bent over, and yanked the heel from the crack, continuing with one shoe on and one off with as much dignity as she could muster. He was probably doubled over, hee-hawing at her less than graceful retreat. Sliding behind the wheel, she finally looked at him.

He was standing where she'd left him, not so much as smiling, as if someone had yelled "Freeze!" She drove off, making the turn onto the main street with a squeal of her tires. That glass of wine waiting at home had just turned into a bottle.

Sawyer wanted to stuff the words back in his mouth. The woman could rile him up like no one else. He hated the way she could make him feel guilty and self-righteous and turned on all at the same time. But, the look on her face . . . Surely, those hadn't been tears in her eyes. And, had her chin quivered? If he didn't know any better, he'd think he hurt her feelings. A stabby pain poked around his chest as if his heart was trying to kick his butt.

He didn't mind her thinking he came to the council meeting to goad her. Let her assume he was behind Ms. Martha's demands. Because the truth was much more damning. She *was* special, and he'd come tonight because he was worried about her.

Damn but she was hot as sin when she was mad. That shot of red in her blonde hair was no lie. The heels she traipsed around in made her legs look killer, and her polished, professional clothes made him feel like a straw-chewing swamp rat.

When she'd cornered him in the dim hall, the same dizzying, off-balance stomach lurch he'd felt the first time he'd ever seen her had him leaning against the wall for support. He'd nearly done something imbecilic like lean in and take her lips. Maybe spin her around and press her against the wall. Thank goodness he'd tamped down the urge. She would have kneed him between the legs and laughed.

After staring at the blank space she'd left for too long, he got himself moving in the direction of his truck. He hesitated on the turn out of the parking lot. Left would take him back across the river and to his farmhouse. Right would take him into the heart of Cottonbloom, Mississippi's, nicest neighborhoods.

He turned right and muttered, "Tally's right. I am losing my mind."

Foolish thoughts reverberated in the silence, and he flipped on the radio. Ever since the pavilion fire in June, he'd been concerned someone was out to sabotage the festivals. Adding in the suspicious letter Monroe had mentioned Regan received and the crayfish basket vandalism in July, and his concern had exploded into outright worry.

He'd lost sleep going over every scenario. The most likely explanation centered around Regan's plans for Cottonbloom, Mississippi's, revitalization. He couldn't imagine any of his people sabotaging crayfish baskets. The parish economy followed the harvest. A good harvest meant increased dollars and more jobs. A bad harvest meant seasonal layoffs or worse. The food banks running out of donations and good people moving to bigger cities for work and never returning.

The reassessments and increased taxes had ratcheted tensions upward on the Mississippi side of the river. He commiserated with business owners like Ms. Martha. It was a challenge to stay competitive, and losing the Quilting Bee would be gut-wrenching. It had been there since Sawyer could remember.

On the other hand, Regan was doing good work. She had turned downtown Cottonbloom, Mississippi, into something special and was poised to make it amazing. Already they were attracting out-of-towners and pulling in money. Her festival was just another piece of the puzzle for her, but she had seriously derailed his modest efforts to bolster the economy on his side of the river.

He needed that grant money for his plans. Financing the restoration of Cottonbloom Park and the baseball fields was impossible with the current parish budget. He couldn't justify taking money away from social and road projects for the park. While flipping through a *Heart of Dixie* magazine in the break room at the auto factory, he'd spotted the call for entries.

Maybe Regan hadn't realized he'd already entered, but she hadn't backed out once the magazine insisted they hold competing festivals, highlighting the already divided, sometimes acrimonious nature of their towns. Apparently, calling dibs didn't work as an adult. He'd been angry, and in his anger had done some immature, debatably insane things to needle her. She'd retaliated with glee. Recent events, however, had tempered his fury into something else.

His drive down streets lined with stately oaks and big two-story brick or Colonial-style houses had him tightening his hands on the wheel. It wasn't the money. He could afford any one of the houses. Fournette Designs paid even better than his position as manager at the auto factory. His discomfort ran deeper.

He was an interloper in Cottonbloom, Mississippi. The disdain from people like Regan's parents had left an indelible mark on him. One he'd tried to erase, but had only ever managed to cover up. Something would happen—a look, a word—and old insecurities would bleed through his confidence. Dating Regan in high school had been reaching for the stars, amazing until he'd been incinerated.

He crossed paths with a rough-looking silver truck

heading in the opposite direction and pumped his brakes. What the heck was his uncle Delmar doing in Cottonbloom, Mississippi, this time of night? The silver truck's one working taillight faded in the distance, and Sawyer put the oddity to the side. His uncle's nighttime activities were none of his business. Never had been. Anyway, Sawyer hardly wanted to explain why he was out and about.

Feeling a little like a stalker or an ex-boyfriend, which technically he was, he turned onto her street, killed his headlights, and sank down in his seat, even though his big black truck was unmistakable.

The old truck she used to haul furniture and her red VW Bug were in the driveway of her house, the garage doors shut. A couple of lights were on in the front of her house, and movement shadowed behind too-thin curtains. Everything was quiet. He blew out a breath and kept driving, flipping on his lights at the end of her street.

She was safe. For now.

Chapter Three

The next night, Regan lounged on her couch eating popcorn and nursing a headache. Whether it was remnants of a hangover or from all the calls and texts and emails about the city budget or the second mildly threatening letter that had been waiting in her mailbox, she couldn't pinpoint. All she wanted was a quiet night of mindless TV.

Her phone vibrated. She rolled her eyes and glanced at the screen, ready to let it go to voice mail. She was officially off the clock. It was her mother. Dare she not answer? Her parents lived four houses down the street and could step onto their front porch and see her car in the driveway. While her interior design shop downtown was in a great location and quaint, it was short on storage and her garage was full of knickknacks and tables and lamps instead of her car.

Sighing, she pasted on a smile—because her mother could tell even over the phone—and answered. "Hello, Mother."

"Thank God, you're there. Someone is behind the garden." The strident panic in her mother's voice had Regan bolting up and spilling popcorn everywhere.

"Geez. Are the police on the way?" She was out the door and running down the sidewalk in two seconds flat.

"I haven't called them. Thought it might be that Fournette boy again." Even over two years of dating, her mother had never referred to Sawyer by name. He'd always been "that Fournette boy" or, when she was really trying to make a painful point, "that Louisiana rat."

Unfortunately, her mother was probably right. She was almost positive she'd recognized the tailgate of Sawyer's truck last night. Who drove down someone's street with their headlights off unless they were planning something nefarious?

"I'm going straight around back. Where's Daddy?"

"At the American Legion playing cards."

"Call the police." She disconnected, slid her phone into the back of her shorts, and jogged on her toes around the backyard fence. Sawyer was in for it. She was going to take him out this time. No mercy.

Two months earlier, Sawyer, his brother Cade, and his uncle Delmar had snuck across the field from the river intending to drop rabbits in her mother's yard. The herd would have destroyed her mother's prize tomato plants.

But her connections on his side of the river had paid off. Rufus, of Rufus's Meat and Three fame, had let something suspicious slip when she'd been picking up her weekly pork barbeque fix.

She'd jumped Sawyer—literally—before he could complete his mission. Their roll around the ground had ended with him pinning her wrists by her head and his body pressing her into the high grass. The rest of the memory she shoved out of her head. She needed to focus.

She slowed at the back edge of the fence and peeked around. A man in dark wash jeans like the ones Sawyer had been wearing at the town meeting and a gray hoodie pulled over his head was running a hand along the fence, searching for the gate latch.

With a rebel yell that would have made her ancestors proud, she sprinted toward him. He startled around, frozen for a moment. Dropping whatever was in his hand, he took off through the copse of pines, heading toward the river.

She followed. A pinecone bit into the arch of one foot and sent her reeling into the rough bark of a nearby tree. The sharp spines of another cone grazed the outside of her other foot. She limped through the rest of the trees like navigating a minefield. Nothing moved, as far as she could see in the dark. Sawyer had escaped.

"Sawyer Fournette, you coward!" Her words echoed through the night.

The pain in her foot paled in comparison with her anger. She skirted the pine trees and found the bottle he had dropped by the fence. Grass killer. Powerful enough to kill tomato plants too.

She let herself in through the back gate. First thing tomorrow, she would buy a padlock. Her mother rushed out of the back door. Deputy Thaddeus Preston stepped out behind her at a more sedate pace.

"Well?" her mother asked.

"He got away, but he dropped this." She handed the bottle over. All Preston did was hum and turn it over to read the back label. "It was Sawyer Fournette, Deputy, you know it was."

The deputy turned icy blue eyes on her. Truth be told, the man intimidated the snot out of her, even if she was mayor and technically his boss. Keith Thomason had been police chief since she'd been in middle school, and she and Keith were on a comfortable, first-name basis. But, with Thomason's retirement imminent, Thaddeus Preston was biding his time to step into the bigger shoes. He was gruff and formidable and more than competent.

"You're positive? You want to come down to the station and file?" A single dark eyebrow quirked.

Regan shifted on her feet, the throb on the arch of her right foot growing more pronounced. "I didn't actually see his face, but it was him. You know about the rabbit fiasco in June. And I'm pretty sure I saw him driving down our street last night. With his headlights off. It's only logical."

Preston sighed. "I heard about the rabbit fiasco, along with everyone else, but no official complaint was filed. Did you call anything in last night?"

"No." She huffed. "He wasn't doing anything but driving."

"Exactly. Seems to me *whoever* this was intends harm to your garden, not to you, Mrs. Lovell." He directed his comments to her mother, which made Regan feel about ten years old.

"Can you at least dust that for prints or something?" Regan asked.

"We can try." His radio beeped and a woman's voice rattled off some numbers. "Another call. My guess is the man won't be back, but make sure you lock up tight and call if you see anything suspicious. Anything at all. My patrols will keep an eye out and drive by more often than usual. Night, ladies."

The hint of condescension in his voice sent her anger-meter to boil. Fine, if he wouldn't pursue Sawyer Fournette, she would. In fact, if he was in his boat, which made sense since he took off toward the river, she might be able to beat him home and catch him with his pants down—so to speak.

"You lock up and call Daddy. I'll talk to you tomorrow." She bypassed the house and made for the side gate. Her mother called out a protest she ignored. If she was going to catch him, she needed to hightail it to his farmhouse.

She grabbed her keys and was on the road in thirty seconds. Counting on Deputy Preston to be tied up with his other call, she drove fast and reckless, skidding to stop by the drooping willow tree out in front of Sawyer's old white farmhouse. Not even the porch light was on, and she fist-pumped. Unless he was playing possum, she'd beat him back.

She turned the car off, but left the keys in the ignition and the door open in her haste. Curses and exclamations and insults rattled through her head as she ran around the side of his house toward the river. She didn't bother being quiet.

A shaft of moonlight reflected off the rippling water. She stopped. Her feet sank into the damp sandy bank. A boat tied to a wooden pylon of a small dock made a thumping sound with the current. Nothing moved. Even the frogs and bugs had quieted in the heart of the night.

Her mind whirled. Sawyer probably had more than one boat and more than one mooring on the river. He owned a large parcel of land. But she was barefoot, and it was black as pitch through the trees farther downstream. It would be foolish to keep going. What now?

"Who's out there?" Sawyer's deep voice boomed in the quiet.

She whirled, pinned by a flashlight. "Turn it off, it's just me." She held a hand up and blinked, but couldn't see beyond the cone of light.

"Just you." He barked a laugh that held no humor. "What are you doing out here? Holy hell, are you looking for more baskets to sabotage?"

"Me? Don't you dare turn this around on me. I'm here because you were upriver prowling outside of Mother's house tonight."

He was silent. The circle of light dropped to her feet before he switched off the flashlight. She was effectively blind.

"I haven't stepped foot over the river today." His voice was softer.

She took a tentative step forward, blinking to regain her sight. "Someone was up there, and he sure looked like you. Who else would be creeping around Mother's tomatoes? With industrial-strength grass killer?"

He muttered, and she imagined him running a hand through his hair, because that's what he did when he was exasperated. "I swear it wasn't me." A slap sounded on bare skin. "I'm getting eaten up out here by skeeters. Come on inside."

Still mostly blind, she took two steps, caught a root with her big toe, and went down. Rocking on her hands and knees, she clamped her lips together and hummed until the acute pain receded.

"You okay?" He wrapped a hand around her upper arm and helped her up. She would have shaken him off if her foot hadn't been hurting like the devil. Her toe throbbed in concert with the pain of the pinecone thorn still in the arch.

He tugged her toward the house, and she limped alongside him. As they got closer, she could see he was shirtless and with her eyes cast toward him, she stumbled again. This time she did twist out of his grasp. "Slow down. I can barely see, thanks to your spotlight, and my foot hurts."

"Why did you run out here without shoes on?"

"I was in a hurry to catch you in the act." She rubbed her arm where his had been, her skin prickly and hot.

"In the act of what?" Was that humor she heard? If her foot hadn't already borne the brunt of enough abuse, she might kick him in his ankle.

"Coming home on your boat." She still wasn't convinced he didn't beat her home and was trying to bluff her. Dangit, she should have checked whether or not the engine was warm. She glanced over her shoulder, but inky darkness hid the path back to the water.

She'd never been inside of his house. It seemed strange considering how well she knew him. Had known him. She hesitated on the steps up to a side door. He entered first and flipped the overhead light on, the soft glow restoring her sight. She stepped inside his kitchen. It was old-fashioned, but functional and cozy.

She finally got a good look at him. He honest to God looked like he'd just rolled out of bed. His hair was mussed and his stubble was thicker and longer than the night before. And his chest . . .

How many years had it been since she'd seem him naked? He had changed. Gone was the nearly hairless, lean boy-chest. His man-chest was broad and thickly muscled with hair a shade darker than on his head covering his pecs and trailing into green plaid pajama bottoms.

They rode low on his hips. A red stripe of underwear peeked over the top and made her think of Christmas and presents and unwrapping things. Time had been good, so very good, to him.

What must she look like? She'd already settled in for the night when her mother had called. Her makeup had been washed off, and she hadn't bothered with a hair dryer or flatiron after her shower, leaving her hair in its natural state, which was messy waves. She tucked a piece behind her ear and tried to smooth a section down her neck, but it sprang back up.

Her old cotton shorts were too short and frayed at the hems. Even worse, she hadn't put on a bra. Not that she was particularly well endowed, but the AC in his house was not her friend. She crossed her arms over her chest and shifted. A yelp snuck out when she put her full weight on her injured foot.

"Sit down. Let me look at your foot." He turned a kitchen chair around and gestured before turning to riffle through a cabinet with a few bottles of medicine.

She sidestepped toward the chair, using only the heel of her hurt foot. Sitting gingerly on the edge, she waited with her hands tucked between her knees.

Sawyer fumbled a bottle of hydrogen peroxide and a box of Band-Aids out of the cabinet. He took a long, slow breath. His heart continued a syncopated rhythm against his ribs like a marimba player.

The adrenaline that had jolted him from sleep to intruder alert in an instant had waned, but the aftereffects had heightened his senses. All his senses. He looked south and gave his twitching half-erection a silent but stern non-pep talk. It needed to be much less peppy.

Although that was asking a lot considering Regan was sitting in his kitchen in a pair of white shorts that showcased her legs, and if he wasn't mistaken—and he'd stared long enough to know he wasn't—she wasn't wearing a bra. After the shock of finding her in his backyard had faded, he'd had a hard time dropping the flashlight. The light had limned every line and curve of her body.

It had been a long time since he'd seen her with bedhead and no makeup. She looked good. Better than good. She looked approachable and sexy and too much like the girl he'd fallen hard for.

Giving himself a mental shake, he gathered the medical supplies, set them on the table, and pulled up another chair, so they were sitting knees to knees. "Let's see your foot."

She hesitated and narrowed her eyes. He narrowed his right back and made a "come on" gesture with his hands.

She lifted her foot, and he wrapped his hand around her ankle. The bottom of her foot was streaked with river mud. He couldn't tell how much of the red on her big toe was polish and how much was blood.

"Can you wiggle it?" She wiggled all her toes. He took her big toe and maneuvered it around. "Not broken. Let me clean it up."

It took several cotton balls to clean her entire foot. When he stroked down her arch, she hissed and jerked her foot. "There's something stuck. A piece of a pinecone, I think. Can you see it?"

Now that it was clean, he could see the embedded thorn and the angry skin around it. "You got yourself good. Did that happen out here too?"

"No, it was when I went chasing . . . that man through the pine trees out back of Mother's." A thread of suspicion still lilted her words.

He harrumphed. "It wasn't me. I promise I was sound asleep when I heard you skid to a stop outside. Hang on. I need tweezers."

He grabbed tweezers from the medicine cabinet in his room. Catching a glimpse of himself in the mirror, he stopped. His hair was sticking up everywhere. He smoothed it down as best he could, but it was hopeless without getting it wet, and that would be too obvious.

He returned to the kitchen. She had maneuvered her leg up and was examining the bottom of her foot in a feat of flexibility that had his southern regions jumping again.

Clearing his throat, he sat down and pulled her foot into his lap. "Okay, this might hurt a little. You ready?"

After a half-dozen tries, he got the thorn out. She had clutched the edge of the chair with both hands and was grimacing. "You got it," she said on a sigh.

He held up the quarter-inch long sliver of pinecone. Blood welled out of the site, and he pressed a cotton ball against it. At the same time, he rubbed her foot with his other hand, his thumb stroking along her arch and pressing into the ball. Her foot relaxed. He couldn't recall ever giving her a foot rub when they'd been together. His teenage hormones had kept him focused on the more obvious parts of her body.

Now though, he could appreciate her slender foot and delicate ankle and the endless length of leg attached to them. His gaze slid all the way up to where her soft thigh disappeared into her shorts and then higher to where temptation called. The outline of her breasts was barely visible under her pink T-shirt, but her nipples were peaked against the thin fabric.

While he rubbed, something she said niggled at him. He quit his semimassage and tightened his hold on her foot. "Hold up. You chased some strange man through the woods? By yourself? Barefoot and wearing *that*?" He gestured over her.

"I thought it was you." She half-shrugged, which only drew his gaze back to her chest. Part of him wished it had been him and that she'd caught him like last time.

"Did you see his face?"

"He was wearing jeans like the ones you were wearing the other night. And a hoodie. But he was built kind of like you. Tallish and—" She shook her head and picked at fraying threads on the hem of her shorts.

"And what?"

"You know"—she rolled her eyes and blew a piece of hair off her forehead with a huff—"not fat. Sort of muscular, I suppose. He took off for the river."

"What were you going to do if you caught up with him?"

"I don't know. Tackle him. Yell at you—him."

"What if he'd pulled a gun or a knife or hurt you, goddammit?" He held her foot in one hand and slid his other hand up her calf to squeeze. The thought of whoever this man was hurting her in any way set his blood on fire and filled him with a fear-tinged anger he couldn't tamp down.

She yanked her leg out of his hands, arched it to the floor, and stood. "It never crossed my mind it could be someone else, okay? First you come to the meeting, then I see you driving by last night. With your lights off. What am I supposed to think?"

He stood, crossed his arms, and bent over to put them face-to-face. "Maybe you could assume that I'm not a douche-bag asshole. Maybe I'm worried about you." For the second time in as many days, he wanted to reclaim his words. He backed away and leaned against the counter.

A hesitancy softened her features as she sat back on the edge of her seat. "*Are* you worried about me?"

"Look, the pavilion was burned down. Crayfish baskets were vandalized. Now this. It all ties back to these festivals, and more specifically to your side of town."

"The baskets were on yours."

His gut told him the baskets had been collateral damage, especially considering the letter she'd received but hadn't mentioned. He wanted her to tell him. Trust him. "Has anything else happened?"

"Nothing." Her gaze skated over his shoulder as she unraveled a thread on her shorts. "So you came to the meeting last night to make sure I was okay?"

The conversation was going south quick. "I need this festival to happen. I've got a lot invested in making it a success. Your side of the river will be fine without it. My guess is you could have a fund-raiser like you had for Monroe and raise the money for your project. I don't have that luxury. Cottonbloom Parish needs the shot of tourism dollars and the hope that coverage in *Heart of Dixie* will bring."

"Of course, it all comes back to the competition." She gave an almost-laugh that he wasn't sure how to interpret and sat back with her arms folded under her breasts.

"That's right." He forced himself to meet her stare so she wouldn't guess he wasn't telling the whole truth. She dropped her gaze first. His entire body deflated now that her brown eyes were no longer boring into him.

"Thanks for the first aid. It's late and I'd better check on Mother. I'll let myself out." She pushed the screen door open and limped out. He let her go before he could do something too telling like insist she call him when she got home.

A car door slammed. The void she'd left seemed to expand like a black hole. A loneliness that he hadn't battled for a long time settled over him. Finally, he moved, flipping the light off and checking out the front window.

Her car was still there. The headlights were on, but flickering. Her battery didn't have enough juice to get her car started. Everything went dark, but she didn't get out. Even if she wasn't there voluntarily, the fact that she was there at all seemed to fill the hollowness that had burrowed in his chest. He didn't want to examine the meaning.

Should he leave her to swallow her pride and come to him for help? She'd probably try to hoof it all the way to town, barefoot. He chuckled until he thought about what could happen to her all alone on a country road in the middle of night.

He grabbed his truck keys and stepped outside. She was sitting in her car with her hands on the wheel, her head back and her eyes closed. He rapped on the window.

Without opening her eyes or moving, she said, "My battery's dead."

"I kind of figured. Pop your hood. I'll give you a jump." His behemoth of a truck could have squashed her Bug. He set up the cables and started his truck. The engine rumbled so loudly he didn't bother trying to speak, only made a hand gesture for her to crank her car.

It fired up immediately. He removed the cables and dropped her hood. She rolled down her window and he leaned over and laid his arms along the sill.

"Thanks again." She tucked her hair behind her ear and kept her eyes focused toward his truck. "I've been a pain in your butt tonight, and I'm sorry."

He grunted. Stringing together the words "thanks" and "sorry" must have cost her dearly.

"As soon as I get this budget through, maybe whoever is causing problems will stop. I'll try to stay out of your way and . . . stuff." She rolled up the window, and he was forced to step back.

Her taillights disappeared. Maybe passing the budget would stop the trouble, maybe it wouldn't. The truth was he was less concerned about the festivals and more concerned about her.

Chapter Four

Sawyer stepped into Rufus's Meat and Three with a two-fold purpose. He wanted to have a word with Wayne, the parish sheriff, and ask him to feel out his Mississippi counterparts for news on Regan's trespasser. If she had mentioned to law enforcement she suspected Sawyer, asking outright might distract from the real perpetrator. Gloria, the sheriff's dispatcher, had let Sawyer know where to find the sheriff. While he was at it, he planned to pick up plates of fresh-smoked barbeque for Cade and Jeremy.

Sure enough, the sheriff was at a side table sipping at a steaming Styrofoam cup of coffee with Sawyer's uncle Del. The two of them appeared to be having a serious conversation.

He took one step toward them when familiar feminine laughter caught his attention. Holding a brown paper bag, Regan emerged through the curtain separating the kitchen from the dining room. A grinning Rufus trailed her. A wary suspicion had him bypassing the sheriff.

"Howdy there, Sawyer. What can I do you for? Your usual?" Rufus wiped his hands on a mostly white hand towel tucked into his apron string. His grin was guileless, the thin planes of his face crinkling with his usual good humor.

"Make it three plates and teas to go, please."

Rufus disappeared behind the curtain. Regan had sidled away and was halfway to the door before Sawyer caught her. "What are you up to?"

"Absolutely nothing besides grabbing some barbeque to go." She shook the bag and spoke in a singsongy, smiley voice.

"You're lying."

"I happen to love Rufus's barbeque, if you'll remember." Wariness replaced her faked innocence, and she quick-stepped out the door.

He did remember. Remembered sharing more than one picnic with her on the riverbank. He glanced over at his uncle as he followed Regan. Delmar nodded at the sheriff but was watching Sawyer. Regan was halfway across River Street, heading to the walking bridge. Instead of her usual heels, she was wearing flat shoes and moving fast.

"Hold up, woman," Sawyer called. She ignored him, and he jogged toward her, catching her at the midpoint, the water gurgling under them. "How's your foot?"

His question seemed to surprise her. "Still hurts a little, but it would be worse if you hadn't gotten the thorn out."

"What were you and Rufus talking about? Does it involve the festivals?"

She leaned back against the rail. "Not really."

He stepped forward to bracket her with his hands on the rail. He didn't trust her not to run, and it was too hot to give chase. "You already went behind my back and hired my blood kin to help you. If you're doing it again with Rufus, I'll—"

What would he do? Take her across his knee and spank her? An entirely inappropriate image flashed. What kind of panties did she have on? Had she graduated to sophisticated lace or were they the simple white cotton she'd worn in high school? He tried to distract himself from thinking about her underwear by staring at her chest. The fabric of her blouse was pulled taut. Her bra was definitely lace. He shook his head and stared down at the water. He could use a dip in the cool water.

"I was asking him if he had an idea who might have been at Mother's last night, if you must know. He tends to hear things."

He returned his attention to her. "When did you and Rufus get so chummy?"

"It's not as if you have dibs on everyone in Cottonbloom, Louisiana, Sawyer. I happen to love the food. I've been going over there for years. Ever since—" She harrumphed.

"It was nothing about the festivals?" As soon as her eyes darted to the side, he tensed.

"Well, I mean, we *might* have discussed a few things revolving around food."

"Like what?"

"Like what you're serving, is all."

"Why were you discussing it?"

"I was thinking about expanding our offerings. Wanted his opinion." She concentrated on picking the paint off the rail instead of meeting his eyes. Their fingers were an inch apart.

"You'd better not expand into crayfish, Regan Lovell."

Her face sparked with equal amounts defiance and mischievousness. "Cottonbloom is not the only parish that harvests crayfish."

The wood of the rail bit into his palms. "You will not serve crayfish in any way during your Tomato Festival. I want your promise."

He'd forgotten how soft the brown of her eyes could be

when she teased him. How her hair sparked in the sun. He was cast back more than a decade to the first time he'd ever seen her and knew his life would never be the same. Of course, that was partly because of the concussion that had ended his fledging football career.

They had both been freshmen in the rival high schools. He was playing football for Cottonbloom Parish, Louisiana, and she'd been a cheerleader for Cottonbloom, Mississippi.

The rivalry between the two schools was unparalleled in both states, perhaps only topped by the Egg Bowl, the annual Ole Miss–Mississippi State matchup. The rest of the season was warm-up for both teams. If one team won every other game on their schedule, but lost the game to their across-the-river rival, the season would be deemed a failure.

He'd noticed her as soon as she'd run out with the other girls. She was tall and thin, her legs amazing in her pleated short skirt. Her hair had been longer then, her beribboned ponytail halfway down her back and glinting under the towered stadium lights.

His first play on the field had sent him to her side as a wide receiver. Trying to play it cool and failing, he'd almost missed the quarterback count. The ball came to him, but he'd been unable to tear his gaze off her to concentrate on getting downfield. The cheers of the crowd had turned into white noise.

His world had tipped and spun on its axis—literally. Next thing he knew he was being carted off on a stretcher. While he'd been staring at the prettiest thing he'd ever seen, a Cottonbloom, Mississippi, linebacker had pile-driven him to the turf. The concussion he'd suffered had convinced him baseball was the less dangerous option.

As much as everyone's parents and grandparents played up the rivalry between the two sides, the kids rebelled and often socialized across the river boundaries. The occasional fistfight might break out, but that just gave everyone something to gossip about in anticipation of the next party. The first opportunity he had, he'd dragged his buddies over the river. Sure enough, she was there and, even better, she'd remembered him. He hadn't cared that her first reaction was teasing laughter. He'd been a goner as soon as her soft brown eyes had met his.

They'd talked all night. It had taken another year of their paths crossing to convince her to meet up with him alone, but he couldn't bring her back to the trailer he shared with Cade and Tally, and her parents didn't approve of him, so they met on the river. He took Cade's boat upriver, and she cut through the field behind her house. Dreams of her running through knee-high golden grass toward him, her laughter trailing, still haunted him.

"I wasn't going to serve crayfish. I'm not malicious," she said grudgingly.

"You hired my uncle and painted graffiti on one of my buildings."

"Kettle, meet pot." She rolled her eyes, but a smile played at her lips. "You want me to pinky-promise you or something?"

He crooked his pinky. This time a true smile lit her from the inside, and she curled her pinky around his. "Say it," he whispered.

"I won't serve crayfish. Promise." Neither of them unfurled their finger. "As long as we're talking toe-stepping, you should know I'm planning a little Mississippi block party for next Saturday night. Can you let us have the night?"

"Sure. We weren't planning anything over on our side for that weekend anyway. I'm curious to see what all you have planned."

"You're welcome to come on over and find out. Starts at five."

"Maybe I will."

She tightened her finger around his. "You know, the last time I did this, I promised Monroe I wouldn't tell Peter Perkins she had a crush on him in seventh grade."

He returned her smile. "Did you tell him?"

"Nope. She lost interest not long after anyway." Her smile tempered, a crinkle appearing between her eyes. "Because of your brother, I suppose."

Cade had only recently confessed his past association with Monroe to Sawyer. "Did you know from the beginning?"

If he hadn't known her so well, the flash of hurt wouldn't have registered. "She only just told me. I get why she kept it a secret. I do."

"Cade only just told me too if it's any consolation."

"I guess everyone has secrets." She pulled her hand away. He stepped back, but she didn't bolt like he'd expected. "What if you win? What are you going to do with the money?"

"Do you have a minute?"

She glanced toward her studio. "Sure. My next appointment's not until two."

He chucked his head and led them back through the wildflowers and onto River Street. She fell into step beside him, and he kept the pace leisurely in case her foot was paining her.

"The flowers are beautiful, Sawyer." Her voice was easy and comfortable, and she bent slightly to let her fingertips skim over the tallest of the blooms.

"Thanks." The word croaked out and he cleared his throat, looking in the opposite direction. "I crept back to the old house and dug up some of the lilies my mama had planted. They were overrunning the front and needed dividing anyway. The rest are some of her favorite wildflowers."

Her fingers brushed the back of his hand, but when he looked over, she was walking with her hands clasped over the folded top of the brown paper bag. She stopped. "What happened here?"

A bare patch marred his manicured bed. "Uncle Delmar took Ms. Leora a bouquet of flowers. Said it was more romantic if he picked them himself."

"Cheaper too." Laughter lilted her voice, and her smile was infectious. "Where are we headed?"

"Old Cottonbloom Park."

She made a knowing humming sound. "You plan to fix it back up."

"Uncle Del said it used to be awesome. A better field than either school. Concession stand. Playground. This was the heart of the town. Now look at it."

They had reached the edge of the decrepit playground, the rusted-out swings motionless in the hot air. Metal stairs reached fifteen feet into the air leading to nothing, the slide long gone. Hardy weeds had encroached into the dirt-packed ground. The abandoned playground reminded him of his own childhood cut short by the death of his parents, but echoes of happiness remained and he wanted to recapture it.

He sensed her stare but kept walking until they reached the overgrown baseball field. A trace of Kelly green paint remained on the nearest dugout, the boards weathered and covered in messages from generations of teenagers who had used the abandoned park as a hangout.

"You want to restart a baseball league, don't you? Relive your glory days?" The tease in her voice held a tentativeness. It had been a long time since the two of them had done anything but throw dirty looks and accusations at each other across the river.

"You know, this park could bring us back together." His words registered a split second after he said them. "By 'us' I mean the two sides of Cottonbloom. Not . . . you and me." Clamping his mouth shut, he rubbed his nape. Why couldn't he control what came out of his mouth around her?

Her little laugh dropped his tensed shoulder down from his ears. She stepped through the tall grass and ran a finger over the nearest board, picking her way over crumbled concrete, weeds, and rotted, falling-down boards. "You brought me out here one night. Do you remember?"

A flash of heat that had nothing to do with the blazing August sun broke a sweat on his back. "Vaguely." A lie. He remembered it like it was yesterday. The dugout hadn't been in such bad shape a decade earlier. They had made out, and it was the first time she'd let him go up her shirt. It had been dark and secluded and he'd written something for her on one of the boards.

She disappeared farther into the dugout. Sunlight slashed through the roof where boards were gone. Part of him hoped the piece of wood in question had rotted into sawdust, but with a desperation he didn't understand, he joined her, searching for the ancient message.

He found it and blew out a sigh. It was faded, a couple of the words erased by time, but it was there. He planned to walk away and claim he couldn't find it, but she noticed his stillness.

"You found it." She stood close. Close enough for him to smell the citrusy scent of her shampoo. "You never let me see it, said I would have to find it later, but I never could."

"You came back to look?" He turned his head toward her.

She sucked her bottom lip between her teeth and her eyes flared. "Maybe."

"When?"

She bent at the waist and leaned closer. "It doesn't matter, does it?"

Silence fell between them while she read the message. For some reason it did matter.

He could recite the message by heart. *Regan Lovell, someday I'm going to marry you. Love, Sawyer Fournette.* It had been his promise to her. His covenant. Until everything went to hell between them.

"Stupid, right? We were what? Seventeen?" A sense of claustrophobia overwhelmed him. He left the dugout for the open air, closed his eyes, and raised his face toward the sun, pinpricks dancing behind his eyelids.

Her voice startled him. "It would be a good thing to bring this place back to life, Sawyer." Her face was serious, but a warmth softened her eyes.

She walked away and he let her go, standing in the abandoned baseball field until she crossed the river.

Chapter Five

With the noonday sun beating down on Monday morning, Regan left her studio for the Quilting Bee. She stopped in the shadow of the brick wall and looked across the river. A few trucks and cars were parked on the opposite side, but not a big black truck. Sawyer's flowers wavered in the breeze coming off the river, making for a pretty picture against the multihued brick storefronts. Her gaze skated over what she could see of Cottonbloom Park.

Her heart echoed the uncomfortable cramping sensation that had made her lightheaded when she read his long-ago message to her. She had gone looking for it several times over the years. Even after they'd broken up she'd felt compelled to torture herself, scouring the planks of wood for his even-handed lettering, never finding it.

Now, she wished she hadn't seen it. Wished she could steer them back into the acrimonious waters they'd been treading for the past decade. The memories and feelings were sharp and agonizing and beautiful all at the same time.

A decade ago, closer to his parents' deaths, his pain had made her physically ache. Then, she could pepper kisses over him and hug him and tell him he wasn't alone. That wasn't her place anymore, yet she'd nearly taken his hand hearing him talk about his mother's flowers. The echoes of the past were strong. As soon as she'd made contact with the bare skin of his hand, she'd come to her senses. Like he'd said, ancient history.

Shaking herself out of her strange mood she knocked on the Quilting Bee's door at the appointed time. A CLOSED sign hung askew in front of a pulled-down blind. She cupped her hands around her eyes and peeked into the darkened interior through a slit.

She knocked again. Shadowy movement not three feet from where she pressed her face had her reeling back. Her heart thumped as she smoothed her skirt down. The locks on the other side of the door jangled, and Ms. Martha gestured her inside.

"Well, hello Regan. Have you been waiting long? I was already in the back with Mr. Rockford." Ms. Martha favored her with a smile, but it looked as forced as Regan's own smile felt.

Regan checked the screen of her phone. No, she was on time. "I didn't get the times mixed up, did I?"

"No, Mr. Rockford didn't want to miss his lunch, so he came early. Come on back."

Regan allowed her smile to pull into a grimace as soon as Ms. Martha's back was turned. Glen Rockford could stand to miss a few lunches. Ms. Martha led her into a large storage room that made Regan almost salivate. This was the kind of space she longed for.

Glen turned, and Regan ran her tongue over her teeth, an old pageant trick to keep her fake smile from sticking. "Hello, Glen. You should have told me you were coming early."

"The missus informed me this morning that she was making greens and ham for lunch. Now, you know I can't miss that." Glen patted the massive overhang of his stomach nearly popping the bottom buttons of his short-sleeve shirt.

Glen was good-natured and downright nice, which is why he was reelected cycle after cycle to be the city manager. It had nothing to do with his skills. Although running a business replacing windows in houses and cars did afford him a certain amount of business acumen, Regan wasn't as confident in his abilities as a builder.

"That's okay. Have you found anything?" She stepped around bolts of fabric and bins of quilting scraps and brown boxes to the brick wall in the back.

"Ms. Martha's right, I think. Looky here." Glen waved his pen like a wand along a crack that ran diagonal from the corner of the cement floor to halfway up the opposite wall.

A faint tapping sounded on the front door. She turned to Ms. Martha. "That will be Mr. Neely. He'll be able to tell us whether this is structural or cosmetic. Could you bring him on back, Ms. Martha?"

Ms. Martha bustled off. Glen had the look of a little boy who'd gotten picked last for the team. "My opinion is that the crack is structural."

No one had warned her a big part of being mayor was smoothing ruffled feathers. "And I value your opinion Glen, I really do. But, Mr. Neely is a builder. He deals with building codes and renovations every day. He'll be able to tell us definitively whether this is structural or cosmetic." She squatted and fingered the crack.

If Glen was correct, it would be like opening a vat of worms. Every business owner in town would want their places reassessed—again—hoping to lower their tax burden.

Mr. Neely entered the room with a crackle of energy. Regan had worked with him on several projects through the region and liked him immensely. Even more important, she respected him. His iron-gray closely cropped Afro and booming voice lent him an air of gravitas that reminded her of a preacher. And, like a preacher, his word on the structural integrity of the building would be accepted as gospel.

They exchanged handshakes before she pointed. "The crack starts in the corner near the floor."

He hummed and stepped over to the wall. Glen dogged his heels while Ms. Martha stood back and called out her opinions. Regan shook her head and left Mr. Neely to his work, mentally calculating square footage. The storage area really was drool-worthy. If Ms. Martha would be willing, she'd switch storefronts today and happily pay the higher taxes.

Regan fanned herself with a hand and looked up. Did the air conditioning not extend to the storage room? No ducts crisscrossed overhead. She moved some bins from the edge of the wall and lifted off a lengthy piece of canvas to check the baseboards. The smell of gasoline wrinkled her nose. A red plastic gas can was on the floor. She scooted it aside with her foot, but there was no vent behind it. She laid the canvas back over it.

Her hands stilled, and a wave of heat that had nothing to do with the close conditions blew through her body like a forest fire igniting. A simple explanation probably existed for the presence of a gas can in Ms. Martha's storage area. Maybe her car often ran out of gas. Maybe she kept it to power a generator in case of emergencies.

She turned back to the trio across the room. Ms. Martha wore a homemade jumper, T-shirt, and sandals. Her legs looked solid and strong, but she wasn't a spring chicken, for goodness' sake. Midfifties if Regan's math was correct. The path her thoughts tread was ridiculous. Outrageous.

No matter how strong Ms. Martha's legs were, she couldn't handle the crayfish baskets, and it had definitely been a man at her mother's house. The two men went out a side door to the alley behind the buildings, and Ms. Martha pivoted around. Had her gaze dropped to the canvas-covered gas can before meeting Regan's?

She was hyperaware of what was behind her and shuffled toward the door to the store. "I don't suppose it's any cooler in the store?"

"I'm sure it is. I've blocked most of the vents to the storeroom. Can't afford to cool it. You're looking a bit peaked. Come on through and let me get you some tea." Ms. Martha patted her arm and opened up the door to the store. A poof of cool air enveloped them.

Her motherly manner, even though she had never married or bore children, set Regan's doubts to fluttering once more. Ms. Martha retreated down a small hallway, opened a small walk-in closet bursting with shelves of fabric, and retrieved a plastic pitcher from a small refrigerator tucked underneath.

The store was homey and welcoming. Cloth and machines crowded the floor, but chairs and a round table took up one corner for the ladies' quilting circle. A half-dozen magazines with names like *Quilting Today* and *A Stitch in Time* were spread on the table, the pages thumbed through and some ripped out entirely. Who knew there were so many magazines devoted to quilting?

Finished quilts hung along the walls. Regan fingered the closest one, sniffing the fabric. The cloth was old and held hints of cedar and pine, the thread along some of the panels unraveling. It brought to mind the log cabins and settlers in her history books from school. It was beautiful. Brown, red, and orange triangular pieces of different sizes gave the impression of the chaos of fall leaves, yet they had been hand-stitched together with an amazing precision.

"My great-grandmother sewed this one."

Regan startled around. Ms. Martha stood slightly behind her, holding two glasses of tea and staring up at the quilt.

"It's beautiful."

"It's a bear claw pattern. It tells escaping slaves to stay in the woods where the bear lives. This quilt isn't that old, of course, but quilts hold history. They tell a story if you're willing to listen."

Regan took the glass of tea Ms. Martha offered and sipped. It was sweet and cold. "Are any of these yours?"

A huff that sounded distinctly ironic escaped Ms. Martha. "Actually, I don't quilt."

"I assumed . . ." Regan gestured around them.

"Yes. Most people do. My mother was the quilter. The storyteller. This place is hers." She ran her hand over the next quilt, the fabric whispering with the movement. Blue and pink circles interlocked on a cream background. "The wedding ring pattern. She made it for me, but I never had cause to use it."

Regan couldn't put a name to the emotion in Ms. Martha's voice, but it was something her heart recognized. Regret? Longing? Sadness?

A companionable silence settled until Glen and Mr. Neely entered the building through the front door. Glen mopped sweat from his eyes with a red bandana.

"What's the verdict, gentlemen?" Regan's hand tensed around the glass, her fingers slipping over condensation.

"It's structural," Glen said with an inappropriate glee and a smug smile.

She looked to Mr. Neely who nodded. Another set of responsibilities weighed on her.

"I don't have the capital to invest in repairs." Ms. Martha set her glass down on a bolt of fabric, a wet ring forming on the light blue cloth.

"The building's not in danger of collapsing, but if you want to sell, it would affect your price for certain. Every seasonal expansion and contraction will grow the problem," Mr. Neely said.

Ms. Martha turned to Regan. "Don't you see? I can't pay these taxes and fix that wall and stay in business. You want me gone, don't you?"

The understanding Regan sensed between them had vanished. Everyone's eyes were on her, and she felt like the Wicked Witch of the West. "Of course I don't want you gone. You have a lovely store, and you're a fixture in Cottonbloom. We can work something out."

It took another few minutes of soothing reassurances from Mr. Neely that the crack wasn't an imminent danger before they stepped outside. Glen waved good-bye and headed to his truck muttering something about a hambone. She and Mr. Neely walked in the opposite direction side by side.

"Shouldn't the assessment people have noted that crack, Mr. Neely?"

"They're more focused on square footage than structural integrity. Anyway, most of them wouldn't have the background to recognize an issue. If they even scooted the bins away to look, they may have assumed the crack was confined to the brick façade."

She rubbed a temple. "Every business owner is going to want another inspection based on this. What's your workload like this week? Can you help me out? I need someone I can trust, but more importantly, someone everyone can trust."

He harrumphed at her not-so-subtle attempt to butter him up, but an uncommon half-smile turned his lips as he shuffled to a stop and pulled a smartphone out of a holster on his belt. He scrolled through it. "I have a few pockets of time. I'll jot you in."

"Appreciate you," Regan called as he walked across the street to his SUV. He gave a wave over his head as his answer.

She meandered back to her interior design studio. The studio was closed on Mondays, as were many of the shops. No customers would be breaking down her door, but she had plenty of work to do. She typically spent Mondays organizing for the week. Efficiency and organization were keys to her success. Fabric and paint swatches, pictures of furniture, gridded layout suggestions were gathered and presented after an initial consultation with a client.

Her studio seemed closed-in and stark after the jumble and roominess of the Quilting Bee. In her small office, she plugged room measurements into her design program, then moved a block that represented a couch around the grids.

The can of gasoline niggled at her. She pushed the mouse aside and pulled out the letter she'd received in June, not long after the assessments had taken place but before the pavilion had been torched. Letters cut from magazines and glued onto a plain white sheet of paper had been waiting in her mailbox at home.

STOP THE FESTIVALS. OR ELSE.

The second letter was much like the first, and she spread them out side by side. Its message seemed more ominous in light of recent events.

STOP THE TAXES. OR YOU WILL PAY.

The first letter had struck her as adolescent and amateurish, as if a teenager had overheard his parents complaining and decided to do something about it. Monroe had told her to go to the police, but citizens aimed their ire at her on a regular basis. It came with the job.

She received texts and voice mails that could be construed as threatening. Things were said when passions got hot. She appreciated the fact people were as passionate about saving Cottonbloom as she was, even if their opinions on methods differed. Anyway, that first letter wasn't an arrestable offense.

The second letter, however, was more worrisome and pointed to a downtown business owner. Only one came to mind. Monroe already thought she was headed straight off the deep end because of the festival competition. If she presented her niggling theory about Ms. Martha, they might haul her to the nearest psychiatric ward.

There was only one person who was as crazy as she was. Sawyer Fournette could be counted on to either shore up or punch holes in her theory. She dawdled another hour, weighing the pros and cons.

He was the last man she should be going to for help of any sort, especially after their most recent run-ins. The sense of camaraderie and understanding building between them would lead to trouble.

He was dangerous. Not that she feared him. Just the opposite. His strength and care and general air of competency made him easy to lean on. But she couldn't afford to trust him. She'd blindly taken that road once and had stumbled back broken and destroyed.

Filled with a sense of inevitability, she locked up and slipped into her red VW Bug. She'd gotten the battery replaced so at least there wouldn't be an embarrassing repeat of the other night. She would duck in, get his opinion, and duck out.

When she saw that his truck was gone and his house deserted, she headed toward the garage he had set up with Cade to make Fournette Designs a family business. Although she hadn't been there, she'd heard enough about the venture from Monroe to know where to go.

She turned onto a recently blacktopped drive off the parish highway. It snaked through tall pines. Clearing the shadows, she emerged into bright sunshine and tapped the breaks. The size of the building jolted her. She expected a poky metal two-car garage. The two-story structure of cement block and corrugated metal was long enough to hold half a dozen cars easily. All the bay doors were closed, but both Sawyer's and Cade's trucks and a motorcycle sat out front.

She pulled in beside Sawyer's shiny black monster. She might've wondered if the size was in compensation for other shortcomings, but she was intimately aware of the fact Sawyer had nothing to compensate for.

She tried not to think of what he wasn't compensating for. The more she told herself not to think about it, the more she could think about nothing else. Like how the faint outline against his pajama bottoms had made her skin feel close to incineration. Or the startling sensation of him inside of her the first time they'd had sex.

Oh God, she had to stop her brain. Or her body. Or whatever was making her hot for Sawyer Fournette. Before she turned the car off, she jacked the AC to max and flapped her shirt to try to cool down. This was strictly about festival business.

She smoothed her hair back in its twist and checked her face in the rearview mirror. Flushed but only a little splotchy. Finally emerging from her car, she wobbled across a mixture of grass and gravel at the edge of the blacktop to a door that seemed small compared to the bay door.

She heard men's voices and a thumping sound of machinery. A knock would go unheard, so she cracked the door open and stuck her head inside. Wearing gray coveralls and rubbing the palm of one of his hands, Cade Fournette was staring at an engine that hung by chains from a steel beam. A blond man in grimy jeans and a blue T-shirt winched the engine higher. Sawyer was nowhere in sight, but the mechanical thumping sound continued.

She stepped fully onto the concrete floor of their garage.

Cool air wafted around her. They'd had the huge space air-conditioned, and fans were mounted to provide crossflow. Everything was surprisingly clean, but then again, they'd only been in the space a matter of weeks.

The speed with which it had been constructed had been the talk of the town. Even her side. But then again, Cade Fournette had rolled back in town with money. Lots of it, if rumors could be trusted. Which generally they couldn't, but Monroe had let slip a few details that corroborated the whispers. Poor boy made good, indeed.

Although Sawyer had tried to keep his circumstances as hidden as possible, she'd gotten hints at how difficult his childhood had been after his parents had been killed by a drunk driver. She was happy for Cade, but even happier her best friend had found love.

"Hello." Her voice echoed and took on a tentative quality in the space. Both men looked over at her. Cade didn't move, so she took a step forward. "I'm terribly sorry to interrupt. I'm looking for Sawyer. I saw his truck outside." She thumbed over her shoulder and shifted on her feet.

Cade cleared his throat but didn't move. "Of course. We don't get too many visitors out here."

Usually, Cade treated her as if she carried the plague, no matter that she was Monroe's best friend. But, surprise lightened his voice, and while she didn't exactly feel welcomed, he didn't seem inclined to toss her out either.

"I'm sorry to bust in, but it won't take long. Festival business."

"Come on back to the break room. Sawyer's buttoning up an engine." He led her to a stark room that was empty besides a dorm-sized refrigerator on the floor, a card table, and three metal folding chairs. "Wait here and let me get him. There's Cokes in the frig. Help yourself."

She paced the room a few times. Uncertainty hammered away at her. What was she doing coming to the one man who wanted her festival to fail so he could win the competition? Maybe there was a back door she could slip out of without anyone being the wiser.

Before she could act, Sawyer blocked the doorway, tugging off black gloves. She took a step backward and swallowed past a huge lump. Her gaze roved despite instructions to stay on his face.

The top half of his gray coveralls had been stripped off, the sleeves tied around his waist to keep them from falling to his ankles. A tight white undershirt was streaked with black grease. His hair was a disheveled mess, his stubble classifying as a beard. She'd never entertained erotic fantasies about a mechanic, but that would change tonight.

His gaze seemed to be drifting up and down her body as well, and she shifted on her heels. He stepped closer. Was he going to back her up against the card table? Was he going to lift her on top and push her legs apart? She wasn't sure whether warnings to flee or entreaties to stay were making her stomach hop like a bullfrog on crack. She pulled in a sharp breath.

He bypassed her by a good three feet and squatted in front of the mini-frig. "You want something to drink?"

"Sure. Okay." Her voice cracked like an adolescent boy's. Litanies to God and Jesus went on repeat in her head. She even threw in a few to Mary. Surely a woman would understand her plight. The curve of his butt in the coveralls was not helping. Did he have on anything underneath them? He rose and her gaze followed.

"Diet Coke still your thing?" He held out a can.

She took it. "On occasion. I usually stick with water. Or wine." She giggled, and then cut herself off when the grating noise hit her ear.

He smiled, pulled one of the metal chairs out, and sat with his knees spread wide. It was like an arrow drew her gaze straight to his crotch. Ridiculous. No, she was beyond ridiculous. Giving herself a mental shake, she joined him, scooted under the table, and crossed her feet at the ankles, her knees pressed together like she'd been taught in cotillion. A classic ladylike stance. Unfortunately, the seventy-year-old woman with perfect bottle-blonde hair hadn't covered the proper etiquette in dealing with unrequited lust for an old lover you were supposed to hate.

"How's your car running?" He took a swig of his root beer. She almost smiled. She'd forgotten how much he loved the stuff. She couldn't stand it.

"Fine. Got a new battery just in case."

"Good. Good. You're back in heels, so I assume your foot is all better." An awkward silence descended. "Is there something else going on you want to talk about?" Hesitancy lurked in his words almost as if he were as nervous and discombobulated as she felt.

"Actually, yes." She toyed with the tab of her Diet Coke, finally pulling it and taking a sip. It burned going down and helped focus her thoughts. "There's no one else I can talk to. People already think I'm taking this festival too seriously."

"I know the feeling."

She looked up from her can to find him smiling. She couldn't seem to stop the smile that came to her face in return. "I met with Ms. Martha this morning."

"Was she right about the structural integrity?"

She dropped her smile to narrow her eyes at him. "As a matter of fact, she was. I had Mr. Neely come down. You know what this is going to mean, don't you?"

"Everyone downtown is going to want a reassessment." Although he sounded sympathetic, suspicion that he'd been the one to feed Ms. Martha her speech tempered her lust and the camaraderie that had briefly flared.

"Exactly." She pointed her finger at him, ready to accuse

him, but stopped herself. Whether he was behind it or not, having Mr. Neely verify or modify the reassessments was the right thing to do. She wasn't out to gouge her neighbors. "But it's neither here nor there. I'm here because I saw something in Ms. Martha's storage room."

He sat forward and laced his fingers on the table. His hands were bigger than she remembered, wider, his fingers thicker. She took another sip of Coke and dropped her focus to the concrete floor.

"A gas can was hidden under a tarp."

He was silent.

"I'm insane, right? You don't need to tell me." She darted a look at his face, stood, and barked a laugh. "I mean, it's Ms. Martha, right? Forget I said anything. Forget you saw me. Forget everything."

He grabbed her wrist. "Hold up. Sit down." His voice was clipped and authoritative. She obeyed, no protest forthcoming. They stared into each other's eyes. He still held her wrist, his other hand pulling at the hair on his chin.

"It's a little . . ." He tilted his head.

"Crazy, I get it." She half-stood, but he didn't let her go. This time instead of pulling or commanding her to sit, he simply caressed the inside of her wrist with his thumb. Every nerve ending sparked and it would have taken an explosion to move her. Actually, her heart felt like it might explode. She sank back down on the edge of the seat. He let go, and as if unplugging from an electrical source, her heart paced slower.

"I was going to say 'far-fetched.' But we can't discount it. Ms. Martha's obviously passionate about her business. It's her life's work. Who knows how far she'd go to protect it."

"I've wracked my brain to think of why she would keep a gas can in her storage area."

"What was in it?" He tapped a finger on the table.

"I'm assuming gas?"

"But was it regular unleaded or kerosene?"

"I'm not sure I could tell the difference. Anyway, right after I noticed the can, she invited me into the shop for a tea, and I had no excuse to go back into the storage area."

"It could be for her car, but she drives a reliable sedan even if it has some years on it. The city takes care of the landscaping, right?"

"Right. So no need for a weed eater or lawn mower."

"A generator? Or a space heater for winter?"

She bit her bottom lip and wrapped both hands around her sweating can. "I didn't see a generator, but her storage area was pretty packed. A space heater would make sense." Now that Sawyer was shooting holes in her theory, her embarrassment factor was rising.

"Do you think she saw you?"

She shrugged. "I have no clue. I wasn't snooping for dirt on her. I'm being silly and paranoid, aren't I?"

He sighed and rubbed his cheek. Was the hair coarse or soft to the touch? She tightened her hold on the can and took a swig.

"Don't get mad at Monroe, but she mentioned the weird letter you got."

She tore her gaze away from his beard. Monroe was going to get an earful. "I told her that in confidence. Just to get her opinion."

"And what was her opinion?"

"She thought I should turn it over to Chief Thomason."

"Why didn't you?"

"Because the letter didn't make specific threats. It was childish even. While an anonymous letter is unusual, I get hang-ups and irate phone calls on occasion. I get that I can be aggressive and my plans have peeved some people off, but I'm going to keep Cottonbloom alive, Sawyer Fournette. Watch me." She jabbed a finger in his direction.

Instead of firing back, a slow smile spread across his face. "I always loved to hear you talk like that, Regan. I thought you'd change the world." His smile crumpled into a more complicated expression, and an unspoken question seemed to fall from his lips. *What happened?*

Her high school dreams had included world travel followed by world domination. She'd planned to graduate with her political science degree, become a Rhodes scholar, spend a year studying abroad, and go to Washington. None of that had happened. She'd ended up with a degree in interior design and back home in a town that most people couldn't locate on a map.

"Maybe I won't change the world, but I can make things better here, can't I?" Emotion roughed out the stridency in her voice.

"You sure can." Was that pity in his eyes? "Do you still have the letter?"

"Of course."

"Can I see it?"

"I suppose. Although, I don't know what good it's going to do."

"Humor me. Is it at the shop or at your house?"

"Shop. It was delivered to my house mailbox, although it wasn't in an envelope."

"This person knows where you live?"

"Most people know anyway, but a thirty-second internet search is all you need."

He muttered a curse that would have her cotillion teacher clutching her pearls. "Do you have a security system?"

"As a matter of fact I do." While technically true, she hadn't actually contracted a firm to monitor it, so it was useless, except for the sign informing any would-be intruders that one existed. She hesitated, knowing another can of worms was about to be spilled. "I got another letter."

He straightened. "When?"

"This week. After the budget meeting."

"Before or after you gave chase to the stranger in your mama's backyard?"

She considered a white lie, but with his hazel eyes boring into her, only the truth emerged. "I found it that morning in my mailbox."

He threw his arms up before crossing them over his chest. Tension made his arm muscles flex. She took another swallow of her drink.

"I'm surprised you're here for help and not to accuse me of writing them."

Strangely, it had never crossed her mind that he might be behind the letters. Not his style to hide behind paper cutouts. The fact he assumed they were handwritten confirmed her intuition. "Anonymous threats aren't your style."

"You need to be more careful, Regan. Don't go running after strangers in the dark." The serious worry in his voice in turn worried her. She was hoping he would dismiss the letters, laugh them off.

"You don't think I could take Ms. Martha?" She forced tease in her voice.

His lips quirked up. "If it came to fisticuffs? Yes. But even little old ladies come packing heat in their pocketbooks these days."

She pressed her fingertips to her forehead. "Are we actually discussing the possibility of Ms. Martha assassinating me? We really are losing it, Sawyer. They're going to lock us in padded cells next to each other."

He laughed, the rich, booming sound filling the small room and reverberating off the concrete. A flutter of wings beat in her stomach and expanded into her chest. More than anything, that's what she'd missed after they'd broken up. His laugh, full of joy and promise and life.

"I think we can evade the little men with straightjackets a little while longer." His laughter faded like the dying rumble of thunder. "Putting an assassination attempt from Ms. Martha aside, she did not cut the crayfish baskets. You might have been able to haul them up and cut them, but not her. The logical conclusion is the same man who was lurking outside your mama's house cut the baskets."

Her gaze met his and held. "Seems like we both have an interest in finding that man."

Chapter Six

Sawyer stared into her big brown eyes. It had been a long time since they sat across from each other at a table and talked. Even though her shop was closed on Mondays, she was in a professional knee-length skirt that hugged her curves and a pretty, floaty blouse with geometric shapes all over it.

Her eyes were soft and pretty, the lashes long and curled and painted black. Doe eyes he used to call them. She didn't need the artificial enhancers. She looked even prettier like she had the other night at his house. No makeup and in a T-shirt and shorts.

She'd look even better naked in his bed. Once the errant thought popped into his head, he couldn't cram it back into his subconscious. All he could picture was her hair loose and her body spread over his mattress. Maybe she'd keep those heels on. His gaze ran down her long legs to the strappy high-heels she wore, pink toenails peeking out the ends.

He ran his scabbed, dinged-up, dirty hands down his legs. His palms had gotten clammy all of a sudden. Like he was nervous or something.

"Have you got any ideas?" she asked.

His gaze shot back to her face. Had she guessed the direction of his thoughts? Because, hell yes, he had ideas. Lots of very dirty, erotic ideas. He shifted on the chair.

"About figuring out who the man is?" This time her question was more tentative.

He had to pull it together before she guessed anything. "The man. Yes. I mean, no. I mean, I've already asked around and no one knows, or else they're staying quiet."

She bit her lip. Again. Did she know how crazy that made him? That straightjacket might become a reality. Or maybe she did know he still harbored a tiny, inconvenient attraction to her and was tormenting him on purpose. One thing she'd never been was a tease. Of course, that was before the nuclear fallout.

Voices carried from the shop floor. Cade was pissed about something. Sawyer craned his neck and could see the shoulder of another man, an emblem on a tan sleeve. Sheriff Wayne Berry.

"What the . . ." He stood and walked out on the shop floor.

Wayne had his hands up as if trying to diffuse the situation. "Now Cade, it was a tip."

"From who?"

"Anonymous."

"Well, now isn't that convenient." Sarcasm turned Cade's voice into barbed wire.

Jeremy, their new hire, looked like the Grinch had stolen all his Christmas presents.

"What's going on, Wayne?" Sawyer smiled and held out a hand for a shake. His role had always been the peacemaker of the family, even before his parents had died. Plus, the hostility that had been bred into Cade through years of run-ins with the law growing up hadn't tainted Sawyer. He actually liked Wayne and, even more, respected him.

"A tip came in this morning that Mr. Whitehurst was seen the night of Thursday, July thirtieth, vandalizing crayfish baskets."

They looked to Jeremy. Bitterness tightened his face and flavored his small smile. "It wasn't me. But isn't that what *everyone* says?"

"Can you give me your whereabouts that night around midnight?" The sheriff pulled out a tablet phone to make notes.

"I was already working here, so I was asleep. Work starts by seven sharp every morning."

"Can anyone corroborate you were at home that night?"

"Nope. I was sleeping alone." Jeremy already looked defeated.

Cade threw a wrench into an open metal drawer on the red toolbox. The clang echoed through the shop. "This is bull—"

"I can tell you he's been on time every morning since he started work." Sawyer laid a hand on Cade's shoulder and patted in an unspoken plea to let him handle things. "And I'll add that he hasn't acted like he's been out all night. He comes in, works hard, and doesn't complain."

He and Wayne stared at each other for a moment. The sheriff sighed, clipped the tablet back on his belt, and turned to Jeremy. "Look, take this as a warning to stay out of trouble, son. If you didn't do it, then someone is out to smear you. If you did do it, I'll track down more evidence that will support a warrant. Understood?"

Jeremy chucked his chin in a knowing, bitter acknowledgment. "Sure. You're saying one way or another, I'm up shit creek."

The sheriff left the way he entered, leaving a heavy silence. Sawyer turned around and bumped into Regan. He hadn't realized she'd followed him. Their gazes met for a heartbeat. She walked around the mounted engine. Her heels clip-clopping, her ass swaying, her calf muscles flexing.

She examined Jeremy like he was a statue while Jeremy looked at her like she'd lost her marbles. "Walk for me."

Jeremy glanced over at Cade, who was watching Regan with suspicion. "'Scuse me?"

Sawyer had no clue what Regan was up to, but somehow over the last half hour, they'd become a team of sorts. "Do it."

Jeremy huffed, but walked from the engine to the bay doors, performed an about-face, and walked back. His fair skin was flushed.

Finally, Regan shook her head. "Nope. Not him."

"You sure?" Sawyer hooked his thumbs in his folded-over coveralls.

"Care to share?" Cade asked, his voice still full of sarcasm but more amused than biting.

"Regan saw a man lurking around her mama's garden. Thought it was me, gave chase, but he got clean away." Sawyer waggled his finger between him and Regan. "We have a theory that whoever cut the baskets is the same man."

Regan looked Jeremy up and down one last time. "The man I saw wasn't as lean. He was built more like Sawyer. Plus, he led with his shoulders. You lead with your hips with a long stride. See?"

She made the walk across the floor in front of them. Her shoulders were back, her hips swinging, but when she turned, she walked with her shoulders forward, faster and with less hip swing. "I learned all about the mechanics of walking during pageant training. I used to lead with my shoulders too, but Mother made me practice until I led with my hips like a supermodel. Since then I've always noticed people's walks. And you don't move like the man I saw."

"Sounds like if things go to hell here, you could move to New York and take up modeling with your pretty face and perfect catwalk." Sawyer tried to tease some trust back into Jeremy's eyes.

At twenty-two, Jeremy was like an abused dog, mistrustful and ready to bite any hand whether it offered help or not. Sawyer hadn't gotten the entire story from their new addition yet, but he'd had a rough start in Alabama, and he knew the boy blamed himself for most of his misfortune. It meant that any bad luck that fell his way took on an air of inevitability, as if he was receiving what he deserved.

Cade harrumphed and picked up his wrench. "An anonymous tip can't stick. You're new to town and an easy mark. I'll let it be known that if people mess with you, they're also tangling with the Fournette brothers."

Sawyer and Cade might fight like two polecats trapped in a sack, but when it came down to it, they had each other's backs. Always had. Cade lifted his fist, and Sawyer gave him a bump with his. "Hells yeah."

"I'd best be going before the testosterone man-love smothers me."

Although he sensed an eye-roll, amusement lightened her voice. She was already halfway to the door when he caught her arm. "You going to be at your shop later?"

"Probably. Got a big job to prepare for tomorrow."

"I want to stop by and see those letters."

She nodded and he let her go.

"Hey, let me see that pageant walk again." He didn't even know why he said it except to watch her backside shimmy.

Her smile was saccharine, and her hand went to her hip. She walked waving her other hand in a parody of a beauty queen during a parade. On the way out, she kicked a heel up behind her and tossed a wink over her shoulder. He threw his head back and laughed. Something hard popped him on his upper arm.

"What the flip is going on?" Cade pointed to the door and tapped Sawyer's chest none too gently with a wrench.

"What?"

Cade mocked Sawyer's laugh with a simpering one of his own. All humor wiped clean in an instant, he jabbed the wrench at Sawyer's chest. "That woman damn near destroyed you."

"I know, but . . ." Sawyer scratched his beard and looked to the ceiling.

He'd never told Cade the entirety of what went down between him and Regan. Whether it was pride or shame or pain that kept the truth bottled up inside, he wasn't sure. All he knew was he'd never gotten the chance to fully explain himself to Regan, and she's the one who'd deserved the truth. But she'd cut him out of her life and her heart with the precision of a scalpel. The trust and love he'd thought they'd built together like an impregnable stone wall shattered like glass.

While he'd humbled himself and begged her to listen, she'd wiped him out of her life like he was the Louisiana scum her mama had always accused him of being. Granted, what she'd walked in on had looked bad, astronomically bad, but things weren't always as they appeared.

Sawyer sighed and braced his feet apart. "Look, if I want our festival to go off without a hitch, then I need whoever is trying to sabotage both festivals caught. Regan has the same goal. That's all this is."

Cade's lip curled with his hum. "Don't forget that you're wining and dining the representative from Nautical Engines Friday night."

"I've already got reservations at the Cottonbloom Country Club."

Cade fit the wrench to a bolt and torqued it, but kept

his gaze on Sawyer. "I know we don't have a dress code around the shop, but . . ."

"I'll shave and get gussied up." Sawyer rubbed his jaw and smiled. "The beard's starting to itch like a patch of cockleburs anyway. Don't worry, I'll close the deal."

Cade's other partner, Richard, had planned to fly in from Seattle, but his son had made a last-minute request for some time with his father. Richard had been torn between business and family, but Cade made the ultimate decision, putting family first and his trust in Sawyer. Even though Sawyer had been successful at the auto parts factory and had full confidence in his own abilities, the little kid inside of him wanted to make Cade proud. For too many years, Cade had been as much a father as a big brother.

He watched the clock the rest of the day, wondering more than once if the damn thing was broken. Once the engine he'd been working on was buttoned up and pressure tested, he ran the back of his arm across his forehead. The shop was air-conditioned, but hard work was hard.

If he didn't care like he'd told Cade, he would head straight over to Regan's shop to look at the letter, sweat be damned. Instead, he pointed his truck back to the farmhouse to get cleaned up.

Chapter Seven

Regan tapped the end of the pencil on the desk, her chin propped in her palm. The rough sketch in front of her was only half-done and covered in eraser marks. Her morning client might not notice, but Regan liked to be prepared with several options, and she'd only completed two.

It was hard to concentrate on whether the couch belonged under the bay window or facing the big-screen TV when so many other thoughts swirled. Mr. Neely had called to let her know he would reinspect the businesses along River Street in the morning and move along to her street the following afternoon.

She prayed they could wrap things up before next Thursday's town meeting. Labor Day was less than three weeks away and she had multiple lists that needed to be completed and too many things that needed to be ordered. Unless she wanted to bankroll the festival herself, the budget had to pass.

A knock sounded, and she bolted upright on the stool. Padding barefoot across the floor, she straightened her skirt and blouse, ran her tongue over her teeth, and smiled as she peeked around the shade. Monroe stood on the other side, her nose pressed against the glass and her eyes crossed.

Regan slumped over with a small laugh and unlocked the door. Monroe grinned on her way in. The woman had turned into a ray of happiness since Cade had moved back. While Regan was beyond happy for her friend, especially after the harsh details of Monroe's childhood and Cade's role as her hero had come to light, the constant smiles and cheeriness could get irritating. Maybe because it high-lighted what a desert Regan's love life had become.

"Saw your car. Thought I'd see what you were up to."

Regan led the way to her cramped office in the back and closed the bottom drawer of her filing cabinet. "Want to come over for popcorn and a cheesy movie this evening?"

Monroe propped herself against the doorjamb and slipped her hands into the pockets of her sensible slacks. "Not tonight. I'm actually meeting Cade for a late dinner."

"Where are y'all going?" Regan leaned back in her cushy office chair.

"We're staying home, actually." A pretty blush tinged Monroe's cheeks. If she had ever entered the pageant cir-cuit, she would have won every competition. But Monroe had never had an interest in such things. Her nature had veered more mature and serious than the rest of the high school girls in their group.

An unexpected jealousy reared up in her stomach. She wasn't jealous of Monroe's nonsplotchy blushes or her long blonde hair. She wasn't even jealous of the claim Cade Fournette had on Monroe's time.

She had once been in love like Monroe. She had walked around pooping rainbows and smiling at the rain. It was a once-in-a-lifetime kind of thing, and she'd lost it. She beat the jealousy back into the closet of her soul that she avoided opening.

"Sounds lovely." And it did sound lovely, but she didn't want to talk about it anymore. "Any word from your mother? Have things gotten easier?"

A hint of sadness crossed Monroe's face. "Better than the first couple of weeks. She didn't do as much crying and begging to come home this past Sunday on the phone."

Any unkind, selfish feeling vanished, and Regan rose to give her friend a bracing hug. Even though Monroe's mother had agreed to attend a residential program for alcoholics, when the day came to check in, she'd changed her mind, forcing Monroe into coercion and threats.

Another shadow crossed Monroe's face. "Sam is fighting the extradition to Georgia. Something about statute of limitations. I don't know. Cade was pissed and yelling at the state lawyer assigned to the case."

"But he's still in jail?"

"For now. Tarwater Senior is pressing hard for bail. There's another hearing next week."

"Will you go?"

"If it helps keep him behind bars, I will." Monroe chewed on her bottom lip. "Kayla is terrified. I talked Tally into giving her a job. I'm hoping between school and work, she'll stay out of trouble, but also be protected, you know?"

Monroe was doing anything not to feel helpless, but if Sam Landry got out and wanted to hurt Kayla, he would find a way. Regan twirled a piece of hair that had come loose at her neck. "Are you taking measures to protect yourself?"

"Sam Landry can't even meet my eyes in court. He's afraid of me. And Cade. Men like him only prey on the vulnerable. Girls like Kayla and women like my mama. Don't you worry about me."

Regan had never heard Monroe sound so hard and intimidating, and she was reminded, despite the outward smiles, her friend was a double black belt and had taught

Sam a harsh lesson in the back alley of the Rivershack Tavern in June.

"You know what? I'm not worried about you one bit. But where was that fire the night of the rabbit kerfuffle?" Regan's tease brought a true smile back to Monroe's face.

"Cade and I weren't exactly fighting over rabbits that night."

"All the greasepaint he transferred from his face to yours kind of tipped me off." Regan winked in her direction.

"Anyway, you had enough fire for the both of us. You took Sawyer down that night as I recall."

A flush of heat spread through her body. She grabbed a brochure of paint colors and fanned herself. She had indeed taken him down. Seeing him holding two squirming rabbits by the ears had enraged her. The speed at which she'd overtaken him had surprised them both, and she'd jumped on his back like a monkey. The rabbits had hopped away.

Her momentum had taken them both to the ground. After they hit the grass, they'd tussled until his strength trumped her fury, and she ended up underneath him, her hands trapped over her head, her hair in her eyes.

She'd squirmed and tried to pull her hands free, her plan to rake her fingernails down his face, but he'd firmed his grip. His touch was rough yet he hadn't hurt her. In fact, his grip, his scent, the press of his body shot a buzz through her. A buzz she couldn't blame on the beers she'd been drinking while in wait.

"Be still, you little hellcat." A complicated mishmash of emotions in his voice had stilled her struggles. Anger was only a small part of it.

Their positions had registered bit by bit. Two of their legs twined around each other while his other leg was jammed in between hers, his heavy thigh pressing at her center. She had wanted to arch into his thigh, maybe even rub herself against it, and she'd had to stifle a low moan of need and lust. God, what was possessing her?

It had been years since they'd been this close. Years since she'd felt a spike of mindless lust. Over the last decade, she'd convinced herself that what they'd shared had been immature and had only been special because he had been her first. Now, her logical barriers against the past tumbled like a house of cards with a puff of his hot breath against her cheek.

Did he feel anything? She needed to see his eyes, but her hair was a veil. She shook her head to try to clear her vision. He'd always been able to anticipate her needs, she remembered as he transferred her wrists into one hand and pushed her hair back with the other. The gesture was unexpectedly gentle and sweet.

Heat lightning flashed, illuminating his eyes for a split second, but she didn't recognize what she'd seen. The teasing Sawyer of her memories was gone. Something more primal and frightening masked his face. Her body thrummed an answer. A resounding *Yes, please*. His thigh pressed harder between her legs. This time she couldn't stop the small whimper in her throat or the slight arch in her back.

He'd muttered a curse and was off her like he'd been shot. She sat up and half turned to where he stood with his back to her, his hands on his hips, facing the river. A man-made whistle wavered in the distance. He turned his head so she could see the strong profile of his face, but he didn't shift to meet her gaze and not a word was exchanged. He took off in a jog.

Another streak of lightning across the sky illuminated him briefly before he was lost to the darkness. The longer she sat staring, the more confused she grew. She didn't like confusion.

One moment didn't erase the past. She'd stood, brushed the leaves, pine needles, and grass from her clothes the best she could, and decided to stick with what she knew, what was easy. Anger.

"Well, the rabbit kerfuffle was two months ago. We've moved past that, I think." Regan tossed the brochure back on the desk, the inconvenient hot flash passed.

"Really? What does that mean, exactly? Are you two combining resources for your festivals?"

"No. Let's not get crazy. But we are trying to figure who is behind the trouble. Whoever is behind the pavilion fire and the crayfish basket vandalism is hurting us both. Plus, I almost caught someone who was trying to get into Mother's garden with a bottle of industrial-strength plant killer."

Monroe stifled a laugh.

"This is not funny in the least. Mother's house is the pinnacle on the Home and Garden tour of Cottonbloom. If her garden is dead, then what?"

"You'd probably sell even more tickets to people wanting to rubberneck at the carnage." Monroe stepped to a chair and sank onto the edge, crossing her legs and leaning forward. "Seriously now, what happened with the possible tomato marauder? You sure it wasn't Sawyer?"

"He got away, I reported it to the police—who did nothing, by the way, except increase patrols for the night— and I confirmed it wasn't Sawyer." Regan picked up the nearest pen and tapped it on the desk.

"Don't you think it's time to show that weird letter to the police?"

A knock sounded on the front door, followed by a male voice. "Regan? You in here?"

Her hand jerked, and the pen flew across the desk and skid under the filing cabinet. "Back here," she called out.

Monroe's eyebrows rose and she mouthed, "That's Sawyer."

"I know," she mouthed back before pasting a smile on her face and rising.

Sawyer filled the doorframe to her office, and her mouth went dry. How could the man look equally as attractive scruffy in grease-covered overalls as he did clean-shaven in nice jeans and a golf shirt? Out of all the errant, inappropriate thoughts ricocheting through her head and body, the one that stuck was regret she'd never gotten to gauge the softness of his beard.

"Howdy there, Monroe."

"Hi Sawyer." Monroe rose, nodding her head and looking back and forth between them. The small, amused light in her eyes told Regan to expect an interrogation later. "I need to get cleaned up before Cade gets home."

Sawyer stepped farther into her office to let Monroe sidle by. The bell on her front door jangled, then silence descended. Sawyer looked too big and masculine for her office. Although she did work setting up spec homes for local builders, women with too much time and money on their hands were her bread and butter. Her office looked like *Southern Living* and *Better Homes and Gardens* had mated and produced a litter of peach and pink and flowered swatches. Had she looked as out of place in his domain as he appeared to be in hers?

"Do you want a drink?" she asked, already swiveling to her filing cabinet.

He stuffed his hands into the pockets of his jeans and shifted on his feet. "Maybe. What'cha got stashed?"

"Some top-shelf Jack."

"Damn, girl. I thought you were a Boone's Farm addict." Humor roughened his voice.

"I matured." She gave him a half-shrug.

"That you did." Any humor was gone, but his voice retained a rough edge.

She didn't know how to take his comment. Normally, she would be put on the defensive, but nerves kept the outrage at bay, and she was happy to have something to occupy her attention. The glasses tinked against each other as she pulled them and the bottle from the bottom drawer. He took the seat Monroe had recently vacated, lounging back and spreading his legs wide.

She poured a shot worth in each crystal tumbler and slid his toward him. "Hope you don't mind it neat."

He picked up the glass, the overhead light fracturing into a cascade of colors against his wrist. He took a sip and she followed suit, hoping the alcohol would impart a measure of calm to her frazzled state.

"That's good stuff." He hummed and fingered the stack of papers on her desk. On top was one of her many lists. "That is quite the to-do list, Regan. Number one, confirm string orchestra. Number two, Coach Hicks's attire." He looked up. "What does that mean?"

With a flick of her hand, she took the paper. "It's for my block party this weekend. Remember our pinky promise?"

"Yes, but what about Coach Hicks?" His lips twitched around the edge of the glass as he took another sip.

She cleared her dry throat and took a sip of her own. "The football players are manning the popcorn machine."

"What about his attire?"

"You know he likes to wear those polyester shorts that are way too short and tight around his"—she gestured vaguely—"you-know-whats. I'm afraid it will put people off the popcorn."

A second passed before Sawyer's laugh reverberated around her. It came from deep in his chest. He had the best laugh, the most infectious laugh, the sexiest laugh of any she'd ever heard. A chuckle shot out of her in response.

With his face still crinkled and his eyes shining, he poked around some of the other papers on her desk. "You got a list with 'catch tomato marauder, gazebo arsonist, and basket desecrater' in here?"

"No, but you might find one titled, 'How to Drive Sawyer Fournette Around the Bend.'" More giggles escaped.

"That checklist is complete and notarized, sweetheart." He picked up a stapled set of papers. "You got Cottonbloom Bakery to sign a contract?"

"Of course I did. They have agreed to provide a service for payment. If something happens, we both need to be protected. Surely you and Rufus have some sort of written agreement."

He tossed the contract back on the stack. "If jotting some numbers down on a paper napkin counts, then yes, we do."

"Sawyer, what if Rufus doesn't follow through for some reason?"

He made a scoffing sound. "Sometimes you've got to take people on faith and trust them." Any amusement drained away as they stared at each other longer than was comfortable. "Now . . . how about those letters?"

"Yep. The letters." That's what he was here for. Not a semifriendly drink or some laughs or an old-new connection that strengthened every time they were together. She reached into the top drawer and handed over both letters. He'd somehow scrubbed all the black grease off his hands and from under his nails, making the small cuts and red blisters more noticeable. Not so long ago, he'd been a paper-pusher at the auto plant and now he was working as a glorified mechanic.

"Do you like it?"

His head startled up from examining the first letter, the

other still folded closed. "Like it? I'd qualify as a first-class a-hole if I enjoyed reading letters that threatened you."

"Sorry, I didn't mean the letters." She took another sip of whiskey. Heat spread through her stomach, but she wasn't sure if it was a result of the liquor or the protectiveness that stretched a mile wide in his voice. "Working in the shop. It must be quite the change from your job at the factory."

"An understatement." He took a sip too. "But mostly different in a good way. You have no idea what it's like to call a man into your office to tell him he no longer has a job. Good, hardworking men with wives and kids. Women too. Single moms." He tossed back the rest of the drink. "And there wasn't a damn thing I could do except pat their backs and give them information about social services, food banks, career training."

Torment and regret lined his face, and she wanted nothing more than to crawl across the desk to kiss a smile back on it. She leaned forward and clutched the edge. An image of him dumping her on the floor and wiping her cooties off flashed. She forced herself to pick up her glass and murmur a simple, "I'm sorry."

He shook a smile back on his face, but it was strained. "Cade is technically my boss, and I'll be honest, he can sometimes be a bastard, but I don't have a problem going toe-to-toe with him. And if we take it to the toolshed to settle a disagreement, there's no human-resources dragon breathing down my neck."

"So you don't mind doing grunt work on the engines?"

"That's my favorite part. It's why I got into engineering to begin with. We've come up with some amazing concepts already. I even filed my first patent."

The pride in his voice tugged a smile out of her. "Congratulations."

He smiled in return, holding her gaze for so long the

silence built to a crackling tension between them. He cleared his throat, set his empty glass down, and unfolded the second letter. She watched his face for a reaction.

Although she'd told Monroe time and again the letter was amateur and didn't bother her, she'd taken the first letter out and read it so many times, the creases along the folds were pronounced. He held the two side by side.

He hummed, his expression one of concentration, not anxiety.

"It's nothing, right? The work of someone with too much time on their hands."

He flipped the sheets over, but the backs were blank. "I honestly don't know. I mean, a lot of work went into this. If the perpetrator only wanted to disguise her handwriting, why not type something up and print it out, right?"

His use of the word "perpetrator" made the whole thing take on ominous tones. "Wait, why do you assume it's a she?"

"This is not a man's work." He laid the second letter down and pointed to the T. "Look how loopy and formal it is. Not from a *Sports Illustrated* or *Car and Driver*."

"Maybe it's a man who likes *Cosmo*." She smiled when she said it, but her mind whirled around the possibilities. "Or quilting magazines? When I was at the Quilting Bee, I was flipping through a magazine and noticed that pages were missing."

"You think Ms. Martha tore them out to cut the letters?"

"I don't know. I tear out magazine pages all the time for ideas or to show a client a piece of furniture or a layout. For all I know, she has binders of magazine pages just like I do." She gestured to the filing cabinet and the stack of three-inch binders full of pages.

"You want my opinion?"

"You're the only one who doesn't think I'm crazy, so lay it on me."

A smile quirked the corners of his mouth. "Take this to Chief Thomason"—he laid the letters in the middle of her desk—"and ask him to keep up the increased patrols on your street. After reporting the man in your mama's garden, he might take it more seriously."

She waited for more, and when none came, she threw up her hands. "That's it?"

"What are you suggesting? We search the Quilting Bee for incriminating evidence against Ms. Martha? Come on now."

The way he said it drove heat up her face, and she took another sip of whiskey to cover the fact that that's exactly what she'd been suggesting. "You're right. That's way beyond the line."

"Miles beyond. I'm parish commissioner and you're mayor. If either one of us was caught . . ." Sawyer shook his head, his gaze focused somewhere over her shoulder.

"Bad things."

"Very bad." The silence that descended was awkward, their eyes glancing off each other twice before she cleared her throat. He stood and rubbed his big hands up and down his thighs. The movement seemed to be born of the same confusion and uncertainty coursing through her.

She darted a quick glance at his face, but it was back to the same impassivity that had greeted her between bouts of annoyance over the last few years.

He led the way to her front door, but stopped with his hand on the knob, catching her eye. "Listen, be careful, all right? Cottonbloom is safe, but . . . until we know what's going on, don't do anything stupid, okay?"

"Like breaking and entering?" She kept her voice light.

"I know you aren't *that* foolish. I mean things like chasing strange men in the dark."

"But that seems to be my favorite pastime this summer."

He half-turned toward her and leaned in until their faces were inches apart. His face was solemn. "I'm serious, woman. Take care of yourself."

He stepped outside and made his way across the street to his truck. She retreated and locked the door with trembling fingers. His words settled a knot of unease in her chest. Peeking through one of her blinds, she waited until his taillights disappeared.

Danger lurked, and she wasn't at all convinced Sawyer Fournette wasn't the biggest threat of all.

Chapter Eight

Two nights later, Regan eased along the brick wall, her heart pounding, her hand clutching the master key she'd filched from the courthouse offices. It was late enough that full darkness was broken only by the streetlights, but not so late that the streets were deserted. Perhaps she should have waited until the wee hours, but practically speaking, she had a full day of work plus a festival planning meeting the next day.

The sound of a vehicle going over the steel-girded bridge stilled her. The flash of a dark-colored sedan passed. Once it was well into Mississippi, she skulked farther along the alleyway wall toward the back door of the Quilting Bee. Her fingers found the crack in the bricks that went all the way through to the inside, and it guided her to the door.

She looked to either side of her. As of yet she hadn't actually done anything wrong—except "borrow" the master key. But once she opened that door and slipped inside, she could get in big trouble.

Sawyer didn't really believe Ms. Martha was behind the trouble, but Regan couldn't shake her suspicions. She needed proof—one way or another. The key was damp from her death grip, and she poked it at the lock, the darkness both a boon and a hindrance.

A hand pressed against her mouth as an arm circled her waist. Panic whooshed through her. The man's hand muffled her scream. She bucked against a big body and chomped down on the fleshy part of his palm.

"For the love of—"

Sawyer's voice was loud at her ear. She eased up on her bite, but didn't release him. "What are you doing here?" Her words were indistinct around his flesh.

He hesitated before saying, "Same thing you are. Acting about as smart as a sack of nails. Could you drop my hand?"

He wiggled his fingers, and she opened her mouth. They were pressed together back to front, his arm catching her close.

"Sorry, thought for a minute you were my man," she whispered.

"Your man?" The words were sharp.

"The one I chased."

"Him. Yeah, well. I'm not your man."

"We established you weren't." She pushed his arm away and dropped to her hands and knees, patting down the sparse weeds pushing through the gravel. "I dropped the key."

"You have a key?"

She hummed. "How were you planning to get in?"

"I was . . . performing reconnaissance. I hadn't planned on actually breaking in."

"Reconnaissance is for sissies."

He squatted and moved a dandelion aside. "Here it is."

The bridge clacked as another vehicle passed over. Sawyer fit the key into the lock without a fumble. The vehicle hadn't passed them yet, and the hairs on her nape stood up. "Hurry."

He had to jiggle the handle before the dead bolt disengaged. Headlights flashed at the end of the alley as a car turned in their direction. Sawyer opened the door, they fell inside together, and he shut it. The darkness was like being trapped in a sleeping bag, oppressive and anxiety inducing. If she hadn't heard Sawyer breathing and rustling around, panic would have had her throwing herself back outside, jail be damned.

The sound of gravel crunching under tires grew louder and stopped outside of the door.

Sawyer mumbled a curse. "Come on." He grabbed her hand and pulled her through the storeroom. While his steps were sure, she stumbled over various objects strewn in her path.

Car doors slammed outside as Sawyer quickened their pace. They passed through the big storeroom and into the main shop. Light was more plentiful here and she took the lead, tugging him toward the narrow walk-in closet. The smell of cloth puffed out but it appeared there was enough room for them both. The sound of voices wavered from the back.

"Damn, I should have thrown the bolt," he whispered.

She backed into the closet and he followed, closing them in. A sliver of light shone from the bottom of the door; otherwise the room was black and small. All she could think about was the lack of space and her need for air.

Her breathing sped up as though she were running, and a fine sweat broke on her brow. It didn't help that she'd dressed in black yoga pants and a long-sleeved black shirt. The voices in the shop grew louder, and Regan couldn't stem her mounting panic.

"Sawyer." She croaked his name and grabbed the back of his T-shirt with both hands.

He shushed her, but turned and wrapped both his arms around her as if sensing her need. Her arms found their way around his shoulders, her face pressed into his neck. Instead of making her even more uncomfortable, the feel of him against her cooled the heat of her panic. She concentrated on the pulse of his heart against her lips. The beat was steady and calm, and her heart sought the same.

Her panic ebbed away and was replaced by something else entirely. The darkness, the intimacy, the comfort all worked to lower her inhibitions. It was as if they were caught in another dimension, one where they hadn't broken each other's hearts.

She lifted her head, her nose brushing against his. His lips were close, very close. She wasn't sure which one of them moved, but their lips grazed. The slight touch shouldn't have started her body throbbing for his—but it did.

Like an addict, she needed more, even knowing the consequences. She touched her lips to his again and sighed. Later perhaps the shame and self-flagellation would come, the questions of what was she thinking and why had she instigated the touch, but the darkness snuffed out any inconvenient thoughts.

So long. It had been so long. If he pushed her away and gave them up because of her foolishness, it had all been worth it for the single blazing memory of his lips on hers once more.

He didn't push her away, though. He skimmed his hand up her spine to cup the back of her head, his fingers winding in her hair. His lips moved against hers, parting and sucking her bottom lip between his teeth and nipping.

She slid her tongue along his upper lip. He released her bottom lip and dabbed his tongue against hers. She was aware enough of the voices still outside the closet door to still the moan that threatened to overtake her.

The kiss was sensual and intimate. It wasn't like any kiss she'd ever experienced, even in her past life with him. Pent-up need and lust had her tightening her arms. The hand in her hair fisted and tugged, the prickles along her scalp registering as pleasure and speeding through her body. She pressed closer to give her aching breasts an outlet. He curved his other hand over her backside and squeezed. The heat from his palm felt like it could incinerate her thin cotton yoga pants.

He shifted them around until she was against the door. The hinges creaked slightly and they stilled, tongues touching, his leg pressed between hers. She fisted a hand in his soft hair, longer than it had ever been when they'd been together. After a few beats when nothing momentous happened, they resumed the mind-numbing tumble into pleasure.

His hips bucked into her, and her pelvis tilted to cradle his hardness. She squirmed, raising her leg to hook around his thigh, opening herself further. Her head lolled against the door and his lips glided down, gently biting the tender flesh. His hands trekked up from her hips to circle her torso, his thumbs close to the undersides of her breasts. She arched, her body begging for more.

An outer door slammed shut, the sound echoing in the empty store. Reality crashed down. He lifted his head, but kept his body against her. His expression was a mystery in the dark, and she wasn't sure if she was grateful or not.

What were they doing? The same question seemed to occur to him because he took a step back and braced his hands on the door, caging her in. Not that there was anywhere to escape to inside the closet. She didn't want to leave anyway.

"They're gone." His whisper sounded strained, and relief made her knees wobble more than his kiss had. At least she hadn't been the only one affected. One thing he couldn't fake was his hard-on.

"Was it the police?"

"Looked like Deputy Preston's cruiser. Let's be thankful he didn't find us. There would be no talking ourselves out of getting arrested. The man is a total hard-ass."

"How in the world could you see? And how did you navigate the storage area with no light?"

"I have good eyes. All the Fournettes do. We were born night hunters, I guess." She felt more than saw his shrug. While her eyes had adjusted as well as they could, there wasn't much light to draw on.

"How did I never know that?"

His chuckle helped to dissipate the sexual currents. "Didn't want you to know I was eyeballing you in the dark back in the day when we hooked up."

"You are so bad." No heat was behind her words. His confession made her feel more nostalgic than anything.

"You were so sweet and shy with me back then. Didn't want to scare you." He tucked her hair behind her ear, and not expecting it, she startled slightly at his touch. She barely stopped herself from nuzzling into his hand.

She needed to get back on solid ground. "We'd better get out of here in case they come back. Those orange prison jumpsuits would not look good on me."

"I don't know, you could make just about anything look good." He opened the door and she stumbled backward, out of the closet. His compliment was just as unbalancing.

"Since we're here we might as well take a gander. It's not like we're going to set the place on fire or steal anything."

The smile he aimed at her made her press a hand over her heart. The damn thing actually fluttered. It had been a long time since he'd turned the force of his charm on her, and it seemed the years hadn't tempered her girlish reaction. If anything, the years without his smile made her aware of how much she'd missed it. Missed him.

She tried to cover her discomfiture with tease. "Well, if they come back and we get arrested, get ready for some good old boy named Bubba to make you his bitch in prison."

He laughed, and the sound coasted through her body, soothing the raw nerve endings. She wanted to record his laugh, put it on repeat, and wallow in the sound. She touched her kiss-swollen lips to find them upturned. Not a pageant-style smile but an eye-squinching grin that would earn her mother's disapproval.

She cleared her throat and firmed her traitorous mouth into a line. "I'll show you where I saw the can."

The meager light from the front window bled only a few feet into the storeroom, but it was enough. The tarp was where she remembered, against the near wall. She lifted it to find . . . nothing. She ruffled the canvas as if to summon the can with magic.

"I swear it was right here." She pointed at the empty spot where not even a ring of dust or moisture remained.

He hummed and sniffed the heavy canvas. "It smells a bit like gas, but it's hard to say."

"I'm not making this up, Sawyer." Her tone veered defensive.

"You are many things, but delusional is not one of them."

"Thanks. I think." She rolled her eyes knowing he could probably see her in the dark. Sure enough, the white of his smile flashed. "I'll bet she moved it. Can't you use your super-power eyesight and search for it?"

He scanned the room. "I'm good, but not that good, and it's too risky to turn on a light. I'm sure they'll be upping the patrols tonight. You still parked out front of your shop?"

"I am."

"Good. They'll assume you're working late. Let's hit it."

He led the way to the back door, and she kept hold of the back of his shirt. He turned the dead bolt, cracked the door open, and checked outside. With a chuck of his head, she slipped by him and pressed herself against the brick wall, trying to make herself invisible. The night teemed with noise in comparison with the pall of the shop.

He locked the door and grabbed her hand. He helped her up and over the hip-high wall that marked the far side of the alley. Behind it was a gravel lot she hoped would turn into more businesses. She'd pushed the zoning changes through the previous year. A line of crepe myrtles formed the boundary of the back of her street.

The dark line of the building that housed her shop along with three other businesses was a stark line. She didn't have a storage area at the back of her shop or the room to pull her truck around to load anything from her office, so she rarely used the back door.

He hesitated under the drooping pink blossoms. "Which one?"

She dropped his hand to fish out her key. The lock turned and the door opened with a loud squeak of disuse. Once they were inside, the adrenaline coursing through her eased, leaving her spent. She flipped on her office light and plopped into the chair behind her desk. Sawyer sat across from her and rested his elbows on his knees, scrubbing his hands through his hair.

Would he mention their impromptu seven minutes in heaven? She blinked, seeing him clearly for the first time. His T-shirt was black, his jeans so worn, the knee was fraying into a rip. His hair was tousled and his shirt was halfway untucked. She had done that. She ran her tongue over her lips in remembrance.

"What a night. I wouldn't turn down a shot of that whiskey you have stashed." He let his hands dangle between his knees and looked up with a half-smile.

"Of course, of course." She blew out a steadying breath and turned to pour them both a shot. If he planned to ignore their epic make-out session, then so would she.

He raised his glass. "Here's to breaking the law."

"Here's to not getting caught."

A knock reverberated. She bobbled her glass, managing to spill most of the whiskey down her shirt. Rising, she brushed at her shirt and shifted back and forth.

"Ohmigoodness, what if it's the deputy? What if he knows?" The sense of safety was shattered and the meteoric rise to panic was steeper with this adrenaline rush.

Sawyer put his hands on her shoulders and squeezed until she stopped shuffling and looked from her wet shirt to him. "Settle down. The police are probably checking on things. That's all. Go answer the door and tell them you were working late and you appreciate their kindness in checking on you."

She nodded like a bobblehead, but his sense of calm spread outward and brought her down a notch. Pageants had taught her to control her nerves, and on the walk to the front door, the trembles in her body subsided. Although nothing could get her heart out of her throat, no one would be able to tell through her smile.

She glanced through the shade. Sawyer was right. Deputy Preston stood like a bear on the other side, feet braced apart and an answering scowl to her smile. He might have been handsome if it wasn't for his air of surliness.

She opened the door, but didn't invite him inside. He peered over her head into her shop. "Evening, Deputy. Did you finally catch wind of the man who was in Mother's garden?"

She hoped to put him on the defensive, but his voice held no hint he was chagrinned. "No, ma'am, and without a description, we're not likely to find him. You haven't seen anyone prowling around, have you?'

"No." She pursed her lips and drew the word out as if really considering the matter. "But I've been back in the office."

His eyes narrowed and coasted down her shirt. He wasn't the ogling type, which meant he was probably making note of her wet shirt and the fact she smelled like a distillery. "I came by earlier and knocked, but you didn't answer."

"I like to listen to music."

"I didn't hear music."

"I use earphones."

"I didn't see a light on."

"In the dark." She tittered an unnatural laugh and tapped her temple. "I find it spurs the old noggin. Helps me with decorating ideas."

He leaned closer, and she leaned away. He took a deep breath. "There's been some suspicious activity."

"What kind?"

"The suspicious kind. In light of recent events, I would advise you to close up shop and head home. Surely"—his gaze coasted down her torso again, and the heat that flared from her body probably vaporized the alcohol into even smellier fumes—"whatever you're working on can wait until morning."

"Certainly it can. I'll wrap things up and head out." She smiled and tried to close the door. His boot inserted itself.

"Are you all right to drive? I can give you a lift home if need be."

The small act of kindness was outweighed by the fact he probably thought she was an alcoholic. "I'm fine. This was an accident. I'll even take one of those breathalyzer things if you want." She schooled her face into what she hoped conveyed a serious, very sober civic leader.

He harrumphed, tipped his hat, and ambled back to his patrol car, parked behind hers. She waited until his taillights turned the corner before turning off the lights and returning to her office. Sawyer was tipped back in the chair, his booted feet on her desk, a huge smile on his face.

"You like to sit in the dark listening to music and drinking, huh?"

"What was I supposed to say? Worst case, he thinks I have a drinking problem."

"He didn't want to give up any info, did he?"

She clasped her hands behind her neck. "You think he thinks I was up to no good?"

"He can't prove anything, but we'd better skedaddle. He'll be back by sooner rather than later if I had to guess. Can I bum a ride to my truck? Not good if he catches me on this side of the river."

She would worry about putting everything to rights in the morning. Right now, she wanted to be safe inside her house. "Where'd you leave it?"

"Outside of Tally's gym."

She stepped onto the sidewalk first, taking a careful look around. No sign of Deputy Preston or anyone else for that matter. She gestured Sawyer outside and locked up behind him. She slid behind the wheel and had the car started before Sawyer managed to fold himself into the passenger seat.

"How can you stand this tin can?" he muttered.

"It's fun to drive and easy to park. It helps that I'm not built like a linebacker."

"I was a wide receiver, thank you very much."

"Not for long." She couldn't stop a burst of laughter. How could she ever forget their eyes meeting over the thirty-yard line before one of Cottonbloom, Mississippi's, linebackers leveled him?

"That hit that was all your fault. Distracting me in that short skirt."

"Ten of us were lined up all dressed exactly alike. Why do you blame me?"

"None of them had legs like yours."

"Please." She shot him a side-eye, but a dark secret place in her heart stretched and sighed as if awakened by the events of the night. She was inexplicably happy, which made her understandably worried.

His truck was the only one on the street. If the deputy had cruised through the Mississippi side, he might add things up and actually get the correct answer.

"Do you still have the master key? I'll need to return it first thing in the morning."

"I don't want to know, do I?" Amusement and apprehension threaded his voice as he held the key out to her. A reddened place where she chomped him was visible.

She took his hand in hers, dropped the key into the cup holder, and brushed her fingers across his palm. "I'm so sorry. I came close to breaking skin."

"I deserved it coming up to you like I did. Was only thinking about keeping you quiet. If something like that happens again, you bite even harder, you hear?" This time only worry registered.

She nodded. She should let go of his hand, but her fingers kept on stroking the callused skin of his palm. His hands had always been rougher than other boys' because his life had been different from the boys in her school obsessed with video games.

The kiss they'd shared squatted between them, as yet unacknowledged but very much alive. He pulled his hand from hers and levered himself out of the car.

Ducking his head down, he said, "Okay. Well, I guess I'll see you around."

"Sure thing. Around."

He disappeared into his truck, and she mashed the accelerator, squealing forward a few feet before getting her foot under control. So that was it. He wanted to act like the kiss never happened. Maybe in a couple of days the feel of his lips and hands and body against hers would fade and she'd be able to do the same.

Chapter Nine

Darkness had fallen over Cottonbloom when Regan crossed the bridge into Louisiana and turned down River Street. The streetlights made the colorful brick fronts glow with a vitality that the Mississippi side couldn't match. Both sides had their strengths, but she couldn't deny the pull of the laid-back charm of Cottonbloom, Louisiana. Too many storefronts sat empty though. If she were Sawyer, she'd offer some incentives to get businesses in and operating.

But she wasn't Sawyer. She wasn't in charge of this side of the river, which is why she was once again skulking around in the dark. She'd driven her work truck instead of her red Bug. Not that she was up to anything illegal or immoral, but being caught might prove awkward.

Since their breakup, she had cultivated a distorted image of Sawyer—cold, untrustworthy, unreliable. It was the only way she could move forward. But over the summer since they'd both entered the festival competition through *Heart of Dixie,* things had changed between them. They'd gone from ignoring each other's existence to adversaries to reluctant partners to . . . she wasn't sure.

The image of him she'd clung to cracked, revealing someone who resembled the boy she'd loved. And the kiss in the Quilting Bee's storeroom had reminded her that some things never die, but they can change. She couldn't stop thinking about him, dreaming about him. He was haunting her. The problem was she wasn't sure which Sawyer had set up camp in her head—past or present.

The bare patch in his flowers had given her an idea. Another really dumb idea. She stopped the truck close to where she remembered the bare area was and got out. No one was around. The whine of the tailgate as she lowered it made her grimace and glance around again. She pulled one of the three pots of flowers to her hip and grabbed a trowel.

The flowers represented more than a beautification project for Sawyer. She remembered lying in the truck bed with him, staring at the stars, and listening to him talk. It was rare he talked about his life in the trailer with Cade and Tally. Looking back, she wished she'd asked more questions about his reality, but she'd been too young and immature to recognize or understand how difficult things were for him. But he loved to talk about his parents and his life before they were killed.

Laughter and love and lazy summers. He'd talked about his mother and how much she reveled in the chaos of her flowers. He'd promised to plant a field of flowers as beautiful and wild as Regan someday.

He hadn't planted these for her, but every time she looked at them, she was cast back to that night under the stars. The love that had burst between them. A love she'd assumed would last forever. The flowers had come to mean something to her, and she wanted to fix them for him.

She'd planted a similar bed of flowers in the back of her house, not wanting to examine the whys behind the sentimental move. Easier on her heart if she'd planted simple hostas. After she finished her glass of red wine that evening, she'd dug up a quarter of her flower bed.

Now here she was, trowel in hand and on her knees, skulking around in the dark like she was a criminal. It didn't take long to uproot the old flower roots and transplant new ones. She watered them from the two cans she'd loaded as well. Besides the disturbed dirt, the bed looked healed, the riot of color restored.

She put everything back in the truck and then hesitated. The abandoned Cottonbloom Park sat at the end of the street. If she was already acting like a fool, she might as well finish on a high note.

Not a single car had driven past her. A crazy Thursday night in Cottonbloom. She ran-walked down the street, slowing only when she reached the grassy section leading to the playground. The streetlights didn't reach this far into the darkness and the moon had yet to rise high enough to light her way.

Her eyes adjusted slowly, and she kept her gaze on her feet to avoid roots and rocks and mole trails. The falling-down dugout was even darker. She pulled her phone out and used the light to find the board. It was her board, and she wanted it.

Putting her phone to the side, she grasped the board and pulled. Nothing budged. Of course, Sawyer would pick the one board that had stood the test of time. She banged on the board with a palm-sized rock to no avail. Considering the wood, she ran her fingers over the inscription, inspiration flashing. Her trowel.

She turned around. A dark mass of a man stood at the exit. Her heart ramped from normal to frenzied so fast she felt lightheaded. Before she could pull in a deep breath to scream, the figure spoke.

"What the hell are you doing out here, Regan Lovell?"

Sawyer. With blatant accusation in his voice. Not that she could blame him. She had gotten a little tipsy and spray-painted *Tomatoes Rule, Crayfish Drool* across his freshly painted, yellow-bricked wall along River Street not two months earlier. Not so far-fetched he would believe she was up to no good. Actually, she would prefer him to think that over the truth.

"I'm just . . . messing around."

"I heard banging."

"Did you?" An uncomfortable laugh escaped, which only compounded her air of guilt. She took a step closer to him to distance herself from the message.

"Are you looking to steal something?" His voice had softened and lost its accusatory edge.

She hesitated, sensing he knew exactly why she was there. She'd given herself away the afternoon he'd finally revealed its location. "It's not stealing. It belongs to me."

"It belongs to the city even if it is falling apart."

"It was written to me, and I want it." The vehemence in her voice took her aback and she tried to mitigate the emotion. "I mean, you know, whatever. It's just that it's been a thorn in my side for a while. And I want it gone."

"What are you going to do with it?" He took a step toward her.

"Burn it."

He huffed, but she couldn't see him well enough to categorize it as amusement or disgust. "You want to wipe me out of your memories, don't you?"

Sometimes she wished she could do just that. Then it wouldn't hurt so bad when she thought about him. He could be the leader of a neighboring town and that's all. Not a former lover who still inflamed her and made her long for unattainable things.

She kept silent. Any answer would reveal too much.

"Are you going to pretend last night never happened?" he asked.

She took a quick breath and matched what sounded like hurt feelings with equal amounts of defensiveness. "You were the one pretending."

He took a step closer. She held her ground even though one of her feet slid backward on the dirt floor. "It's almost like it was a dream, isn't it?"

At least he hadn't said "nightmare." She rubbed her lips together. He took another step. The heat of his body and fresh scent enveloped her. He'd showered recently. Maybe he'd worked late. Maybe his hair was still damp. Maybe the stubble from the night before was growing into a beard.

"It was dark and secluded and we were kind of forced into one another. It had nothing to do with you and me. Just like the night of the rabbits. It was the situation, right?" Why had she asked instead of stated? And why had she mentioned the night he had pressed her into the sweet-smelling grass and left her a puddle of lustful confusion?

"Exactly. It's dark and secluded now too." Another step and his chest grazed hers. She lifted her face toward his, every nerve ending straining for him.

"It is that. And we're close."

"How do we keep managing to get ourselves into these dark and secluded situations?" He circled her nape with his hand. It was all the encouragement her body needed. She pitched into him, her arms rising to circle his shoulders. Her fingers wound in his damp hair, the faint scent of his shampoo niggling at her memories. It was the same one he'd always used even though he could probably afford a salon brand. Practical, solid, sexy Sawyer.

His lips coasted from her temple to her jaw, laying small

kisses along the way. She arched against him, turning her head in search of his mouth. Finally, he kissed her. A stuttering sigh escaped her on contact.

His one hand tightened on her nape while the other coasted down to cup and knead her backside. She whimpered, the noise coming unbidden from her throat. His tongue made gentle forays inside of her mouth, twining with hers. She sucked his bottom lip into her mouth and nipped it. He pulled back with a growly sound that veered humorous.

"You missed this haven't you, baby? I'll bet none of those Mississippi boys made you feel like this."

His words were a dunk in the ice-cold waters of reality. She had spent too long getting him out of her system to regress over one short summer. Pushing off his chest drove her pelvis into his, and she nearly succumbed to temptation. His hard length pressed into her.

The truth was she had missed him. Terribly. Not only physically, but the emotional connection that sparked so readily between them. She twisted against him and he let her go, leaving her stumbling backward two steps before she caught her balance.

Her lips felt swollen and tender and craved more. "This is crazy."

Sawyer tried to calm the storm raging in his body. She was right. One slipup that she had chosen to ignore afterward was one thing. Twice made it seem planned or deliberate or inevitable.

He wouldn't lie to himself and say that he wasn't a little hurt she'd acted unaffected by their epic make-out session in the closet. If the cops had busted them, he wasn't sure he'd have been able to summon anything resembling regret, much less an apology. That kiss had been brewing all summer. Unfortunately, instead of sating his thirst for her, a desperation like a man wandering the desert in search of an oasis had taken hold of him.

Thank goodness she assumed his interest was purely physical and hadn't guessed why he'd run across her two nights in a row. Sleep had been elusive for weeks. Only a drive-by verifying that she was home and safe settled him down. Last night, seeing her car parked in front of her shop so late had settled a hollow worry in his stomach. Seeing her sneaking through the dark had made him want to alternatively shake some sense into her and laugh. Regan Lovell was something else.

And tonight her truck had been gone, leaving him to grip the steering wheel too tight and drive too fast in his search for her. After scouring downtown Cottonbloom, Mississippi, and finding no trace, he had resigned himself to either no sleep back in his bed or watching her house until she was safely home. The anxiety and protectiveness wasn't entirely foreign. It was part of the stew of emotions she'd incited when they were young.

"You're right. Crazy. This festival has obviously screwed with our ability to make rational decisions. We'll either end up in bed together or committed by Labor Day." He froze, trying to pretend the words had only scrolled through his head and hadn't actually come out of his mouth.

"We're not going to end up in bed together." Her voice wavered, but he couldn't pin an emotion to it. Her eyes were wide and her lips still parted. She ran her tongue along her bottom lip for the second time. Crazy. He was being driven crazy. By her.

"Of course we're not. I was joking. Here, if you want that board so bad, I'll get it for you."

"It's down—"

"I can see it." He gave it a yank from the top, feeling it give a fraction.

She chuffed. "I forgot you can see in the dark."

He tugged twice more before the wood splintered where it met the frame of what was once a bench. What came away was a three-foot-long narrow board. He could make out the pen marks but not the actual words. Better really that she take it and burn it. End it.

If the written history of them was destroyed, did that mean it would cease to exist? Would she laugh at him if he insisted on keeping the splintered piece of wood? Would she guess at the sickness that had invaded him over the summer? A sickness that kept her constantly on his mind and in his worries.

"Here. Take it." He forced himself to hold out the piece of wood. Their fingers brushed on the exchange.

"Thanks," she said softly as she wrapped her arms around the piece of wood in a mock embrace.

"Come on. I'll walk you back to your truck."

He led the way back to River Street. The soundtrack to the night was the soft gurgle of the river, the town like a Rockwell painting. Her hair was loose around her shoulders and glinted in the streetlights, looking fierier than normal. Her attire was unusually casual. A silky-looking pink T-shirt, a pair of tight ankle-length jeans, and lace-up mint-green canvas shoes.

The hands that held the board were dirty along with the knees of her jeans. As they approached her truck, her pace quickened and she pulled ahead of him. His gaze went straight to her ass. Beyond the seductive sway, something registered as different.

She was halfway behind the wheel when "the something different" clicked into place. The gouge in his flowers had been repaired with white and purple zinnias. The dirt freshly turned and still wet.

The truck's engine cranked, sputtering. He turned around and knocked on the window. She stared straight ahead and pumped the gas until the motor settled into an even idle. He knocked again, and her gaze darted toward his, her bottom lip pulled between her teeth.

Finally she lowered the window and graced him with one of her pageant-fake smiles. "Is there something else you needed?"

"Anything you want to tell me?"

"Yes." Her gaze searched the sky. "Your hair is sticking up. You don't want it to dry that way, do you?"

She'd been the one running her hands through it while they'd been kissing. He shifted so they could both see her handiwork. "The flowers?"

"They're lovely."

"You filled my bed." He closed his eyes and wrangled his tongue. "I mean you filled the gap in my flower bed."

"No." She lilted the word into a question. He took one of her hands off the steering wheel and turned it over, rubbing his thumb over her dirt-streaked palm and quirking his eyebrows. "All right, maybe I did."

They held gazes. A look he hadn't seen in a long time softened her face, and her hand twitched in his as if she wanted to take hold of him. What would she do if he pulled her in for another kiss? It had nothing to do with where they were or how dark and secluded it was. It had everything to do with her. He whispered her name. "Regan."

"It's to make up for the wall thing a couple of months ago." She jerked her hand out of his. "I have to go. It's late and I have a long day tomorrow."

The truck moved forward, forcing him to drop his hands and step back. He watched her make a U-turn and head over the bridge into Mississippi. He stared at the flowers and rubbed a hand over his chest.

Maybe it was to make up for vandalizing his wall, but he hoped not. He squatted next to the flowers and fingered a delicate bloom. Had whatever infected him infected her too? The passion that exploded whenever they were within eyesight was familiar yet completely new. They weren't kids fumbling in the back of a truck or in a boat anymore.

Life had changed them, made them wary and protective. But the flashes of her sweetness were tearing down his walls. He wasn't sure if either of them could handle exhuming the hurts buried in the past. But for the first time in a long time, he wanted to try.

Chapter Ten

Sawyer adjusted his blue and silver tie and smoothed a hand down his charcoal gray suit jacket. After spending his recent days in coveralls, he'd forgotten how constricting a suit could be. It felt like he was wearing a costume. Maybe that was good, because Sawyer had a part to play this evening. Charming but not creepy, knowledgeable but not a blowhard, tough but not an asshole.

He checked his phone one last time. He was meeting with Terry Lowe, VP of Innovations for Nautical Engines. Nerves akin to a final exam tumbled his stomach. This was a test. If he failed, then Cade and Richard might rethink bringing him into the partnership.

He lounged in a leather chair in the entry of the Cottonbloom Country Club, tapping his fingers against the armrest. A woman with dark hair cut into a severe bob pushed through the front doors. She wore a curve-hugging dress in dark blue and high heels and appeared to be in her midthirties. She was attractive in a fierce way.

Although Regan was typically in skirts or dresses, her eclectic style, strawberry blonde hair, and frequent blushes gave the impression of a barely restrained passion. Like she didn't mind getting a little wild and dirty with a country boy in a dark closet or a dugout. He wasn't sure which one of them had instigated the kiss in the closet, but he'd been the one to touch her first in the dugout. He hadn't been able to help himself. Lord knows, ever since their roll in the grass earlier that summer, he hadn't been able to get the feel of her out of his head. Soft curves and sweetness.

He gave himself a mental slap. Thoughts of her were becoming increasingly frequent and distracting. He needed to concentrate on tonight.

Sawyer stared beyond the fierce woman to the doors, willing Lowe to show up. The waiting notched up his anxiety. He didn't notice the woman approaching until she was nearly at his side. "Excuse me"—her voice was clipped yet husky—"are you Mr. Fournette?"

Sawyer rose. "I am."

The woman extended a hand, her nails tipped hot pink. "I'm Terry Lowe from Nautical Engines."

He pasted a smiled over his shock and took her hand in a firm shake. "Ms. Lowe. A pleasure to make your acquaintance. How are you enjoying Cottonbloom?"

"Charming, but hot." She laughed a throaty laugh. Several people glanced in their direction.

"Fall is the prettiest season, and the most pleasant temperature wise." He gestured her toward the entrance to the restaurant. He wasn't a member of the club, but for a premium, nonmembers could dine. And until Rufus's Meat and Three upgraded from paper napkins to cloth, the country club offered the only fine dining on either side of the river.

The maître d' led them to a table overlooking the golf course and the sunset, giving the feel that this was a date and not a business meeting. In fact, couples, some married some not, seemed to occupy most of the tables. Out of habit, he pulled the chair out for Ms. Lowe and helped her scoot under the table.

She smiled as he rounded the cozy table to his chair. "Why thank you, Mr. Fournette. I suppose it's true what they say about Southern gentlemen." Was it his imagination or had her tone been flirty and her eyes appreciative?

"My mama made sure my brother and I knew the basics. Open doors, always give up your seat for a lady, never steal a kiss on the first date." He cursed his tongue. Why had he said that?

She folded her arms over the menu. "I must say, you didn't seem surprised that I was a woman. That either means you did your research or you're good at hiding your reactions, which should make our negotiations lively indeed."

He should have dug further into her bio, but he hadn't. Not that he was going to admit that. If she was already talking negotiations, then she was interested in their design and he needed to stay on his toes. He sensed a tiger behind her casual, flirty manner. He spread his hands, shrugged, and matched her tone. "I like to be prepared."

"So do I." A single, overly plucked eyebrow arched upward. "Your brother recently relocated to Cottonbloom, yes?"

"Yes. Although, our shop is actually not in Cottonbloom, Mississippi, but outside of Cottonbloom, Louisiana, in the parish."

"I see." She drew the words out, obviously blind to the situation. "What does that mean exactly?"

On comfortable ground, Sawyer took out his phone, pulled up a map, and explained the lay of the land— literally. Outsiders often didn't realize Louisiana was divided in parishes and not counties. He explained his role as commissioner overseeing the entire parish, not just the city of Cottonbloom.

While they sipped on an expensive white wine Richard had recommended he order, he regaled her with old folk stories of rivalries and family feuds and even Romeo and Juliet–type love stories. By the time he'd finished and she'd asked all her questions, a good half hour had passed and the atmosphere between them was comfortable and friendly. They had even progressed to first names.

In the break, they placed their orders. The waiter emptied the bottle of wine into their glasses and promised another bottle with their meal. He sat back wondering if he should bring up the engine design now or after they ate.

"So you grew up on the Louisiana side of the river." She trailed a hot pink–tipped finger around the top of her glass, a faint tone coming from the crystal. He nodded. "Did you ever cross over and try to date one of the Mississippi girls?"

He swallowed a too-large gulp of wine and sputtered a cough.

Terry leaned back, her long crossed legs bumping his. "I'm taking that for a yes."

He opened his mouth to deny it when a flash of red caught his eye at the entrance. Regan weaved her way through the tables, coming inexorably closer. She had yet to notice him.

Pain shot through his jaw where his teeth were grinding. She wasn't alone. Andrew Tarwater, Junior had his hand on the small of her back and was following close enough to whisper in her ear. The man's blond hair gleamed in the brilliant rays of the setting sun. He looked like an old advertisement for Coppertone. All good-looking sunny smiles.

Sawyer wasn't sure if his antipathy for the man was born from Cade's resentments or if it was Andrew's general air of smarminess. He was the Mississippi golden boy, given everything and not faltering, becoming a successful, sought-after attorney. Sawyer wasn't aware the man was courting Regan, but it made sense. Once Monroe rebuffed Andrew for Cade, why wouldn't he try to catch

Regan? She was successful in her own right and needed to be carrying a damn fire hazard sign in that sexy red dress.

Their tables were catty-corner and less than twenty feet away. Andrew treated her as he would a date, pulling out her chair and leaning down to say something in her ear. The jerkwad might have even touched her ear with his fish lips. Her laugh carried through the soft murmur of conversation and piano music and seemed to grab his necktie and tighten it.

Terry put her hand over his, making him aware that his fingers had been involuntarily attempting to tap a hole through the table. "Is everything okay, Sawyer? You look ill."

Regan chose that moment to sweep her gaze around the room. The residual smile that curved her lips from whatever asinine thing Andrew had whispered fell into a tight line. Her gaze took everything in, including Terry's hand over his. He didn't move. Let her think he was on a date with another woman. After all, she hadn't said a single word about seeing Andrew Tarwater.

Two hot-as-sin kisses notwithstanding, she and Sawyer weren't dating. Not even remotely. They were only seeing each other so often because of the festivals. He'd made the mistake of getting all warm and gooey over her planting the flowers, and now he felt like a fool. A sickening feeling twisted his gut.

He forced a smile to his face and pulled his hand away, tucking it under his leg. "No, I'm fine."

Terry half-retuned her smile, but her eyes were suspicious. The woman was sharp, and Sawyer needed to fucking pull it together. Luckily, the waiter delivered their meals and the second bottle of wine. Sawyer had ordered steak, and Terry, wanting to eat local, ordered crayfish and grits. He sawed at the rare cut of meat with grim satisfaction. Some of the primal frustration he didn't want to examine appeased.

"Tell me about the local economies."

He was grateful for the distraction and described the blue-collar workforce and the crayfish and catfish industry on his side of the river. He lost his train of thought twice. Once when Regan leaned over her arms and showcased the top curves of her breasts in the V-neck dress, and once when her laugh drew his gaze, her head thrown back, flickering candlelight illuminating the pale column of her neck.

Terry regained his attention by pushing her plate away, leaving half her grits but having eaten the crayfish. He had no idea what he'd been saying and hoped he'd at least been communicating in complete sentences.

"That was delicious but I can't eat another bite."

As he'd only been stabbing his baked potato the last few minutes, he pushed his back as well. The atmosphere changed in an intangible way that had Sawyer's brain perking up. This was it.

"I reviewed your proposal, and I'll admit I'm impressed."

"Impressed enough to license the design?"

"Let's not get ahead of ourselves, Sawyer." She leaned forward, her husky voice dropping into Kathleen Turner sexed-up regions. "There are some modifications I wish to discuss. Also, the exclusivity of the design."

"As in you want exclusive licensing?" He did a mental fist pump. Exclusivity meant a much higher price.

"We don't want to license the design. We want to buy it."

Sawyer didn't immediately say no, even though that would be the eventual answer. "We don't sell our designs, we only license them."

"Up until now." She leaned back, took a sip of wine, and aimed a look he could only interpret as sultry over the rim. A foot grazed up his calf. He shifted. "Everything has a price."

"Not everything." He meant to say more, but Regan drew his gaze for the millionth time that evening.

She was standing and adjusting a ridiculous—make that a ridiculously sexy—red high heel, one hand on the table for balance. The top of her bodice gaped and even from the distance, a strip of black lace was visible. Sure enough, Andrew Tarwater was transfixed, a hungry, gaping, village-idiot expression on his face. A couple of feet closer and his face would be buried in her cleavage.

When had Regan gained such an impressive rack, anyway? If he recalled—and he could picture them in infinite detail—her breasts had been small, but firm and tipped with the prettiest pink nipples. They were, in a word, perfect.

Terry's voice lilted in a question, the words garbled and lost forever. He swiveled back to her and hummed something that could be interpreted as an affirmative or as a negative, and she appeared suitably confused.

He half-rose and tossed his napkin on the table. "Would you excuse me? I won't be a moment."

"Certainly." Her eyebrow arched in a quizzical, ironic way.

Probably she thought he needed to discuss something with Cade or Richard. And he did. But right now his thoughts were consumed by the swaying red backside that was slipping away.

Regan pushed her hair around with trembling fingers and stared into the bathroom mirror. It was next to impossible to concentrate on Andrew's proposal with Sawyer sitting a few tables away with one of the most beautiful, sophisticated women Regan had ever seen.

Not that it mattered who Sawyer Fournette was getting busy with. It hadn't mattered in a decade. It certainly hadn't mattered when she'd walked into his dorm room to find a naked woman in his bed.

The anger and pain of his past betrayal that had been slipping away in the light of their tentative partnership and unresolved lust tightened around her heart like a chain. Sawyer hadn't changed one bit, but she had. She was no longer the lovestruck girl who thought he was different from all the other boys. Special. Trustworthy.

She'd never made that mistake again. No man was worth getting hurt over. Why had she gone and planted those flowers and kissed him . . . again? He probably thought he had the upper hand after her sentimental act. No more getting too friendly, and definitely no more kissing. A two-time mistake she wouldn't compound a third time.

She needed to pull it together so she could confidently discuss upholstery and color schemes and hardwood choices with Andrew. Redoing the Tarwater and Tarwater offices would be a big project, one she could use in her advertising if everything went well.

She blew out a breath, stretched her neck, put a hand on a jutted hip, and smiled. It wouldn't have even put her in the running for Miss Congeniality, but it would have to do. Feeling less frazzled, she pushed the bathroom door open.

A hand circled her arm and tugged. Sawyer Fournette was leading her down a hallway. Surprise kept her compliant. Dishes and the calls of "order up" echoed from the kitchen. He continued on and rounded the corner, the short arm of the hall dead-ending into a janitor's closet.

Sawyer's eyes were glittering and hot, his mouth pulled into a frown.

"What the hell—"

"Why are you—"

They spoke on top of one another, cutting off at the same time.

"Why'd you pull me out here?" She crossed her arms under her breasts, and when he didn't immediately answer, she asked like a taunting third-grader, "Huh? Huh?"

"Thought you should know you're flashing the whole damn restaurant." He wagged a finger a few inches from her chest.

Involuntarily, she splayed a hand over the V-neck of her wrap dress. The push-up bra had been overkill, but when she'd looked in her full-length mirror at home, her "normal" boobs had not done the beautiful dress justice.

"I have not."

"You're wearing a black lace bra. Am I right?"

Dear Lord, he was right. And he'd noticed that from four tables away. She gasped and covered her mouth. Was her décolletage the reason Andrew's attention kept wandering and why he had been unusually flirty?

She stepped back and leaned against the cool cement-block wall. Sawyer followed and bracketed her with his hands on either side of her shoulders.

"Are you seriously dating that jackass?"

"Dating." Instead of coming out like a question, her shock made it sound more like a statement.

"Ah, hell, Regan. He's a snake. You know his daddy is defending Sam Landry. And, didn't Monroe and him go out for a while? What happened to girl code?"

"He and Monroe never dated."

"Be that as it may, I've been watching him watch you, and it ain't pretty."

The sophisticated, smooth-talking, suit-wearing Sawyer had been replaced by a rough-and-ready redneck. Danger crackled. Her body responded in the exact way she wished it wouldn't. Her nipples had tightened against the rough lace of her bra, and her back arched. God, she had no control over the primal call. It was embarrassing.

"What's wrong with him looking at me?" The defensiveness edging her voice had little to do with his line of questioning and more to do with hiding her physical response.

"The man looked like he wanted to bury his face"—his gaze dipped and held—"down there in front of everyone in that restaurant. He wants you for dessert."

"So what? Doesn't mean I'm on the menu." She paused for full effect. "At least not yet."

He slapped a palm against the wall. "Are you and Tarwater fucking when you couldn't seem to get enough of me last night?"

Even as his question offended her on so many levels, a zing of satisfaction sped through her blood straight into her heart making it beat faster. "That is none of your business, now is it? Anyway, you and Cruella de Vil out there seem to be mighty cozy. Are you—" She couldn't bring herself to use the F-word. The thought of that woman with Sawyer drove a spike into her chest. "Are you taking her home?"

The Cruella de Vil comparison was petty and mostly untrue, except for the severe cut of her gleaming black hair and her sultry, evil air. The woman waiting for Sawyer was probably perfectly nice. Hadn't stopped her sudden urge to take the woman down like a linebacker when she'd seen the bright pink–tipped hand on top of Sawyer's. But Regan had been taught better than that. Anyway, as mayor, she had an image to uphold.

Scant inches separated their bodies. She could pull him closer or he could press her against the wall like he had in the closet. His gaze coasted over her face as if searching for answers. Emotional fissures cut the taut mask of his face, startling in their intensity. Frustration, anger, longing. Or was she only projecting the stabs of her own feelings onto him?

The air around them grew stormy, dense with portent. The crash of a tray of plates around the corner cut them apart like lightning. He stepped away and ruffled his hair, checking his watch. With a muttered curse flung in her direction, he stalked off, out of sight in two seconds.

Whoa. She wasn't sure what had even happened or what it meant, if anything. Without a watch or her phone, she wasn't sure how much time had even passed. Two minutes? An hour? How long had they stood there not touching?

She skirted the mess of broken dishes and the workers in white cleaning it up and strode back into the dining room, her gaze magnetized to Sawyer, who was back at his table with his date. He didn't seem to feel the same pulse of residual energy from the hallway, every iota of his attention directed at the woman across from him.

She rejoined Andrew and took a surreptitious glance at her phone. Twelve minutes had passed. Disorientation assailed her, as if she'd travelled through a black hole and been spit back out. What had she and Andrew been discussing?

"So sorry about that. Ran into someone I knew."

"No worries. I know how you women like to gab in bathrooms. Always go in pairs, don't you?"

She smiled and hummed at his slightly misogynistic comment and predatory smile. Did she have Sawyer to thank for pulling off her blinders, or was she misjudging Andrew. "So, can I talk you into bamboo flooring?"

"I believe you could talk me into anything you want."

Nope, he said that with a definite suggestive tone. She ran a finger over her bottom lip, debating her move. His gaze dropped and his tongue darted over his lips as if he really was considering her for dessert.

She adjusted the bodice of her dress and his gaze dropped lower. "Andrew, it's been delightful discussing your needs. I mean your firm's needs. In terms of flooring and lighting and things." The words fell on top of one another, and she calmed herself with a long, slow inhale before continuing. "It's been a long day, and I have festival business and a block party to handle tomorrow. Should we split the check?"

"Already taken care of." He rose and she followed suit, leading the way out. His hand splayed on her back a bit lower than was proper. "An early night, it is."

She stutter-stepped, not sure what to say. Had she inadvertently given him the wrong idea? They'd known each other since grade school. She hadn't thought anything untoward of him inviting her to dinner to discuss a job.

She cast one last look over her shoulder at Sawyer, but he was immersed in his lady-friend. Andrew was at her side. Maybe she should rethink her friendly relationship with Andrew. Maybe she should consider him now that he'd shown a marked interest in her. Why not?

They were both single. He was good-looking in a superficial way. He was successful and driven. She admired that about him. His parents were social-climbing parasites, but the same could be said for her parents. The mere thought of the Lovells and Tarwaters aligning themselves through marriage would send her mother to the hospital in happy shock. She'd quickly recover to plan the wedding though.

Laughter threatened at the absurdity. While she might have ended up back in Cottonbloom after college, she went out of her way to upend expectations. Her mother had been aghast when Regan had run for mayor and horrified when she'd won.

Her red VW Bug stood out like stinkweed in a flowery

patch of BMWs and Mercedes. Andrew had parked next to her and they stood between their cars.

"Thank you for dinner, Andrew. I'll need to stop by your offices next week to take measurements before I work up options. I'll be in touch." She held out her hand.

He hesitated, but clasped her hand. Instead of shaking it, he sandwiched it between both of his. "I don't suppose you'd be interested in a nightcap at my place?"

Sawyer exited the country club with the woman on his arm. His big black truck was tucked at the end of a row. He guided the woman toward it and helped her inside. For some reason, she felt a little—okay, a lot—like crying. A sound somewhere between a grunt and sob came from her throat.

"So is that a yes?" He squeezed her hand slightly between his.

"Not this evening. I'm . . . sorry." Her voice was thick, but she managed a smile like she always did. And part of her *was* sorry. Andrew was the easy choice. The one who would make everyone but her happy. She pulled free of him and fumbled the door of her Bug open. The interior was muggy, but silent and comforting. She left Andrew standing at the bumper of his car with his hands stuffed in his pockets and let her smile fall into nothing.

She was weary of putting on a front. Weary of pretending to be happy and capable and confident when inside she felt like the same shattered girl she'd been after Sawyer had broken her heart.

Chapter Eleven

Sawyer escorted Terry Lowe out the front door and into the still-warm night. Andrew's high-end silver Mercedes would have blended like a chameleon with the other cars, but Regan's red Bug glowed under the parking lot lights.

Regan and Andrew were standing close together and holding hands unless he was mistaken. Were they headed to his place or hers? Aggression snaked through his body, tensing his muscles.

"Well, Sawyer, I'm not sure what we've agreed to." Terry's voice veered into a giggle. She'd consumed a majority of the second bottle of wine on her own. Richard would advise pressing his advantage now while she was vulnerable. But that wasn't his style.

"Only one thing for sure. I'm driving you back to your hotel."

He offered his arm and she slipped her hand to his elbow and leaned into him. He helped her navigate the running board, and she plopped into the seat. He revved the engine, the throaty growl a manifestation of the animalistic urges impelling him.

"I've never been in a big truck like this before."

He hummed and was pulling up to her hotel five minutes

later. Leaving the truck running, he hopped out and helped her down. She hesitated on the running board, her hands on his shoulders for balance.

"I don't normally . . . but do you want to come up?"

The invitation was clear. She was a beautiful woman, sexy, sure of herself, experienced. The sex would probably be amazing. Not only was he too much of a professional, he couldn't summon the smallest hint of desire for her.

"I don't think mixing business with pleasure, especially since we haven't settled the business yet, is wise." He managed to inject regret into his voice even though he felt none.

"Perhaps not." She didn't sound convinced.

He lifted her off the running board and put her down an arm's length away. "I'll make sure you have a ride back to your car in the morning. You should plan to head into the shop tomorrow. Cade and I can address the concerns you have about the design and we can discuss terms, if you're still interested."

He should have pressed for a commitment earlier in the evening, before she'd had so much to drink, but he'd been distracted. Nevertheless, it wasn't a loss unless his rebuff soured the deal.

She harrumphed, clopped up the steps, and weaved through the automatic doors and out of sight. He shed his coat, rolled up his sleeves, and loosened his tie, missing his coveralls.

He shifted into drive, but didn't move. Cade would be expecting a report. He didn't feel like talking, he felt like fighting. On a mission to torture himself, he found himself on Regan's street. This time he didn't sneak down with his headlights off, but coasted forward slowly.

He steeled himself to see either Andrew's car parked out front or her car gone. His hands tightened on the steering wheel the closer he got. He hit the brakes hard enough to lock his seatbelt at her curb. Her Bug and the old truck sat in her driveway. No sign of Tarwater's Mercedes. That didn't mean he wasn't in there, although he had a hard time picturing the man shedding his dignity and riding in her Bug.

Her garage door was open. Did she know? What if the prowler from her mother's garden came around? He might steal things from her garage or worse. The worse he imagined clinched his decision. The woman should know better. She should take better care of herself, dammit.

He turned the truck off. His agitation reached new levels the closer he got to her front door. The simmering stew of discontent and resentment had reached a boiling point.

He almost hoped Tarwater was in there so he could punch him in the face for no reason other than the cutting memory of every flirty look and smile she'd aimed in his direction. Instead of pressing the doorbell, he hammered a fist against her front door. Regan Lovell was going to get an earful.

He heard chains rattle on the other side and the door swung open. She was still dressed in the red wrap dress and shifted on her high heels, her hair loose around her shoulders. He didn't wait for an invitation, but stepped inside and slammed the door shut with the heel of his shoe.

They faced off. If she was surprised to see him, she masked it with an intensity he couldn't place, but that seemed more complicated than anger.

"Is Tarwater here?" he asked even though he didn't see anyone else. For all he knew, Andrew was tied up spread eagle and naked on her bed.

She huffed and put her hands on her hips, which pulled the fabric across her bust and deepened the V. "As if it's any of your business—which it's not—no, he isn't."

Satisfaction tempered a small amount of his anger, but

other emotions welled to take its place. Emotions he didn't want to acknowledge much less examine. The irrational frustration she engendered was easy. His current state of insanity was due entirely to her.

"Your goddamn garage is wide open. What the hell, Regan?"

"I needed to load some things for work tomorrow into the truck, you jerk. It's open for a reason."

"You're planning on hauling stuff around dressed like that?" He skimmed his gaze up and down her body. She was sexier than any woman had the right to be. The way her long legs played peekaboo in the dress's slit only sent him further over the brink.

"Where's your new girlfriend? Is she waiting in the truck for you?"

It actually took him a few seconds to tease out who the hell she was talking about. He didn't answer and instead stepped toward her. With each step he took, she retreated one until he'd backed into the hallway wall, the harsh overhead entry light muted by shadows.

He placed his hands on the wall, caging her in. This was the conclusion to their confrontation at the country club. The overwhelming desire to kiss her had nearly overtaken him then. Now there was no clumsy kitchen staff or waiting client to interrupt him. Only a small area of his conscience protested, but her scent, sweet and light, and her lips, soft and inviting, muffled the warnings.

Her hands came up and he tensed, expecting her to shove him away, maybe even knee him in the balls, but they circled his tie. Was she was going to choke him? She tugged him forward.

Their mouths met and everything went still and silent. The silky skin of her lips slid over his, faint memories surfaced of the hours they'd spent making out on the bench seat of the old truck. Everything in the here and now was exciting and new, yet their shared history sheared away the need to go slow.

After watching her from a distance for years, their lives running parallel on opposite sides of the river, close yet miles apart, the past weeks had closed the gaps and fate had entwined their paths until he couldn't get away from her. Didn't want to get away from her. He just plain wanted her. Had always wanted her.

Pure, primal need drove his next actions. He pressed his body into hers, the wall forcing her to accept his dominance. Cupping her face, he deepened the kiss, driving his tongue inside her mouth. Her moan echoed into his chest as she wrapped her arms around his neck.

The feel of her tongue tangling with his and her soft breasts against his chest and her hips cradling his erection was both relief and torture. He rocked into her and she wrapped her leg around his, her knee at his hip.

He found her knee bare, the slit of her dress parting to reveal most of her thigh. The calluses along his palm rasped against the softness of her skin, and he pulled back, worried his coarseness was a turnoff.

Her head lolled against the wall, her lips parted and red and her eyes closed. She didn't seem turned off, in fact, she arched against the wall, driving her pelvis into his erection. Her dress begged to be unwrapped, and he was too far gone to deny the temptation.

Thankful her eyes were closed so she couldn't see the tremble in his fingers, he tugged on the tie holding the two sides together. One snap stood in his way and he pulled hard, fraying thread but not caring.

She opened her eyes and lifted her head, her expression one he'd never seen. Need and want and regret and fear all shone from her brown eyes. Wondering if she saw something similar in his face, he dropped his gaze and the worry was forgotten.

Her breasts were pushed high in the sexiest scrap of satin and lace he'd ever seen. His mouth worked, coherence an impossibility. Her panties matched, an impractical scrap of lace that begged to be removed by his teeth.

He'd been wrong earlier. *This* was the conclusion to their roll in the grass outside her mama's house and their kiss in the closet and the dugout. Or maybe this confrontation had been brewing for even longer. Like a volcano at rest, the hot, dangerous undercurrents had been there waiting to explode. The festivals were the seismic change that had set the explosion in motion.

His survival was still in question.

"I'm gonna fuck you." It seemed eons since he'd spoken, the words coming out hoarse and cavemanlike.

"Yes." Her breathy acquiescence was accompanied by the pull on his waistband by her hands. God, she was acting as frantic as he felt.

He brushed her hands aside and attacked the fancy closure and zipper with less finesse and more desperation. He pushed his pants and underwear to his knees and pressed back into her, thrusting against lace.

She wrapped her hand around him and skimmed her thumb over the tip. His hips bucked. He wasn't going to last even as long as he had their first time together. Her pretty, sexy bra was in his way. He yanked the cups down until her breasts jutted over the fabric.

He blew a long, slow breath through his clenched teeth, trying to maintain a semblance of control. Her breasts were spectacular. His dreams of late hadn't done them justice. They were fuller than he remembered, but her nipples were the same delicate pink tight little points. While his body ached to feel her breasts rubbing against his bare chest, he couldn't take the time. He would have to content himself with touching her with his hands and mouth.

Palming one, he squeezed gently and tested the weight

while he dropped his lips to graze the other. Another of her throaty out-of-control moans urged him on. He teased her with his tongue, flicking the bud. She drove her hands in his hair, her grip tightening, the tug ratcheting up his arousal. When he closed his mouth around her and sucked, she writhed between him and the wall, her throaty little cries driving him wilder.

He raised his face. He wouldn't do this unless she understood where he stood. Which was firmly on his side of the river. "This won't change anything. Agreed?"

"I'll still hate you, Sawyer Fournette." With her breasts exposed and her lips swollen from his kisses, she launched the words as if making her final stand.

Even as the sentiment jabbed at his heart, his erection jumped against her. He hooked a finger around the lace shielding her from him. His knees trembled. She was wet. So effing wet for him.

With his fingers holding her panties to the side, she took his erection and guided him to her entrance. Their gazes held as if magnetized. He pushed inside of her an inch. She gasped and her eyes clouded with what he hoped was pleasure. Slowly, savoring the welcome of her slick body, he pushed until finally he was buried inside of her.

He was slipping into a place where the past didn't matter, where his perceived betrayal and her heartlessness ceased to exist, stamped out by their joining. That limbo was dangerous.

Letting his lips fall to her temple, he took a single hard thrust when he wanted to be gentle and slow and continue staring into the depths of her.

"I'll still hate you too," he whispered, taking a hard thrust.

She answered by clutching him closer, not pushing him away. He lifted her thigh until her leg was curled high on his hip, opening her to him even more. God, he wanted to look, wanted to see her body taking him, yet knew the sight would signal the end.

He nuzzled his lips along her temple and down to her jaw. "You're so damn tight and sweet, baby. Does this feel good?"

"I've wanted this for so long." Her voice bordered on begging. "Make it last."

Her admission spiraled through him, the meaning clear. This one moment of insanity might be their last. The eruption of a volcano that would once more go dormant.

He wanted to make it last all night, but when she tensed and moaned in his arms, her body's pulses were a call he couldn't deny, and he let go. Even knowing it deepened the unwise intimacy between them, he kissed her, curling his tongue languidly against hers and taking small sips on her lips.

The aftershocks of his orgasm left him leaning into her, the wall and her body the only things keeping him upright. She didn't seem to be in any hurry to break the physical and emotional connections, her hips undulating against him, her nails biting into his back muscles.

But nothing lasted forever. Cracks shattered the bubble that cocooned them from reality. He wasn't sure which one of them moved first, but she pushed him back, both hands fisting in the cotton on his chest.

"That was . . . that was . . ." Her voice wobbled, and he anticipated what she would say even as the word snapped at his heart.

"A mistake." He kept his voice distant and applied a chill. She would try to work his vulnerability to her advantage if she could.

Yet, something else flashed in her eyes before she dropped her gaze to the floor and pushed harder at him. He skimmed his hand down her thigh to her knee before dropping her leg. A last weakness.

He pulled out of her, the loss of her warmth like getting thrown in the river in January. He tried—and failed—not to watch her adjust the scrap of her lace panties and cover her still budded nipples with the sexy bra. It was only when she pulled the dress around her like a robe that he became aware his pants and boxer briefs were around his knees. He yanked them up and managed to get his pants zipped.

She was still leaning against the wall, her knees pressed together, her hands clutching her dress closed, and her hair mussed. She did not look like a happy, satisfied woman, and part of him wanted to go to her, take her in his arms, and make sure he left her with a smile on her face.

He didn't. Obviously, she regretted their encounter, and he was painfully aware it had been all at his instigation. He'd followed her out of the bathroom at the country club, followed her home, followed her like a damn dog in need of a pat.

He pointed at her and picked up their inane conversation. "Close your garage door and set your alarm. You can load whatever you need in the morning."

He stormed out the door, not sure what he was feeling. Halfway to his truck, he risked a glance behind him. The door was still half open and she was exactly where he'd left her. He stopped and pivoted. What was he doing? He'd invaded her house, taken her against a wall, and stormed out like she was the one at fault.

Before he could take another step in any direction, she moved and slammed the door. Lights went out. The noisy creaking of the garage door lowering shook him out of his reverie. He trudged the short distance to his truck and climbed in.

He needed to get moving. After his monumental asshattery, he wouldn't be surprised if she called the police to report him loitering outside of her house. He drove back over the river on autopilot.

The crazy thing was that his body wasn't sated. Screwing each other's brains out had only whetted his appetite. Underneath the embarrassment and regret and hurt feelings, he imagined her naked on his bed. Naked for him to do whatever he pleased. All night long.

They'd never had that in the years they'd dated. It was all stolen moments in the truck or on the boat or the ground. He pulled up to his house. Cade's truck sat by the willow tree. He banged his head against the steering wheel a couple of times to rid himself of thoughts of Regan Lovell. There would be no next time with her.

His phone was on the dash and blinking with five messages. All from Cade. He didn't bother to listen to them. Loosening his tie, he made his way around to the kitchen door on the side of the house. Sure enough, Cade was sprawled at the table as if he owned it, flipping through a boating magazine.

At one time, it had been their family table. Sawyer didn't know why he kept the old thing. Good memories and bad lingered in the wood. His parents, Cade, Tally, and him squeezing around it for family dinners. Laughter, a few fights about eating vegetables, but mostly love. It came with them to the trailer and it was where he did his homework and where they ate the food Cade had caught or trapped, sometimes supplemented by the no-brand macaroni and cheese from the food bank.

As hard as Cade had tried to keep it a secret, Sawyer had found out about the charity in the hardest way possible. A classmate whose mother volunteered at the food bank had confronted him in the halls with malicious laughter. He'd punched the kid's teasing smile off his face. Pride had him holding his head up on the way home that day. No way were the Fournettes accepting charity.

As he got closer to their ramshackle trailer, doubts wormed their way into him. Small things had added up into one big truth. Sawyer had sharpened his eyes, and sure enough found evidence crumpled and buried at the bottom of the trash.

He'd waited up that night to confront Cade, throw the evidence in his face and tell him to never go back to the food bank. But when Cade had stepped through the door, the weariness on his face had stilled Sawyer's tongue. His brother had dropped out of school and seemed to have aged a decade in six months. That night Sawyer had crossed from selfish adolescence into adulthood.

Sawyer went to the frig, grabbed two beers, and handed one over, joining Cade at the old, scarred table. Cade tossed the magazine aside and took a swig. Neither of them spoke until half their beers were gone.

"Please tell me you didn't sleep with her," Cade said.

Sawyer startled. "How . . ."

Cade dropped his forehead to the top of the beer and spoke to the table. "Your pants are undone."

"Look, we both agreed it was a mistake. It won't happen again, I swear." Sawyer wished his promise held a little more conviction. He tried to summon regret for what he'd done with Regan. Tried and failed. Even as his head acknowledged the monumental mistake, his body remembered the pleasure. In fact, his only regret was that he hadn't had more time. Time to strip her bare and reacquaint himself with every inch of her body.

"It doesn't matter. You've screwed up the whole deal by screwing her."

Had he comprised the festival? "I don't see how what I did—"

"I thought I could trust you. Told Richard I could trust you." Cade's green eyes glittered with fury and Sawyer understood why he played the bad cop during negotiations.

Cade shoved out of the seat and paced. "Holy hell. You can kiss your partnership good-bye. Of all the asinine, adolescent things you could possibly do—"

"Hold up." Sawyer held up a hand, everything becoming clear. He wasn't sure if he wanted to laugh or plead with God to strike him dead. "I didn't have sex with Terry Lowe. Even though she propositioned me. And that's Richard's fault for recommending the wine, by the way."

If he wasn't sure what was coming, he might enjoy the confused shock on Cade's face. Cade plopped back in his seat, sent a probing look toward Sawyer before killing his beer. Sawyer picked at the sweating label of his.

"Let's back up a minute. So, you didn't sleep with Ms. Lowe?"

"That's right. No hanky-panky with the rather gorgeous Ms. Lowe. Thanks for the warning, by the way. I was expecting a Mr. Lowe."

"I didn't realize either until Richard called this evening to check on things or I would have given you a heads up. Did you close the deal?"

"Not quite. She's set on discussing a couple of modifications and broached the subject of buying the technology instead of licensing it."

"That's not going to happen."

"Told her that, but I think she'd still going to try to push her agenda."

Cade harrumphed. "Wouldn't respect her if she didn't give it a shot. I hope to God you misread her signals."

"I didn't. I let her down gently, and she was too buzzed to take offense at the time. She's coming to the shop tomorrow, so we'll need to make sure she isn't embarrassed about it."

"Maybe we can use it to our advantage. My guess is she won't want to hang out negotiating for too long with a man who rejected her."

"You are brutal, brother." Sawyer rose, set his half-empty bottle in the sink, and fake-stretched. "Well, it's late and I'm sure Monroe is waiting anxiously for your return."

"Don't think you're getting off that easy. If it wasn't the lovely Ms. Lowe, then whose bed have you come from?"

"No one's." No guilt at all came from admitting the truth.

Cade tried to bore to the facts with his intense stare. It probably would have worked on anyone else, but underneath the smiles, Sawyer was as tough as his brother.

Cade broke the stare and rose, this time more sedately. "Actually, Monroe *is* waiting up for me. But I'll find out." A fair amount of curiosity tempered the threatening words.

"You're as bad a gossip as the Quilting Bee ladies. It doesn't have any bearing on Fournette Designs, so let it go. Please."

"Fine. What time should I expect Ms. Lowe to make an appearance?"

"Not sure. Her rental is at the country club. I'll call her in the morning. Maybe offer her a ride. Tour her around and act as if nothing happened."

"Might work." Cade stepped out and Sawyer followed him around to the front of the house. "Text me in the morning when you're heading to the shop. Monroe likes to laze in bed and make pancakes together on Saturdays."

"Dang, are you whipped or what?" Sawyer forced a disdain he didn't feel into his voice. In truth, lazing in bed with a beautiful woman and making pancakes sounded amazing. A snapshot of a tousled-haired strawberry-blonde beauty in his bed punched his heart and made it skip a beat. He resolutely blanked his mind.

Cade flipped him the bird before sliding behind the wheel of their daddy's old truck. The engine coughed to life, and Cade revved it a couple of times before heading down the lane.

Sawyer stood there long after the taillights faded. He stood for so long, an owl hooted and the scurry of a prowling possum or raccoon shook the bushes. He was a man no longer, but one of them. The night took on a dreamlike cast, the moon rising over the tree line.

When he had bullied Cade back to Cottonbloom to recover from his climbing accident, he never foresaw the life-altering shifts that would result from his brother's homecoming. Seeing their daddy's old truck live on through Cade refilled a well of optimism and hope that had grown dry over the last few years.

At first, seeing Cade behind the steering wheel of their daddy's old truck had been painful, and he'd lashed out at his brother, maybe because Cade had finished something Sawyer had been unable to bring himself to touch.

But Cade had breathed new life into the truck and into Sawyer by coming home. Working side by side as Cade's equal at Fournette Designs was invigorating. His staid job as the plant manager of the auto factory had sucked any happiness out of his life, yet he'd been unable to leave Cottonbloom behind like Cade had done so many years ago.

The hunk of rusting metal had turned into more than a monument to their parent's death. It had come to symbolize everything he'd lost, including his big brother for far too long. And Regan. Too many of his memories of her had been etched into the metal and leather.

But the truck was alive once more. What did that mean for him and Regan?

Chapter Twelve

The next morning, Regan rolled out of bed, bleary-eyed and still in her underwear from the night before. She wasn't normally a crier. From a young age on the pageant circuit, she'd learned to cover her disappointment and hurt feelings with a smile. Nothing like hearing someone else's name get called as the winner while hundreds of eyes watched to test your resolve.

But last night she'd fallen apart. As soon as she closed the front door, she'd dissolved into a splotchy puddle of tears. She'd made sure to close the garage door so he wouldn't come stalking back to catch her in a weak moment. For all she knew, the woman he'd had dinner with was waiting for him somewhere. Or maybe she had been in his truck while he had pressed her against the wall and rocked her world.

Idiot. The word went on repeat. She'd collapsed onto her bed, facedown into a pillow, and let loose. Sometime during the night her dress and shoes had ended up crumpled on the floor, her panties still damp from Sawyer.

She wadded up the underwear and buried it in her laundry basket as if her mother might dig through like she had in high school. Good thing she was on the Pill. Neither one of them had even thought about protection.

The shower brought a semblance of order to her thoughts. Like he'd said, their impulsive wall sex had been a mistake. If that wasn't exactly what she'd been about to say, she was grateful he'd filled in the blank of her mind with the appropriate word. Because what she'd been thinking had been very, very inappropriate.

God, he'd felt amazing—big and hard and hot and commanding. She didn't remember that about their frantic couplings in his daddy's truck. They'd been more concerned about getting caught in those days, which had lent its own special excitement. Last night had been different. Amazing. But a mistake. Definitely a mistake. A one-time, amazing mistake.

Her routine eased her back into a normalcy Sawyer had blown to smithereens. She pulled on dark wash jeans, ballet flats, and a cotton blouse. Today she was meeting one of Cottonbloom's "ladies who lunch" at her house to work on furniture placement and new wall art. Even though it would be tiring hard work, she still had to look professional. The block party would occupy the rest of her afternoon and evening. A dry run for the festival.

She loaded the covered pickup with an assortment of items from her garage and headed out. The morning passed quickly in spite of how often her thoughts drifted to Sawyer. Finally, after moving things back and forth and back again, her client was happy, and she'd sold several pieces. Even though this type of work could be tedious and it took her away from the office, once clients saw her vision on their walls or in their houses, a sale was inevitable.

Maybe she wasn't changing the world, but she was making it a better place. Her mother had told her time and again her job was to decorate the world. Of course, her mother had meant it in terms of becoming an arm accessory for an ambitious man. Her mother was old-school subservient to her father. If she and her mother hadn't shared the same hair color, Regan might wonder if she was adopted.

Back at her studio before noon, she checked her phone and scrolled through a multitude of calls and texts to return about the block party that evening, but nothing from Sawyer. Loneliness took up residence in her stomach, hollowing it and making her head feel swimmy.

What was her problem? She had a full life. No man—that was true—but after going through the annihilation with Sawyer, she hadn't craved drawing a big fat bull's-eye on her heart ever again. Anyway, the sex hadn't been tender and sweet, it had been tinged with anger and frustration. That kind of sex probably didn't necessitate a follow-up call.

She mentally shook herself and got back to checking things off her lists. The string quartet had been confirmed as had the ice cream shop and the Cottonbloom Bakery. In addition to ice cream and an assortment of baked goods, the high school was manning their lemonade cart and popcorn stand. They would raise money for their programs while feeding the masses.

At least, she hoped to attract masses. She'd hung fliers all over town, even by the university, although summer school meant things were quiet on campus. Adolescent fear of no one showing up to her party had her pacing while she handled the last-minute details.

The bells over her door tinkled, and Nash Hawthorne stepped into the studio. The director of public works was updating her on the progress of the setup. She made a face at Nash and held up a finger while interjecting a few "uh-huhs." Nash wandered around.

Everything seemed to be moving along with minor hiccups, and she thanked the director before disconnecting. "What's up, Nash? Looking for some new pillows?"

He tossed the fringed, flowered throw pillow aside and looked anywhere but at her. "Not exactly."

"What's wrong?"

He winced and cast a glance over the top of his glasses. "Thought you deserved fair warning."

"Of what?" Her lips had gone numb as if she'd pressed them against ice for too long.

"Sawyer put together an impromptu block party on the other side for tonight."

"He wouldn't."

"He did." Nash was solemn. She believed him. It wasn't his nature to stir up trouble or drama.

Even though she and Sawyer had both sort of agreed the sex has been a mistake, they'd also pinky-promised. Betrayal burned away the loneliness. This is why she would never trust a man again. Ever.

"How'd you find out?"

Nash sent her another look, this time with more amusement. "Tally, of course."

Nash had succumbed to the dark side along with Monroe, becoming involved with a Fournette of Cottonbloom, Louisiana. Regan had been there, done that, bought the T-shirt.

"If it's any consolation, I don't think it's a dig at you." He added.

She snorted.

"It has something to do with a deal they're trying to close. Cade decided she needed to be treated to Louisiana hospitality."

"She?"

"Some muckety-muck from a big boat company on the East Coast."

Had Sawyer been wining and dining this boat woman the night before? It sure hadn't looked strictly business. She hadn't missed the woman's foot grazing up Sawyer's leg. Focus. She had to focus on the problem at hand, which did not include who Sawyer might or might not be doing—besides herself.

"Does Tally know you're here warning the enemy?" Regan wasn't sure how far she could trust Nash and Monroe anymore.

"As a matter of fact, yes. She feels a little bad."

Regan studied him, surprised. He returned her probing gaze. Tally disliked her. Intensely, if years of cutting glares were any indication. Even before she and Sawyer broke up, Tally had regarded Regan with the same distrust Regan's mother aimed toward Sawyer. And afterward, she might as well have been caught torturing puppies, given the level of virulence Tally had held toward her.

"Tally hates me."

"She doesn't."

"She used to."

Nash broke their study of each other as he walked around the pillow display, trailing his finger along the different fabrics. "You were always nice to me in school. You and Monroe weren't like some of the others. I don't know if I ever thanked you for not treating me like a freak."

Monroe had been the one to convince Regan to take the Louisiana boy under their wings. At the time, Monroe's motives had been murky. Now Regan understood; Nash had been a stand-in for Cade. If Monroe couldn't help Cade, then she'd done her best to protect a different Louisiana boy. And because Regan had Monroe's back, she had Nash's back too.

Anyway, with her wavy hair, smattering of freckles, and wild notions, she'd often felt like an outcast among Cottonbloom's homogenous, perfectly coiffed society girls. Even Monroe couldn't betray her genes. She could have been the poster child for Southern womanhood, a blonde haired, blue-eyed beauty.

But, Regan had learned to cover it all with a learned, practiced smile and a blustering bravado. The only times she'd been truly herself were around Monroe and Sawyer.

She joined Nash at the bin of pillows. Both of them kept their gazes on the tumble of patterns. "Thanks for letting me copy your calculus homework." She hip-bumped him. "Freak."

He barked a laugh. "Is there something I can do?"

"I don't suppose you want to put those fighting skills to use and go beat up Sawyer for me?"

"That I can't do."

"Figured." She gave a half-shrug and pasted on a smile. "Too late to do anything about it anyway. I'll do my thing, and Sawyer will do his. I guess we'll have an idea who has the upper hand for the competition."

Nash was halfway out the door. "I'll bet turnout on both sides will be great."

She chucked her chin in his direction and forced a smile. As soon as he was out of sight, she closed the shop early and pulled the shades.

The tentative moments of harmony between her and Sawyer had been derailed by last night's encounter and blown to bits by the underhanded way he was trying to ruin her first block party. A wave of heat coursed through her body. Soon enough, she would be too busy to think, but for a moment, she wallowed in her hurt feelings and cursed Sawyer.

Sawyer rubbed his temples. This spur-of-the-moment party was a monumentally poor idea, but Cade had offered it up before Sawyer had a chance to do more than open his mouth to protest. Terry Lowe seemed flattered and excited they were putting together a party for her. The negotiations had gone well, and Cade wanted to send the scanned, signed contracts to Richard that night.

Cade slapped him on the back, emphasizing the throb in his head. "Why so glum? This is another opportunity to stick it to Regan Lovell."

Sawyer guffawed. The irony of Cade's choice of words was lost on everyone but Sawyer. Thank God. Dreams of sticking it to Regan—over and over—had made for a restless night, leaving him slow-witted and groggy all day.

"Why a block party? Why not take her to Rufus's if she's after local flavor."

"Look, people like Ms. Lowe expect to be entertained. They want to be impressed. We might not have the finest restaurants or the attractions of a big city, but what we have in spades is charm. What we can offer is a unique experience. Champagne parties at art museums are the norm for women like her. But, a down-home, bluegrass, slice of gooey Southern hospitality? She'll be talking about this for the next year."

Sawyer tilted his head back and stared at the white-pocked ceiling tiles. "Are you saying we're going to have to trot out the local flavor every time some Yankee comes down looking to make a deal?"

"Nah. Only the big dogs. You saw the number of zeroes on that deal, right? Let's celebrate." Cade walked out of the break room.

No matter how many zeroes on the deal, Sawyer couldn't celebrate. He had pinky-promised Regan not to interfere with her first attempt at a block party. He'd seen her cute little fliers advertising the string quartet and the ice cream social. It sounded sophisticated and sweet, just like Regan.

Cade's head popped around the doorjamb. "You got the beer truck lined up, right?"

Heaven help him. "I did."

"We're going to steal every man and woman over the

age of twenty-one to our side." Cade fist-pumped and disappeared.

Whatever self-respect he had left after walking out on her the night before drained into the concrete under his boots. Cade was right. They would steal a good portion of Regan's crowd. Beer would be a strong draw on a hot August night. He felt like a worm. No, he felt like the dirt worms pooped out.

There hadn't been much to do except make a few calls. Everyone knew the drill. The beer truck was new, and Wayne Berry had some concerns about public intoxication and drunk driving, but once Sawyer had mentioned the portion of sales that would be allocated to the police department, the sheriff had decided the force could handle it.

Sawyer got to the riverfront as his uncle and the rest of the bluegrass band were tuning their instruments.

Terry Lowe was standing with Monroe and Cade, a beer in hand and a smile on her face. "Why Sawyer, this is just the cutest. And it looks like both sides of the river will be hopping."

Sawyer had avoided even looking across the bridge, but now he did. Regan had decorated the pavilion in red and blue bunting and set up chairs along the grass. The faint strains of a cello carried on the slight breeze.

"They'll be ice cream over the bridge. Not something to miss," Sawyer said slowly.

The toe of Cade's boot made contact with his ankle. Cade's green gaze lasered into him. "We have beer."

"True." Sawyer transferred his attention to Terry, giving her a wide smile. "The church ladies usually sell pecan pies, but they didn't have enough notice. I heard that Cottonbloom Bakery will be selling pie and cake by the slice over the river, and the high school is selling lemonade."

"We have beer." Cade repeated forcefully.

Sawyer returned Cade's frown with a grin, backing up and holding his arms out. "If you folks will excuse me, as Cottonbloom Parish commissioner, I have duties to attend to."

He mingled with the crowd, pointing out the corn hole games Regan had set up for the kids to families and the lemonade stand to people he knew were teetotalers. By the time his uncle Del fired up the bluegrass music, there was a steady stream of people crossing the bridge in both directions. As more single, legal-aged adults made their way to the Louisiana side, the families and older folks found their way to the Mississippi side.

After an hour and with the band taking a break, Cade found Sawyer standing at the edge of the river drinking beer from a plastic cup.

"I know what you're doing."

Sawyer startled, but stayed silent.

"You've been talking people into crossing over. Are you actually feeling guilty?"

He was. Extremely guilty. Not only had he not called or texted her today—even though he'd picked his phone up a dozen times with the intention—he'd demolished the tentative partnership they'd formed.

At least Cade hadn't guessed Regan still had a hold on him. He couldn't deny it any longer. What-ifs and might-have-beens had reared in his conscience more and more often since the beginning of summer.

The urge to dredge up the past was strong. He wanted to explain himself, clean the slate. Maybe they were distanced enough that she would finally listen. Would his behavior last night compounded with today's fiasco make any future impossible?

A future. Was that what he wanted? A future with her? The more he was around her, a hard truth wrapped itself around his heart. He missed her. He had been missing her the past decade. The resentment and hatred that had filled the space had seeped away over the summer, leaving an ache he was just now identifying.

"What we did was pretty low," Sawyer said finally. "She's been planning this for weeks."

"She deserves it for trying to steal your Labor Day thunder. And for everything else."

"The magazine insisted we hold them the same weekend. She wants to help her side as much as I want to help mine. Can't fault her for that." Sawyer killed his beer and rubbed his nape. "Our breakup wasn't entirely her fault, you know."

"Sure seemed like it at the time." Cade crossed his arms over his chest, his gaze on the river. "Her mama talked her into breaking up with you."

"True. And I was pissed." The pain of hearing her tell him they should take a break from each other, see what else was out there before committing themselves forever still had power over him. He crumpled the cup in his fist. "That night a bunch of guys from my frat took me out. I drank too much. Way too much. Blacked out."

"Whoa. Real responsible." Cade did not look amused. He'd been shoved from adolescence to manhood in a single, terrible night.

"It gets better. Or worse. Regan showed up that morning to make up, I think. All I remember is coming to with her standing over my bed. Only I wasn't alone. My friends had decided what would cheer me up was another girl."

Cade ran a hand over his jaw and winced. "Some friends you had."

"I was still drunk with a strange naked girl in my bed and Regan looking like she wanted to disembowel both of us. I couldn't even assure her nothing had happened, because I couldn't remember a damn thing."

"Poor Regan." Cade looked back over the river. For the first time, sympathy laced his words when referring to her.

"She ran off. I followed her, but like I said, I was still drunk from the night before. No way could I drive."

"At least you weren't as dumb as your buddies. Did you?"

"Did I what?"

"Sleep with that girl?"

"Turns out I was too drunk to get it up. Which only adds to the humiliation."

"I assume you told Regan that."

"Tried to tell her a hundred times. She cut me off. Cut me out of her life, her heart. I would have gotten a signed affidavit from that girl if I thought Regan would have believed me."

"So you two broke up over a misunderstanding?"

"If it were only that simple. Everything was against us from the beginning. Her parents hated me, you thought she was using me." When Cade tried to stutter out some words, Sawyer held up a hand. "I get you were trying to protect me. Like you always did. No one understood what we had together. But I betrayed her trust, and once that was gone, we couldn't survive all the rest."

"Technically, you were on a break."

Sawyer's laugh was humorless. "That excuse has failed through the ages. I didn't even attempt it."

Cade sighed and ruffled his hair. "I can't believe I'm saying this, but maybe now you're grown-ups and on equal footing, you could try again. You obviously still have the hots for her."

Hearing the crazy notion put into words by his brother shot accelerant through his body. "You think? I—"

"Holy. Shit." Cade swiveled to him, his green eyes wide. "You hooked up with Regan last night."

"Do not tell Monroe." Sawyer poked his brother in the chest. Cade held his hands up and attempted to look innocent, but Sawyer had the feeling he and Regan would be the hot topic during their pillow talk.

"Wow, so you *really* screwed her over with this little shindig tonight, huh?"

"*I* did? This was all your idea, you chicken-livered dickweed." Sawyer shoved his brother's shoulder, but Cade only burst into laughter.

"I swear if I had realized or if you had told me last night . . . Listen, go on over and apologize. Throw me under the bus. I deserve it."

"You totally do." Sawyer couldn't help but return Cade's smile. It was good to have him home.

"I'm going to close down the beer truck after the next set on your authority. My guess is the crowd will clear out pretty fast after that. I'll handle cleanup."

"Thanks man." He and Cade clasped hands and bumped shoulders. Halfway across the bridge, he looked back. Cade was on the bank, his hands shoved into his pockets, an almost fatherly expression on his face. It was both painful and heartening to see. The river seemed to whisper of past regrets, and Sawyer strode toward the rebuilt pavilion to escape the wave of nostalgia.

Chapter Thirteen

Regan's cheeks hurt from her pinned-on smile, but shockingly everything seemed to be going well even with Sawyer's attempt at sabotage. In fact, many Louisiana families had crossed over to enjoy the wholesome entertainment. Kids played tag while trying to keep their ice cream from dripping, older people took to the chairs, the music a soft background to their conversations and laughter.

Granted, she'd lost some of the younger couples and singles to Sawyer's side, but the mass migration she'd feared hadn't come to pass. In fact, the turnout was even better than she'd anticipated. *Because* of the Louisiana block party and not in spite of it.

A pagan rhythm thumped her temples, and heat prickled her face even as a shiver coursed down her spine. She retreated to the brick wall of the first row of shops, close to the Quilting Bee, and massaged her cheeks, her smile relaxing. Forcing herself to appear happy and enthusiastic was hard work. Satisfaction at the squeals of laughter and buzz of conversation was gratifying in its way. Not enough to erase her recent humiliations or her headache, but tempering both.

Oh God. Sawyer moved through the crowd as if he were

the mayor and not her, shaking hands and inciting laughter. Did she have the power to ban someone? It sounded more medieval than modern, but she might just scour the law for a loophole. Talk about satisfying.

The moment his gaze found her, a jolt that was a stew of anger and embarrassment with a dash of something indefinable yet magnetic rushed her body. She wasn't sure if she wanted to run to him or away. Flight instincts took over, and she slipped into the narrow alley behind the shops.

It was wide enough for a regular-sized pickup but partitioned from the nearest parking lot by a hip-high brick wall topped with tea rose bushes in full bloom. Part of her beatification project. Except now she was regretting the choice. The cloying scent made her stomach roil.

She rubbed her arms, her skin almost painful to the touch, and dropped to a squat, feeling faint and flustered with the ebb of adrenaline. Sawyer rounded the corner and stopped. Full dusk was upon them and the parking lot lights leaked weakly through the thick bushes, leaving her in deep shadows. Maybe he wouldn't see her and move on.

His gaze latched onto her immediately. But of course, she couldn't escape his superhuman Fournette sight. He stepped closer, tentatively as if she might spook. "What's wrong?"

"Nothing." It was a lie. A sweat had broken out on her forehead in contrast to the shivers making goose bumps pop up in the cooling air. She dropped to her butt and stretched her legs out in front of her. Her hands shook as they smoothed down her shirt. She needed him gone so she could get her game face back on and wrap up the block party. Only then could she collapse in bed and sleep. Her soft sheets called like a siren's song.

He squatted next to her. She traced the straining seam of his jeans with her eyes. He had nice legs. Muscled and covered with hair. Manly. At least he used to, she hadn't even gotten a glimpse of them last night.

"I didn't even get to see your legs last night, Sawyer." The words bypassed her brain, emerging from her mouth straight to her ears for processing. She covered her mouth before something even worse could come out.

"We could remedy that." Surprise, but also amusement, sparked in his voice even though it was too dim to see his eyes. "I figured you'd be more upset with me."

"I'm really freaking mad." She tried to work some outrage into her voice, but the effort required was too great. Behind the ungodly thumping, her brain wanted to launch into a lecture about civic duty and pinky promises. Instead she mumbled, "You didn't call or text or anything today. I know it was a mistake, but . . ."

She stopped herself from admitting her feelings were hurt. What kind of loser admitted something like that to a man who had barged into her house and took her against a wall? A pathetic loser.

"I should have. I meant to."

"By the way, I'm on the Pill. Thanks for your concern." Anger lent her strength and she pushed off the ground. Vertigo skewed her perception. She listed and grabbed hold of whatever was near. The solid muscle of his biceps flexed under her grip.

"I'm so sorry, Regan. I really . . . Jesus, you look terrible."

"Nice wrap-up to your apology." She ran her tongue over her dry lips but was afraid to let go of him. The wall supporting her butt and his arm were the only things keeping her upright. The law of gravity seemed to be betraying her.

"When did you last eat?"

"I had an iced coffee and a bag of chips for lunch. Things got busy." Had a cold front moved in? Any residual

heat from the day had dissipated, leaving her shivering. "I'll
go get some popcorn or a cookie or something. I'll be fine."
She forced herself to loosen her grip on him, but before
she could push off the wall, he moved in front of her and
tucked her hair behind her ear, brushing her forehead.

"You're hot."

"Thanks, but even if I was inclined to give you another
shot, it would not be up against another wall. Especially a
brick one." His muffled laughter had her batting away the
hand grazing along her face and neck. "Quit it."

"I mean, you have a fever, woman. Not that you aren't
hot in other ways too."

She touched her forehead with the back of her hand, but
couldn't interpret heat from cold.

"I'm taking you home and putting you to bed."

"No. I can call Monroe or my mother or someone." She
should push him away and crawl to her car. All she needed
was some medicine and a good night's sleep.

"Let me help you, baby." His voice had dropped and
roughened. "Let me take care of you."

Exhaustion swamped her. She was beyond arguing.
Voices echoed down the stretch of alley. Sawyer shushed
her even though she hadn't spoken. Forming words required too much effort. His arm slid around her shoulder,
and she leaned into his chest, her cheek squished against
his T-shirt. His warmth wrapped around her, and the thump
of his heart soothed her into a state between wakefulness
and sleep.

He tensed, but didn't say anything. Voices too far away
to knit themselves into words drifted to them. She blinked
her eyes open. Delmar Fournette and Ms. Martha were illuminated by the headlights of his old truck. Why didn't
Sawyer call to his uncle?

She snuggled closer and closed her eyes. Sawyer would

handle everything. Take care of her. Dangerous thinking but she didn't care. His chest rumbled against her cheek. Words hung but, as if they were foreign, she couldn't decipher them. It didn't matter because he was talking on his phone, not to her.

Time passed. His heat helped control her shivers. A bright light invaded her consciousness. She squinted. A truck moved closer. She was lifted in his arms and set on soft leather, the support not as welcome as her bed would be but better than the brick wall.

She slit her eyes open. Sawyer and Cade stood in the open driver's side door. Cade actually appeared concerned. Must be a trick of the shadows. Cade had never liked her, even when things had been good between her and Sawyer.

Sawyer climbed behind the wheel and shut them in. He backed out of the alley, leaving Cade standing in the wash of the headlights, the bright light making her head swim. She closed her eyes.

When she opened them again, they were at her front door and she was in his arms again. "Regan. Regan, baby, I need a key. Do you have one on you?"

She fumbled in her pocket and handed her keys over. He managed to unlock the door and open it with her still in his arms.

"What about your security system? Is there a code I need to enter?"

She vaguely waved a hand, not lifting her head off his shoulder. "It's not hooked up."

"What am I going to do with you?" His voice held a note of exasperation, but was soft, almost affectionate. Her fever must have spiked higher. "Is your bedroom up or down?"

"Down."

Without turning any lights on, he picked his way to the master bedroom. It looked over the garden toward the river. The drapes were open, moonlight reflecting off the whites and creams of her bedding.

He set her down, so she was sitting on the edge of the bed. Tossing pillows over his shoulder, he mumbled something about naked birds and suffocation. When he was done de-pillowing her bed, he stood back and put his hands on his hips. The moonlight limned his body but threw his face into deep shadow.

A question hung in the air between them, unasked and unanswered. Finally, he moved to her dresser and opened and closed drawers before coming back with an old college football T-shirt she only wore when doing chores.

"Do you want me to . . . ?" He held the shirt out, the tentativeness in his voice and manner in contrast to his normal behavior.

"Turn around." Her voice was scratchy, as if it had been days since she'd last spoken. He turned. It didn't matter that he'd seen most of the good parts already, she felt more vulnerable than she had last night.

The buttons of her blouse were like little puzzles to her clumsy brain and fingers. After exchanging blouse for T-shirt, she unhooked her bra and worked it out of one sleeve. Then she laid back and shimmed her jeans off. They landed next to his boots, and he shifted as if ready to turn around.

"Hold up." She scooted back and slipped under the sheets. Between the softness of her old T-shirt and the warmth of her thick comforter, she let out a soft little moan of relief.

He took her noise as his cue and loomed over her, his palm over her forehead. "Where do you keep your medicine?"

"Kitchen."

He disappeared and she closed her eyes, drifting off. The mattress dipped and something wet landed on her arm. "Sit up and take these."

She was beyond arguing and swallowed the pills without a peep, settling back into her nest, falling asleep within minutes.

Sawyer kept watch over her for a long time. Her restless movements and little whimpers ceased after a half hour. He cupped her cheek and she nuzzled into his touch, her lips tipping up. What or who populated her dreams to make her smile so sweetly? Was it wrong to hope it was him?

She was still too warm, but the blaze of her fever was under control. Damn, she had scared him. She'd been working too hard, not eating well. No wonder she was sick. The budget, planning the block party and the festival, an on-the-loose arsonist, the letters had stressed her out. He was loath to add himself to the list, but he probably hadn't helped matters.

I'm on the Pill. Thanks for your concern. Her words gouged another path of guilt though his heart. He hadn't even considered protection last night. His only thought had been to get inside of her—fair means or foul.

He promised himself if he had the chance, he'd make it up to her. This was a start, even though he wasn't a hundred percent sure she would appreciate his efforts once she was feeling better.

He wandered back into the entryway, stared at the unlit control box for her security system, and shook his head. How could he keep her safe when her independent streak was a country mile wide?

Other worries inserted themselves. He pulled out his phone and hit his brother's name.

"Everything good?" Cade asked in place of a greeting.

"She's in bed and her fever seems down."

"Good. Monroe offered to come over, but I told her you got it covered. Am I right?"

Sawyer glanced toward her bedroom and settled into one of her overstuffed couches. "I got it. Listen, something happened while I was waiting for you to bring the truck around. I'm not sure what to make of it."

"Shoot."

"Uncle Del and Ms. Martha went through the back of her shop. He came out with a gas can." He briefly outlined what Regan had seen the day of the reassessment.

Shuffling came from Cade's end, then quiet. Finally, he said, "You think Uncle Del is the arsonist?"

"I couldn't hear what they were saying." Silence followed his non-answer.

"Let's assume the same person or people are responsible for burning the pavilion down and cutting the baskets. Would Uncle Del mess with the livelihood of his neighbors?"

"I don't know." His uncle had never been picky in terms of what jobs he'd taken as long as money was involved. Still . . . "I don't even know that Ms. Martha is involved. It could all be very innocent."

"But?"

"I got a bad feeling, is all."

"You sure your feelings for Regan aren't clouding the issue?"

He hesitated. His knee-jerk reaction was to deny he had any feelings whatsoever for her, but after his earlier confession and Cade's witness to his need to care for her, he was beyond denials. "Maybe so."

"Only one thing to do."

"What's that?"

Cade harrumphed. "Ask Uncle Del what the hell is going on. How about we go fishing tomorrow?"

Sawyer stared once more into the dark bedroom. "If Regan is better."

"I'll send Monroe over in the morning." Cade disconnected.

"Dammit," he muttered, not sure if he was mad at his brother's high-handedness or disgusted with his own pathetic urge to sit at Regan's bedside until she was better.

Restlessness kept him from settling down on the couch. Instead, he wandered her house, searching for clues to understanding present-day Regan Lovell. He picked up one of the pictures on the mantle.

The frame still had the fake display picture inside. A happy family frolicking at a picnic. Weird. The frame at the other end held an old picture of Monroe and Regan from their college days based on their hair and Ole Miss sweatshirts. An eye-pleasing grouping of candles was in the middle of the mantle. Next to it was a thin flat object wrapped in white gauze. He lifted the edge.

Recognition coursed through him as he unwrapped the piece of wood. She had cut the top half off and smoothed the edges, leaving his decade-old message to her in the middle. Maybe she was planning some voodoo ritual before tossing it into the fire. He glanced down at the enclosed gas fireplace.

She was keeping it. On her mantle. Taking a deep breath and still holding the piece of their past, he stepped through the sliding glass doors and onto her spacious deck. Pots of colorful geraniums and petunias were placed at different heights drawing him around the space. Her subtle yet elegant touch was becoming more familiar. No wonder she was in demand as an interior designer.

He propped his hip against the rail and faced the river. Although he couldn't see or hear it at this distance, the flow was as unmistakable as the blood through his veins. More flowers were interspersed in beds along the bricks of the house.

Except in one spot by the French doors leading out of her bedroom. A barren swath of turned soil and nothing else. She'd dug up her own flowers to give to him. He had no idea how it all fit together, but something resembling hope flickered somewhere around his heart.

Chapter Fourteen

The next morning, while Monroe waited to wake up Regan for another dose of medicine, Sawyer pulled off onto the old grassy track to his uncle's house. Tally's car was parked next to Cade's truck.

As Sawyer was passing by his uncle's ramshackle house, Tally stuck her head out the door. "Hey. Come here a minute."

She disappeared back inside. Cade and Uncle Del's voices drifted from the river. How much had Cade told her? She and Cade were the same side of the same coin, distrusting and protective by nature. Her dislike of Regan had reached epic proportions after their breakup.

He trudged up the sagging front steps and found his sister in the narrow galley kitchen. "What's up?"

Tally chewed on the inside of her cheek. "I found something last month when you called me to check up on Uncle Del, remember?"

"I remember."

She opened a bottom drawer and pulled out a roll of cash.

"Ah, hellfire." He thumbed through the bills. At least five hundred, maybe more.

"I should have mentioned it earlier, but . . ." She shrugged.

He understood. Uncle Del was their only family, besides each other. While he hadn't been the most reliable of caretakers, he did care. There was never any doubt of that.

He handed the money over. "Put it back. Does Cade know?"

She shook her head. "I got here after they were already down at the river. You'd best head down. They're waiting on you."

Sawyer scrubbed a hand over his face. He'd dozed fitfully on her couch between forays to check on Regan. Besides waking her up once to take more medicine, she'd seemed to sleep well. Better than him for sure. He and Tally stepped off the porch.

"How's Regan feeling?" The sympathy in her voice surprised him.

"No clue. She was still asleep when I left. Why do you care?" Although the question sounded harsh, he was more curious than defensive.

"She was nice to Nash when they were in school." She scuffed her shoes in the rocks, her eyes downcast. "Not that I'll ever forgive her for hurting you."

"I wasn't her victim. I hurt her too. Maybe even worse." It was the first time he'd really admitted the truth. Playing the wronged party had been easier than acknowledging his own weakness and stupidity had led to the ultimate heartbreak.

She hummed. "You know sometimes the past is just that. The past. The future is what matters."

He put his arm around her shoulders for a squeeze. "When did my all-black-wearing, kick-ass sister become an optimist?"

The smile she aimed at him was lighter and full of a joy he hadn't seen on her for too long. "Since Nash."

She ducked out of his hug and skipped to her car. He waved her off and kicked a rock, wanting to simultaneously delay and get the confrontation with Del over. Shoving his hands into the pockets of his pants, he joined his brother and uncle at the river.

"There he is. How's Regan?"

"Better, I think," he said shortly, an unasked question in his voice. Cade gave him a small headshake. The boat was loaded, and they set off downriver.

Cade slowed the boat where the river widened, and Uncle Del pulled out his fishing gear. The dread of the moment pressed on Sawyer.

"Uncle Del, there's something we need to talk about."

Del shifted his gaze up as he continued to thread a live worm on his hook. "You look like shit, Sawyer. You ain't sick too, are you?"

The way his stomach crawled up his throat made him wonder if he wasn't going to throw up over the side. "Not really. Listen. I saw you last night with Ms. Martha. In the back alley."

"We weren't doing nothing." The defensiveness in his voice only increased the pressure.

"She gave you a gas can."

"Yep. Kerosene." His uncle's shoulders rolled forward, and his voice resumed its normal, easy cadence. "Said it was stinking up her storage area. It'll be good for my space heater this winter."

His uncle threw a cast and hummed a tune. Sawyer and Cade exchanged a glance.

"I saw you driving over on the Mississippi side the other night. Close to Regan's neighborhood. What were you doing over there?" Sawyer asked.

"What were *you* doing over there?" Amusement flavored his uncle's voice. "Every time you're in the same airspace as Regan Lovell you can't keep your eyes off her."

Cade guffawed from the back, but it was obvious by the way he cut his attention back to the engine, he would be no help in navigating the tricky waters with their uncle.

"What about the wad of money in your kitchen drawer?"

His uncle muttered a curse and adjusted the collar of his denim button-down.

"What the heck is going on, Uncle Del?" Sawyer scooted forward and propped his elbows on his knees.

"Delmar Fournette." Cade's voice boomed between them like a scolding teacher. Del winced. "You promised me to use that money to fix the well. The sulfur's gotten worse. It might not kill you, but you put everyone in mind of Lucifer every time you enter a room."

Sawyer sat up and swiveled around. "Wait. That money was from you?"

Cade's eye-roll was answer enough.

"And the kerosene?'

"Thought Ms. Martha was doing me a favor." Del tugged on his line.

"And why were you sneaking around Cottonbloom, Mississippi, so late at night?" Cade asked.

"I've been courting Miss Leora. Not a state secret. If we want to get up to no good in the moonlight, then I think we've paid our dues." A seriousness hid behind their uncle's smile. "Life's short, boys. I've wasted too many years thinking I wasn't good enough for my Leora. Don't go repeating my mistakes." After aiming the nugget of wisdom in Sawyer's direction, Del recast his line and hummed the *Jeopardy* theme song.

Sawyer tried to shake the image of his ne'er-do-well uncle and the paragon of polite society getting up to no good. "So, just to be clear, you had nothing to do with any of the festival sabotaging?"

"No, and I'm mighty disappointed in both of you that you would even suspect I was up to something so underhanded and lowdown."

Sawyer and Cade's tripping apologies were cut short when Del hooked a fish and they worked together to bring it in, leaving behind festival business and their various love lives. The talk veered from fishing and hunting to the upcoming football season.

Once the sun reached its zenith, they headed back. Del trotted up to his house to get the fish on ice, while Sawyer helped Cade secure the boat, their walk back more circumspect.

"Thank God Uncle Del's not involved." Sawyer kept his voice low.

"How serious do you think things are getting between Delmar and Ms. Leora?"

"Serious enough that we'll have to start calling her *Aunt* Leora." Sawyer shot a side-eye and grin toward Cade.

"I've always got the impression Fournettes were below pond scum in her eyes."

"They were sweethearts. Things went to hell because of the war and she hated him—and us—because of that. Not because we were Louisiana swamp rats."

"Were?" Cade gestured between them. Both were covered in mud and fish scales and smelled of river water. But a smile was on Cade's face.

The shots of humor and sarcasm had been the biggest shift in Cade's personality since coming home. It harkened back to their life before their parents had died. Back before the struggle and responsibility had landed squarely on Cade's shoulders. Only now could Sawyer understand and appreciate how hard he had tried to keep Sawyer from following his path.

Sawyer threw an arm around Cade's shoulders, much as he had done to Tally earlier. "Things were hard for a long time, but we made out all right, didn't we? Thanks to you."

"Not because of me. You worked hard."

"You worked harder." Sawyer gave him one last squeeze.

As if of the same mind, they stopped at the line of pines and looked toward their old home.

"I want to bring a backhoe in here and bury that piece of shit," Cade said.

The trailer had never haunted Sawyer like it had haunted Cade and Tally. It had been a place to sleep and study and eat and even laugh on occasion. In his heart and in his dreams, his home had been on a quiet street with a swing set in the backyard and his mother making cookies after school.

"Burying it won't help. It's a pile of metal and wood. It's not evil. It hasn't hoarded our bad memories. Anyway, I have lots of good memories from there."

"Like what?"

"Like the night we ran out of kerosene and had to huddle together to stay warm."

"How is that a good memory? It was so cold we couldn't even sleep."

"I know." Sawyer smiled. "We stayed up all night talking and playing word games and laughing. Don't you remember?"

"That's right," Cade said on a soft chuckle. "And the time the chipmunk got loose."

"I'll never forget Tally jumping on the bed with that old tennis racket and screaming like a banshee." Sawyer's laugh faded into the stillness of the afternoon, and he whispered Tally's words from earlier, "The future is all that matters."

Cade clapped him on the shoulder and turned his back on the trailer. "I'll see you tomorrow at work, bro."

With Tally's words on repeat in his head, Sawyer stopped by his house to shower and change before heading to the grocery for the vegetable soup fixings. Pulling to the curb in front of Regan's house, he cut the engine but didn't move. Monroe's SUV was gone.

If only the future mattered, he needed to man up, get his head out of his ass, and own his part in their demise. Shifting the bag of groceries on his hip, he knocked. And waited. And waited. Cupping a hand over his eyes, he looked through the wavy glass on the side of the door.

Maybe she'd seen him and decided not to answer. Or maybe she had passed out somewhere and needed help. He tried the door. Unlocked. Of course it was. The woman had no sense of personal safety. He eased inside, the only sound the crinkle of the brown paper bag in his arms.

"Regan? You okay?"

Nothing. He tiptoed farther into her house and set the bag on the big, granite-covered island in her kitchen. He could see the den and up to the second-floor landing. She wasn't lying in a heap anywhere visible. Her bedroom door was halfway open. He approached on soft hunting feet and toed the door open, expecting to find her asleep in bed.

The sheets were rumpled and the pillows still in disarray on the floor. A noise came from his right. He swung around as the bathroom door opened and a glistening, completely naked Regan walked out.

Their gazes clashed. For what felt like an eternity, he was frozen, taking her in. From the top of her damp, wavy hair down past the beauty of her breasts and through the sexy dip from waist to hip, all the way down her long, slender legs to her bare feet.

Her scream and scramble to grab the corner of a sheet off her bed for covering prompted him to emit some stuttering grunts and word fragments. The corner of the sheet barely covered her breasts and the juncture of her legs, amping the sexy factor up past a hundred—on a scale to one from ten.

"Ohmigod, get out!"

He turned on his heel and retreated to the kitchen. He closed his eyes, but all he saw was her body. Her naked, delicious body. His memories and their quick coupling the other night hadn't done her justice. She'd only ripened over the years.

Not thirty seconds later she was stalking out of her room in shorts and a loose Ole Miss T-shirt. "How did you get in here?" Her voice was sharp with surprise and fear.

"Your door was unlocked. If you actually had an operational security system, this wouldn't have happened."

"Yeah, sure. Make this my fault too."

Her jab was subtle, but he felt it like an electric shock straight to his heart. "I didn't mean to scare you. I was worried."

"About me?" Her suspicion transmitted through her scrunched-up face and tone.

"You were feverish and ready to pass out last night." He let some of his exasperation show as he leaned against the island and crossed his arms and ankles.

"Yeah, that. I feel better. Fever's all gone. Headache too. You don't need to stay."

Although she did look better than she had last night, no color flushed her cheeks and her brown eyes were flat. He didn't move.

"What's in the bag?"

"Arsenic," he deadpanned.

Her gaze startled back to his. The animosity that crackled around them lost its potency with the small laugh that snuck out of her. She sauntered closer, her movements more relaxed. "You wouldn't poison me. You'd dump me kicking and screaming in the swamps with a bunch of gators."

He made a scoffing sound. "You'd stumble out weeks later wearing alligator boots. You're a survivor."

She laughed a full-bellied laugh this time and came close enough to brush his arm as she pulled the bag closer. "Chicken, broth, vegetables. Am I making soup?"

He tugged the bag back toward him. "No. *I'm* making soup. Go lay down."

"But—"

"Woman, let me do this. I feel bad enough already."

"Why do you feel bad?"

For a multitude of reasons he couldn't admit to her. Not yet, anyway. "I think the Saints are playing a preseason exhibition game."

Her gaze probed deeper, but he resisted. "I'm a Cowboys fan, I'm afraid," she said with faked regret and flopped on the couch.

He sucked in a breath. "So do you want me to go heavy or light on the arsenic?"

Her giggles echoed over the back of the couch, and he smiled as he pulled down a stockpot hanging from the ceiling and found a cutting board and knife.

The TV transmitted the sounds of football as the smell of chicken noodle soup filled the air. He left it simmering. She was lying on the long side of the L-shaped couch under a blanket. He pressed the back of his hand against her cool forehead. Before she could protest or bat it away, he moved to the short end of the couch.

"Diagnosis, doctor?"

"You'll live."

They watched the game progress in companionable silence. Her feet stuck out of the blanket close to his hip. "How's your foot? All healed up?"

Before he could consider his action or she could protest,

he scooted closer and pulled her feet onto his lap. He examined the bottom, the place where the thorn had pierced—still visible but healing. Her toes were painted a mint green today.

He rubbed both thumbs down the sole of her foot and massaged the ball. She flipped to her back, a soft whimper coming from her throat. He looked up, but her eyes were closed, an arm thrown over her head.

He worked his thumbs down her foot again, watching her face. A sigh accompanied a slight smile. Her enjoyment was obvious so he continued, moving back and forth between her feet. The sexy, little sounds and her squirms drove him on. What kind of sounds would she make if he had access to her entire body?

His mind went back to the moment she stepped out of the bathroom. That image spurred him on and with his gaze on her face, he slid his hands up her legs, taking the blanket with him. They were smooth and soft. Her arm had moved to cover her eyes, her breaths coming faster between her parted lips.

He leaned in to kiss the side of her knee as his fingers caressed the delicate skin underneath. Color flushed her cheeks. He stayed attuned to her body's reaction and moved closer, her knees shifting apart as if they were partners in a dance.

He pulled the blanket off and dropped it to the floor at the same time he levered himself on top of her, between her legs, his arms on either side of her head.

"Regan," he whispered. "Can I kiss you?" After the last time, he needed to ask, not wanting to push himself on her.

Her lashes fluttered open, her eyes as dazed as they'd been the night before in the throes of her fever. "Yes."

His lips met hers in a gentle caress. The blistering need for her simmered in the background, overtaken by the desire to take care of her, but when her tongue touched his bottom lip, he caved to his baser instincts, slanting his mouth over hers, pressing her into the cushions with his weight.

Her legs wrapped around his hips, and he rocked against her. Their tongues sparred, aggressive yet playful. One of her hands slipped under his T-shirt to graze the skin of his side, inciting a raspy moan from his chest.

He shifted to run his hand up her leg from knee to hip, slipping his fingers under the hem of her shorts to the lacey edge of her panties. Her shirt was already bunched around her torso, exposing a line of skin above her shorts. He pushed it upward, exposing her bare breast.

He stared like a teenager getting his first glimpse of the female mystery. He'd been crazed the other night. Now, he would go slow, savor and explore and appreciate.

He cupped her breast and cursed the calluses along his palm. She didn't seem to mind his rough hands, arching her back. The weight and fullness drew his mouth closer. Her small nipple was peaked and begged for attention. He flicked his thumb over the tip before soothing it with his tongue.

She speared a hand through his hair, her pelvis bucking into his erection. Need superheated his body. He squeezed her breast, shifting so he could pull her shirt up and off.

She grabbed his wrist after he'd exposed her other breast. He stared at the pert nipple, wanting to give it the same attention he'd applied to the first.

"Stop."

The single whispered word froze him. Confusion was overtaking the desperate need on her face. He waited for her move.

She let go of his wrist and covered her breasts. Friendly teasing had turned into a sensual foot rub that morphed into a full-on make-out session. Her skin prickled, overly sensitive where it rubbed against the cotton of his shirt or the denim of his jeans. Was her fever returning or was it simply desire?

She should push him off, but his weight felt good. No, better than good, he felt incredible. She had to stop herself from wiggling and rocking under him. Her mind and body were both weak from the fever, leaving her vulnerable, physically and emotionally. He was staring as if waiting for a guilty verdict—expectant yet morose.

"What are you doing?" Her voice was raw and cracked.

He cocked his head as if it were a trick question. "Kissing you. Don't you want me to?"

Her body wanted him bad. Her body didn't care if he took her again and walked out. But the rest of her cared. Too much. "I mean, what are *we* doing, Sawyer? If you're here to get your rocks off with an old flame, then leave. I don't need a fuck buddy."

"I swear I didn't come over here with the intention of . . . getting my rocks off." Although his expression stayed serious, humor lilted the words. Anger burned a path through her, incinerating the lingering desire.

She bucked her hips against him. "Get off me."

He pushed off, and she sat up. The pillow acted as a shield at her chest.

"I don't know what we're doing, but I don't want to go back to the way things have been," he said.

She squelched the leap of hope at his words. "We both know where this will lead, and it's not pretty."

"Maybe the past isn't as important as the future."

God, she wanted to believe that. Wanted to believe they could wipe everything clean and start over. But even if the past wasn't as important, it shaded every future decision. It was how people learned. Past mistakes were not to be repeated.

"I don't trust you, Sawyer." She stared at the fringe on the pillow as the truth of her past emerged. "I want you to leave."

His head dropped and his sigh was heavy. Tension grew tight in the stretched silence. He rose. "You've been sick, and I'm sorry I took advantage. I'll go. But sometime, I want to talk to you about that trust problem."

She stayed on the couch. He'd shown himself in, he could show himself out.

"The soup's ready. Enjoy and rest up." His voice echoed from the entry. The door snicked closed.

She didn't even have the energy to cry. She flopped back down, pulled the blanket back over her, and slept.

Chapter Fifteen

Regan was fully recovered by the time Tuesday's budget vote rolled around. Mr. Neely presented his results of the reassessments. Although Ms. Martha was in attendance and squirming in her seat, she didn't argue. Considering she'd come out the best of any business owner, she had no right to complain. The slight changes to tax income had already been incorporated into the budget, and it was adopted by a seven-to-four margin.

With the budget passed, she could move forward and finalize details of the festival. Most of the vendors were local, but some were from out of town and required a substantial down payment. The festival committee was meeting the next afternoon, and she needed to have her list ready.

Through the relief and the lists scrolling through her head, disappointment lurked. She glanced at the double doors on the side for the umpteenth time. No Sawyer. She exited through the side door and into the cool marble hallway. It was deserted, just like it should be.

A cacophony of voices crested as she turned the corner. The meeting attendees had poured out of the stuffy room to discuss and gossip in the atrium.

Deputy Preston's six-foot-four, former linebacker body scythed through the crowd. Their gazes met and he made a "come-on" gesture with two fingers. He retreated toward the door without looking over his shoulder to confirm her compliance.

The crowd closed the path he'd made, so she skirted around the edges, giving out smiles and sound bites, but not stopping. The deputy wasn't waiting at the door, but she could see the red and blue lights of his cruiser casting bright circles.

He was sitting in the driver's seat with his legs out, talking on his phone. She shifted on her heels and looked to the sky, but the stars hid behind dark clouds tonight.

"She's right here." The deputy garnered her full attention. He didn't look up, only checked his watch and said, "We'll be there in ten." He disconnected and slipped the phone into his belt holster.

"What's going on?" Her stomach tumbled and rolled like a rock kicked down an endless hill.

"Your shop's been vandalized."

She grabbed her throat. "Not set on fire?"

"No. Ransacked. We need you to identify anything that's missing."

"Of course." She stumbled to her car in a dream state. While the pavilion fire and the basket cutting had caused damage, neither had been aimed directly at her, but at the festivals in general. Even the man outside of her mother's had been after her tomatoes.

This seemed personal. Her shop was her livelihood. She drove the route on autopilot, passing by so she could prepare herself before going in. A jagged hole marred the plate-glass window in front. The breeze swung the drawn blinds forward and back. The door stood open and light poured out.

She took a spot in front of a black and tan cruiser. She considered going home and crawling under her covers.

Deputy Preston rapped on the driver's side window, making her squeak. He chucked his head toward her shop and walked off.

She turned the car off and followed, her ankles wobbly in her heels. Her head circled all the possibilities and problems. How big a loss? Would her insurance cover it? How soon would the security system people be able to hook up her house alarm? Who would do this? Was it the man from the garden? Had Sawyer heard?

Broken glass crunched under her heels. She took in a bracing breath and stepped into her studio. Everything was in disarray. Down feathers covered everything in a layer of white, small pieces floating in the air like snow.

"Try not to touch anything," the deputy said.

Her gaze darted around the room, taking an inventory from memory. It appeared as if her display of pillows had taken the brunt. She walked a circle around the room. Everyone was quiet. She poked her head into her office.

A woman in plain clothes and wearing gloves sifted through the swatches on the back table. STOP THE FESTIVAL OR ELSE was written across the wall in red spray paint. The irony was not lost on her even though the message contained a threat her stunt with red spray paint on Sawyer's wall back in June didn't.

Her bolted-down safe appeared untouched. Not that there was much to steal inside. Saturday morning was her deposit day. The cabinet drawers hung open, files scattered on the floor. And her whiskey bottle was gone. It had been three-quarters full.

"Can you open the safe? Verify the contents?" Deputy Preston's voice came over her shoulder.

Regan squatted down and opened the safe. Everything was how she remembered it, but she pulled out her petty cash box and counted the money.

"Everything's here. And, it appears most of the damage was superficial. The pillows made a big mess, but they're honestly the cheapest things in the shop. Where's the chair he used to break the window?"

"Why do you assume it was a man?" Suspicion colored his tone.

Regan shot a side-eye toward the deputy. "I assume the chair that went through the window was the oak armchair in the display. It's solid. Not that a woman couldn't lift it, but did you forget about the man I reported out at my mother's? Seems a little too coincidental, don't you think?"

The deputy hummed, not giving away anything. "We found the chair on the sidewalk and moved it out of the way. Beyond the damage, is anything missing?"

Reporting a mostly full bottle of Jack as the only missing item would no doubt be a story for the ages. "The important stuff is still here."

The deputy herded her toward the door. "We're going to be awhile finishing up. No need for you to stay. You can contact your insurance tomorrow and begin cleaning up."

She had a niggling feeling the deputy wanted her gone and whirled on him. She was on the sidewalk while he had his hands braced on the doorjambs, blocking her reentry. "I had nothing to do with this. You were in the budget meeting tonight same as me."

"True." A sharp nod accompanied the single word.

"So . . ."

"We're not sure when this happened. I'm not accusing you of anything, Miss Lovell, but I need to stay impartial and keep non-police personnel to a minimum while conducting the investigation."

He might not be accusing her, but he certainly wasn't clearing her either. "I expect a call in the morning with anything you discover."

"I'll file my report and Sheriff Thomason will follow up with you in the morning." He stepped back and closed the door. Before she made it a dozen feet, he cracked the door back open. "Miss Lovell, why don't you stay at your mama and daddy's tonight?"

She glared over her shoulder and didn't answer. Dealing with her mother was the last thing she needed tonight. The woman was a drama magnet and gossip queen. By the time the sun was up, she'd have told everyone a serial killer was roaming Cottonbloom, and Regan was his target. The excitement would trump the worry. Then she'd have to hear yet again about how inappropriate her role as Cottonbloom mayor was.

Stubbornness, pure and simple, had kept her from calling the security company already. Giving Sawyer the satisfaction of possibly being right had stuck in her craw. She should have listened to him. Hindsight was an evil bitch.

She drove by her house, but nothing moved. Her parents' house was dark. It was ten. They were in bed watching TV or maybe even asleep by now. She drove around the block, pulled into her driveway, and sat in the car with the doors locked.

The longer she sat, the stuffier the air inside became and the more paranoid she grew. It was how she felt after a scary movie, as if everything held sinister portents. Only this time it was real life.

She fumbled her phone out of her purse and dialed Monroe. It went to voice mail. She and Cade were probably getting busy. She scrolled through her contact list. Mostly clients or government officials. No one she trusted to protect her from boogeymen.

She could call Sawyer. Her conscience ticked off the many reasons why she shouldn't. But the deep-down truth was he was the only one she trusted—even though she didn't trust him. The conflict made no sense whatsoever.

The finger that tapped his name trembled. It rang once. What was she doing opening this door? Worse danger than the boogeyman waited behind it. It rang twice. She should hang up.

"Regan. What's wrong?" His voice was sharp.

"Why does anything have to be wrong?" She tried a laugh, but it trailed off as she stared at a bush near the corner of her house. It moved, but not with the wind. She tightened her hand on the steering wheel. She should head to her parents'. Deal with the fallout in the morning.

"Because you're calling me at ten on a weeknight. Did the budget not pass?"

"No, it passed," she said absently, the movement growing more violent. A bird flew out of the top of the bush followed a heartbeat later by her neighbor's black cat. "Holy hell!" The words were out before her brain registered the harmless events. Well, maybe not harmless for the bird.

"Where are you? Tell me right now what's going on?"

If she wasn't mistaken, panic that neared the level of her own crackled over the phone. "I'm at home in the driveway in my car. I'm fine. It was just a cat." She sank down in the bucket seat, feeling lightheaded in the aftermath of the pulse of adrenaline.

"Don't you fucking move." The line went dead with a double beep.

Probably she should feel pathetic and weak for sitting there. She didn't. Relief loosened her hands, and she gathered her purse to her chest and waited. Eight minutes passed. She tensed at the sweep of headlights on her street, but the sight of his truck settled warmth in her chest.

She slipped out of her car. The truck jerked to a stop, half on the curb, and he was out and running around the front. He grabbed her upper arms and skimmed his gaze down her body and back up, relaxing when he met her eyes.

"You scared me," he whispered. "What happened?"

Her gaze performed a similar trek. The same pajama pants he'd worn the night she'd accused him of tomato mischief hung low on his hips. A plain white T-shirt covered his torso. He hadn't even stopped for shoes, his bare feet covered in dewy grass.

She clutched her purse tighter when she really wanted to throw herself in his arms. He'd come because she'd needed him. No explanation necessary. A lump of emotion that beat the same rhythm as her heart clogged her throat.

"My shop was broken into tonight."

"Robbery?"

"Vandalism. And a warning spray-painted in red across a wall in my office. *Stop the festival or else.*"

"Let's get inside." He put an arm around her shoulders, and she relished the weight and security.

She unlocked the door and pushed it open. He glanced toward the still-defunct control panel and back at her, but didn't comment. As he made his way into the house, he flipped lights on, checking her bedroom and even upstairs. But now that she was inside and with him, she wasn't worried. No one had been there.

She went to the frig and pulled out two beers, uncapping both and handing one over when he returned. "Everything looks fine. Now, tell me everything."

She did and realized how little information the deputy had imparted. "Honest to God, I think he suspects me."

Sawyer's lips twitched around the rim of the bottle before he took several swallows. The strong column of his throat worked, and she laid her cold bottle against her cheek. He set his bottle on the counter and her gaze transferred to his lips.

The feeling of them on hers and teasing her breasts made her fan herself with a hand. Why did he have to attract her like a gnat to a bug zapper?

"Now that I'm inside, everything will be okay," she said.

"You were just sitting in your car waiting for someone to walk you to the door?" He leaned back against the counter and crossed his feet at the ankles. "Your mama is four houses down."

"You know what Mother's like."

"Yep, I know." While her voice had contained a fair amount of exasperation and amusement, his had been all bitter.

Regan broke his gaze and tore at the label on her bottle. The wave of guilt was as strong as it was unexpected. Her mother's vitriol and prejudice against Sawyer had poisoned their relationship. Regan had been desperate for guidance in those harsh days after their breakup. Her mother had provided comfort but also a way forward that included cutting Sawyer out of her life. At the time, it had seemed the wisest path.

"I called Monroe, but when she didn't answer . . ." How could she put her feelings into words without opening herself to him? The events of the night had left her feeling raw and exposed. She forced a smile even as she kept her gaze focused over his shoulder. "You and Monroe are the only ones who wouldn't think I was a whack job for being scared."

"You own a gun?"

"No." Her smile dropped.

"I'm staying on your couch."

"You don't have to. Really." Her protests were weak. She wanted him to stay.

He smiled, not in a smirking knowing way, but in a sweet, rock-solid way that had her choking out thanks.

She retreated to her bedroom and riffled through her pajama drawer. Her choices included a silk teddy set with the tags still on. Too sexy. A holey, soft T-shirt. Too pathetic. A cute yet comfortable tank with matching striped shorts. Just right.

She went through her nightly routine, hyperaware he was in her house. She grabbed a new toothbrush, an extra blanket, and a pillow from her bed.

He was lounging on the couch, his knees spread wide and his hands over his head, SportsCenter at a minimum volume. He appeared comfortable and at ease.

"I brought you some stuff." She set everything on the nearest cushion and shifted on her feet, her gaze directed at the TV even though she wasn't paying attention. Every nerve ending seemed to strain toward Sawyer. "If you want to use one of the upstairs rooms—"

"I'm fine on the couch." He reached for the toothbrush. "Anyway, I don't want to be too far away. Just in case."

"Look, I really do appreciate you coming over. You've been great about everything, considering . . ." Her words were weak and unsure.

"Considering what?"

"Considering our past. We haven't exactly been friends the last few years. And the festival competition didn't help matters."

He tapped the toothbrush against his palm. "Things have been weird, but I've never stopped worrying about you, Regan. Even when I didn't want to." The last came out as a whisper.

Their eyes met. The resentment and dislike that had grown over the years had changed sometime in the past few weeks. Or maybe the complicated range of emotions on his face and rushing through her had always been there. Dislike was easy. Whatever was sprouting between them was not.

She retreated step by step until her back hit the doorjamb to her room. Feeling like a coward, she said, "Good night," and closed her door—the physical barrier a poor substitute for the emotional one that was being bulldozed down a little each day.

She closed her eyes and forced herself to remember why they'd ended things for good. The picture of a sleepy, tousled-haired Sawyer in bed with the naked big-boobed brunette with smudged mascara was branded onto her brain.

Tears burned her eyes, as if it had happened yesterday and not a decade ago. Could the present make up for the past? Could she forgive him? Could she forgive herself? She had set the awful events into motion. She fell asleep with "if onlys" scrolling through her head. Restlessness plagued her as she relived alternate futures in her dreams.

A bang startled her upright in the bed, the covers clutched to her chin. Sawyer burst into the room, and she let out a short yelp.

"Are you okay? What was that?" Dawn leaked through her partially drawn curtains, highlighting his bare chest and low-hanging pajama pants.

She stumbled over a few uhs and ahs. He stalked to the French doors that let out onto her back patio and ripped the curtains open.

The orangey light from the sunrise outlined his body. An answering flame lit in her belly. She dropped the covers and almost reached for him. Damn the past and the future. She wanted the in-between. That slice between night and day.

"A bird. Poor fella broke his neck chasing the sun in your window." He drew the curtains closed, and the moment was snuffed out along with the light. If she wasn't careful, she would end up like that bird. She flopped back onto the pillows. He joined her, stretching out on top of her covers, his hands linked under his head.

"Quiet night except for errant birds."

"Yep. Guess I didn't need you after all." She hoped he'd put the roughness in her voice down to sleep. "You'd best head out soon. Mother is up at the butt-crack of dawn to walk her dogs."

He shifted and propped himself up on an elbow to look down at her. "And you're worried about what she'd say? Thought you were a grown woman, Regan."

"I am." She pushed up slightly on the pillows to even their faces. "But appearances still matter around here."

"Not to me, they don't. I came over last night because you called me. Because you needed me. Anyway, I didn't lay my dirty, swamp rat hands on you, did I?" His bitterness made her stomach roll.

"I'm not ashamed—I was never ashamed of you, Sawyer."

"Why didn't you take me to your prom then?"

Her mouth dropped, but all she could do was shake her head. The question was so unexpected, she could only reach for the truth. "You tried to hide it from me, but I knew."

"Knew what?"

She swallowed hard. "I knew how poor you were."

He stilled. "I doubt that."

"I went to your place once."

"What place?" His question was tentative, probing.

They'd never gone to her house or his. Their places were the bed of his brother's truck, the skiff he'd take up-river to behind her house, the soft moss under the trees on the bank. Snatches of time in the neutral zones between their lives. It was understood he wasn't welcome at her house, and he'd made it clear his place was off-limits.

"The trailer in the woods."

"When?"

"Your birthday." She sat cross-legged and shifted to face him. "I was going to surprise you."

He rolled to his back. "I guess you were the one surprised."

"Yes and no."

"What does that mean?"

More light snaked into the room, the bright sun promising another scorcher of a day. It also highlighted the defensive set to his face.

"People like to talk. Especially once it was common knowledge we were together. I heard all kinds of stuff from girls who thought I should know that your brother was a poacher and that your family got clothes and food from the church charity bank."

"Did you believe them?"

The shame on his face told her it had all been true, and she spoke her own truth. "I didn't care if it was true or not. It didn't change how I felt about you."

The tight lines around his eyes eased as he cast them toward her. "But something changed how you felt about me or you wouldn't have broken it off. Was it your mama?"

Her own shame welled up from an ugly place she tried to deny. Maybe it was time to excise the poison. "Yes," she whispered. She cleared her throat and continued. "Even before I left for Ole Miss, she planted doubts. And, once we were apart . . . I was young and she was my mother. I thought that she had accepted you were good enough for me. You were in college studying engineering, for goodness' sake."

"You went along with her plans and broke up with me." His resignation and disappointment fed her shame.

"She made it sound so logical. I felt smart and mature. A break to see what else was out there and if neither of us found anything else, then we could get back together and she'd support us a hundred percent."

"Pretty smart of her really. She shoehorned us apart,

and then worked on pushing us so far from each other, we could never find our way back."

"Yeah, except, I realized in less than twenty-four hours that being smart and logical shouldn't hurt so bad. I tried to find my way back to you." Under the shame, her anger grew. Anger at her mother, at Sawyer, at herself. The combination was potent and devastating.

"Regan, baby." He touched her knee, but she jerked it back, pulling her knees up and wrapping her arms around her legs. She was close to shattering and no amount of superglue would put her together again.

"I called and called. When no one answered, I left before dawn and drove down. You found something else pretty quick." She wanted to rise up and scream like a pressure cooker releasing steam.

"There's something I tried to tell you so many times, but you wouldn't, couldn't hear me. That morning you found me . . ."

His words stalled on a sigh, and in the expectant silence came a hard knock and three quick pushes of her doorbell. The yip of dogs carried all the way into her bedroom.

She muttered a curse that would have half the ladies of Cottonbloom Church of Christ gasping and the other half hiding giggles. She swung off the bed, knowing ignoring her mother was futile. Another thirty seconds would have her coming around the back and peering into her windows.

She stalked into the entry, turned the locks, and flung the door open. "What?"

After the walk down memory lane with Sawyer, the sight of her mother, makeup and hair perfect, in kitten heels and struggling to keep the two Pomeranians from wrapping their leashes around her ankles reared up a suppressed resentment.

Her mother craned her neck, the sagging skin the

only concession to her age. "What is that truck doing out front?"

Regan made a show of looking over her mother's shoulder. "Looks like it's just sitting there."

"You know very well what I meant. Where is he?"

Regan propped a hand on the doorjamb and forced a smile, although it felt barbed. "I left him in the bedroom."

The dogs applied themselves to getting inside her house. She liked dogs in general, but her mother's spoiled, yippy purse dogs were more than she could handle. Marie set up a continuous bark while Donny stared at Regan, hiked a leg, and peed down her front door. She wouldn't be at all surprised to find out her mother had a telepathic bond with the little terrors.

"Nice manners, you little—"

"Regan. It was an accident. You must understand the situation has them overwrought."

"Why would your dogs care, Mother? Let's not pussyfoot around. You're the one who is overwrought, but might I remind you I'm a grown woman who can invite the entire Cottonbloom Barbershop Quartet for a sleepover if I want."

"That sort of crass talk is never appropriate, young lady." Her mother's reprimand still had the power to jab through her adult façade to the insecure child beneath.

Sawyer chose that moment to saunter up in his pajama bottoms and T-shirt. Regan almost wished he'd stayed shirtless for the shock value alone. "I'd best be going. I need to shower before work. Thanks for the toothbrush."

When she went to take the toothbrush he held out, he grabbed her hand and pulled her close, laying a mint-scented, close-mouthed kiss on her lips. It was gentle and sweet and left her heart pounding.

He brushed a kiss along her cheek to her ear. "We're going to finish that talk later."

He let her go. The smile he bestowed on her mother was all Dixie Crystals sweet. "Mrs. Lovell. Nice to see you. If you'll excuse me." He inclined his head and headed to his truck with as much dignity and aplomb as a barefoot man in pajama pants could muster.

She and her mother were silent as he disappeared into his truck. The loud rumble of his engine prompted another round of yips and Marie to poop on her entry rug.

"Mother, go home and take your ill-mannered dogs with you."

"I want to know what's going on."

"Too bad." She tried to close the door, but her mother wedged a kitten heel in the door with surprising strength.

"Sawyer Fournette broke your heart. Don't you remember? You were a wreck. Almost flunked out of school."

"I remember," she said softly. "I also remember how I let you talk me into breaking up with him in the first place. The truth is I have no idea what's going on between Sawyer and me, but whatever is happening will happen without your influence. Is that understood?"

Her mother huffed, but Regan didn't allow what was sure to be a negative answer. She shut the door in her mother's face. *When one door closes, another opens.* The old saying popped into her head.

She gathered cleaning supplies and put her entryway back to rights, tossing the rug into the washer. Sawyer wanted to talk later. Well, she'd let him. She'd hear him out and let her heart do the answering. Right now though, she had more immediate problems than Sawyer or her mother. A mental list scrolled. She had to deal with the police, her insurance company, and all the gawkers downtown who were sure to ask questions. Plus, she needed to call a security company and finally get the system hooked up.

Yet, even with the other things churning through her

head, she paused and ran a finger over her lips. The very fact his good-bye kiss hadn't been sexual made a crater-sized impact in her chest. What did it mean? Would he have planted a kiss on her if her mother hadn't been standing there? Yes, she rather thought he would. That kiss had been a declaration to her and her mother. Sawyer Fournette had been out to make a statement.

Chapter Sixteen

Besides the broken front window, most of the damage to her shop was superficial. She bought paint to cover the red slash of the vandal's message in her office. She filled three garbage bags, but the down feathers and stuffing seemed to reproduce. She would no doubt be finding remnants for weeks to come. A few decorative knickknacks were broken, but nothing of value had been stolen. It seemed to be the work of someone who meant to intimidate and scare her, not to steal from her. She honestly wasn't sure which scenario was more worrisome.

Monroe stuck her head in, shaking a takeout bag and cradling two drinks. "Could you use a lunch break? I have forty-five minutes until my next client."

"Yes, please."

They retreated to her office where the spray-painted message loomed over them. They ate chicken salad sandwiches and sipped on sweet tea in silence.

"Ironic, don't you think?" Regan gestured at the wall with her drink.

"On purpose irony or accidental irony?"

"It's common knowledge I painted Sawyer's wall. It was

there for all to see a good twenty-four hours before I re-painted it."

"Someone who doesn't like you picking on Sawyer? Someone who wants his festival to go and not yours?"

"If we assume it's the same person who cut the baskets as did this"—she waved a hand around and took a sip of tea—"then it seems like whoever it is doesn't want either festival to be a success."

Another knock sounded on the front door. Regan wiped her mouth with a napkin and went to the front. Ms. Martha stood on the sidewalk, looking at the broken window. At least she could be assured Ms. Martha hadn't been the vandal. Regan flipped the lock and forced a smile. The last thing she wanted to discuss was property assessments, but the break-in would worry other business owners and it was her job to reassure them.

"Hello, Ms. Martha. You can come on in, if you want."

The lady stepped over the threshold, her eyes wide and darting. "Goodness me. Was there considerable damage?"

"Nothing too costly, besides the window, of course. It was mostly a pillow massacre." Her laugh seemed to surprise Ms. Martha.

"I expected you to be more upset. I don't know what I'd do if my place were vandalized."

Regan shoved another handful of stuffing into one of the trash bags. "I don't think you have anything to worry about, unless you run for mayor next term."

Ms. Martha fiddled with the fabric she held. "What do you mean?"

"This seemed to be a personal attack." She led Ms. Martha back to her office and presented the defaced wall with a flourish.

"Oh my." Ms. Martha stared at the threatening message. Her face had paled and she swayed on her feet.

Monroe hopped up. "Here, why don't you sit, Ms. Martha? You're looking a tad peaked."

Ms. Martha aimed a wan smile toward Monroe and patted her hand. "Thank you, dear."

Regan sank into the chair behind her desk.

Ms. Martha had returned her attention to the wall. "Are you scared?" she finally asked.

Considering she'd taken refuge in her car until Sawyer could check her house for boogeymen, she'd qualify, yet she sure as tooting wasn't going to admit that to Ms. Martha—or Monroe for that matter. She still felt at odds with Ms. Martha over the tax assessment, and something about her attitude put her even further on guard.

"Not really. I'm taking precautions, and whoever is behind the incidents will be caught soon enough. The police were all over the shop, dusting for fingerprints and searching for hair they can analyze." The half-lie came from watching too many crime dramas, and Regan tensed, waiting for Ms. Martha's reaction.

"I hope none of the rest of us become targets because of your festival."

Regan relaxed back in the chair. Ms. Martha was only interested in how this would affect the Quilting Bee. Selfish but understandable. "Again, I don't think you should be worried, but if it settles your mind, both Sheriff Berry and Chief Thomason will be mounting extra patrols."

Color returned to Ms. Martha's cheeks and she stood, murmuring her good-byes. In the doorway of the office, she pivoted back. "I almost forgot. I made you a new pillow. I know it won't replace . . ." She gestured vaguely.

Regan took the fabric she held out and spread it open on her desk. It was a patchwork of plaids in blues, greens, and reds. Guilt that she suspected Ms. Martha of any wrongdoing warred with the warm feeling of being part of a community that cared about each other.

"It's lovely, Ms. Martha. Thank you so much." She skirted the desk and gave the woman a hug. It wasn't the warmest or most comfortable hug, but it was a start. "I hope once the festival is over, you'll find that it benefited you and the town."

Ms. Martha pulled away. "And if it's a disaster?"

"Then we won't waste our resources on another one next year, I promise."

"I am sorry about all of this. Truly."

"It's hardly you're fault. We're all in this together." Regan followed her to the door. Ms. Martha nodded, but didn't meet her eyes on her way out.

She watched until Ms. Martha made the turn onto River Street. Monroe joined her at the door. "That was weird."

"Was it? I took it like a peace offering of sorts."

"I read a book one time about serial killers. Did you know that they get a thrill out of revisiting the scene of their crimes? Even better if the police are around."

Regan retrieved the pillow casing from her desk and used stuffing from one of the garbage bags to bring it to life. "Are you comparing Ms. Martha to a serial killer?" While it wasn't her usual taste, the pillow was very homey and sweet.

"All I know was the vibes she was putting out were odd."

"She's worried about her shop. The Quilting Bee is her life."

"Exactly. And you are interfering."

Regan hugged the pillow to her chest. Monroe was dead serious. Her blue eyes were crinkled. Doubts inserted themselves once again. "She couldn't have broken in here and thrown that chair out the window. It weighs a ton."

Monroe's face smoothed, but a frown remained. "True. It was definitely a man you saw outside your mother's garden?"

"Definitely."

More knocks sounded, followed by a wavering voice. "Regan-honey, are you here?"

Ms. Leora and Ms. Effie stood inside the door, looking around. Ms. Effie wrapped an arm around Regan's shoulders. "We're just so sorry about what's happened."

"It's not your fault." She repeated the same thing she'd told Ms. Martha.

"No, but it's our town, and it's abominable that something like this should occur. Do the police have any suspects? Did they steal anything?" Ms. Leora asked.

"Not that they've said. You ladies have nothing to worry about. Cottonbloom is entirely safe. This wasn't random. Someone doesn't want the festival to happen."

"Why do you say that, dear?" Ms. Effie cocked her head, her eyes sharp.

Regan led them into her office where Monroe was finishing the last bite of her sandwich and gestured to the wall. Both the ladies made appropriate sounds of shock and dismay. Debating for a moment, she rounded the desk and pulled out the two letters.

"I also received these." Regan handed one to each lady, carefully gauging their reactions.

Ms. Leora did a pearl clutch and gasp while Ms. Effie muttered something a bit less ladylike.

"You got a second one?"

Regan ignored Monroe's accusatory tone and said nothing. The two old ladies exchanged a glance and something unspoken passed between them.

"This sort of behavior is unacceptable." Even with the waver in Ms. Leora's voice, her strength was palpable. She was not a woman to be trifled with.

The two ladies retreated to the door. Ms. Leora stopped with her hand on the knob. "You let me know if I can help with the Tomato Festival in any way, Regan. We'll win that grant."

Heretofore, the ladies of the quilting circle hadn't thrown their considerable influence behind either festival. Ms. Leora's sudden support gave Regan a shot of much-needed confidence. "I will, thanks so much."

The ladies made their way to the café across the street, their heads close. Monroe tapped her on the shoulder and waved the two letters in her face. "When did the second letter arrive?"

"Right after the budget meeting."

"Did you show these to the police last night?"

"I didn't. Sawyer is the only one who knows."

"What the heck is going on with you two?"

"Nothing." Regan cleared her throat and focused on a few scraps of stuffing that had worked their way under an antique chest.

"Please. He calls Cade in a tizzy because you have a fever. Spends the night. And looked like a kicked puppy when I pushed him out the front door the next morning."

"I can't imagine Sawyer in a tizzy about anything." Regan straightened but couldn't meet her best friend's eyes. "I showed him the letters because he's as invested as I am in finding whoever is doing this. That's all."

Maybe it was all. She wouldn't know until she and Sawyer had a chance to finish their talk. She glanced up. Monroe's blue eyes cut through her lies. Or at least her half-truths.

"I understand more than anyone what it is to protect yourself from being hurt. Just remember that living is laying your heart on the line for someone else to protect." Monroe gave Regan's arm a squeeze and left her alone.

Before any more well-meaning friends or business owners or gossips could stop by, she closed up, turning the key in her newly installed lock even though the gaping hole in her front window had only been secured with a battened-down tarp. Even after everything that had happened, she trusted nothing would be stolen. A police car rolled slowly by and she waved. Chief Thomason was following through on his promise to step up patrols.

She didn't feel like dealing with the shop or the festival. All she could think about was Sawyer. The danger of making someone or something the center of your world was that when it self-destructed, everything was ruined.

Yet, Monroe's words resonated. Could she trust Sawyer to protect something he'd destroyed once?

Doubts circled, the uncertainty casting him back to his adolescence. It had been a long time since he'd been nervous and excited about a woman. Since Regan as a matter of fact.

Before he had the chance to question himself, he made his way to the river and set off. He tried not to think too far into the future. Whatever was growing between them was a seedling he had to nurture. Any storm could flatten it.

He was used to travelling a little farther upstream to her parents but guessed he was near enough. Seeing a navigable section of bank, he ran the skiff aground. The past seemed both close and a different lifetime. Hauling himself up the bank, he could see the faint outline of her house in the distance.

He ran his hands down his shorts before pulling his phone out. He'd gotten in trouble for not calling her after their fiery encounter against her wall. A mistake he wouldn't repeat. He hit her number.

She answered on the fourth ring with a tentative "Hello."

"Hi, yourself. Checking on you. How are you?"

"Fine. Fine."

He rubbed his nape and stared toward her house. "Are you home?"

"I am. Hard to get anything done with half the town stopping by to see the damage. What about you?"

"I'm out and about, actually."

"Do you want to come over here maybe?" A shy hesitancy softened her voice. "We can throw around some theories about whoever is behind the festival shenanigans."

He leaned against the trunk of a water oak. "I'm already at your place."

A pause before she said, "I don't see your truck."

"Meet me at the river? I'll be waiting under the big oak."

The silence stretched and he barely heard her whispered "Okay" before she disconnected.

He had no idea how long he would have to wait. Or if she would change her mind and call him back. Or just leave him hanging. It took all of five minutes. Movement caught his attention and had him pushing off the tree and stepping forward.

She was run-skipping toward him, her hair loose and sparking in the hot afternoon sun. His heart tried to claw out of his chest and perform a kamikaze-style suicide. Or maybe it was more of an offering to the gods of fate. The truth broke open inside him.

He still loved Regan Lovell.

Always present just muffled by layers of complications and pains. Philosophers say the truth will set you free, but he was fearful the truth might destroy him.

She slowed to a walk a dozen feet away. Her sleeveless sundress was white and covered in small red flowers, poppies maybe, and she was barefoot, flip-flops in her hand. The smile on her face rivaled the sun.

"I was surprised you called," she said as she stepped

into the shade with him. "Especially with an invite to the river. I assume . . ." She craned her neck toward the water.

"I came by boat." His voice sounded like it had been run through a grinder. "How about a ride for old times' sake?"

"Why not?"

She slid on the flip-flops, and he helped her down the bank to the boat. They slipped into old rhythms. She took the seat in the bow, tucking her skirt under her legs and swinging to half-face the front.

He pushed them off, jumped in before his feet got too wet, and started the motor. It was one of Cade's first designs and quiet. He got them moving, letting the river current do most of the work. Her hair blew around her face, the wind undoing whatever magic she'd performed to straighten the natural waves.

She raised her arms and twisted her hair back, holding it off her neck. Her arms flexed, toned and graceful. Her breasts stretched the top of the dress. She arched her back and tilted her chin, showcasing her long neck. Her every movement seduced him like a choreographed dance.

He bypassed the section of river that bisected downtown Cottonbloom. It was too shallow and too public. He had no idea how public she wanted to take whatever it was that they were doing. In all their time dating, he'd never taken her out to eat or to the movies.

It had been hard to justify such luxuries when his family struggled to even put food on the table or clothes on their backs. Regan hadn't seemed to mind. Or maybe it was more that the clandestine nature of their relationship had suited her fine. She'd wanted to keep her parents—especially her mother—in the dark as much as possible.

They passed into Louisiana and entered a narrow section of the river. The trees leaned low, the branches reaching for one another. After the bright sun, the shadows were deep. He killed the engine and let them drift. The current kicked the back around, setting them into a slow, arching circle.

"It's beautiful out here. I'd forgotten." Her tones were hushed, reverent.

"I don't guess you had much cause to get on the water after we—" He didn't want to talk about the pain of their breakup. Not yet. "I remember my daddy and Uncle Del taking me and Cade on the river to fish. We couldn't stay quiet. Back then we were more like best friends than brothers."

Now they were moving slow, she'd turned to face him and a genuine smile turned her lips. He'd always hated her fake, pageant smile. "Guess you didn't catch any fish."

"Daddy put us out on the bank, told us not to mess with any gators, and left us." The memory made him smile even as she gasped.

"Sawyer, that's terrible."

"Naw, Cade and I had fun that day. We went looking for a gator but only found a couple of lizards. Daddy and Uncle Del came back for us a couple hours later with a cooler of fish."

"I can't even imagine . . . my days were managed to the minute."

An eddy pushed the boat alongside a fallen tree, and they came to a relative stop, the water rocking the boat slightly.

"I'm surprised you had the time for me. Actually, I'm surprised you ever gave me the time of day." He asked something he'd wondered about over the years. "Why did you?"

Regan stuttered a breath in. When they'd been kids they'd never talked in-depth about their feelings and whys or why nots. Her love for him had been a fact, not something she'd spent time examining. Then, afterward . . . her hate had been just as factual. But as an adult she understood how simple and childish they'd been in their love.

"You were pretty cute, if you weren't aware. And you definitely made a big first impression."

"So that's it?" He seemed disappointed and maybe even a little hurt.

How honest was she willing to be, considering she had no idea where they were headed? "At first, flirting with you at the parties was exciting and made me feel rebellious. I knew Mother would have a fit even then." She got tangled in his hazel eyes and continued without censoring herself. "You were the first person to really see me."

"What do you mean?"

"My mother saw herself in me. Or who she'd wanted to be maybe. The pageants, the cotillions, the cheerleading. The push to look the right way, act the right way, date the right boy. At first, all that was fine. I liked to win. I liked the attention." She shrugged. "It's nice to hear you're pretty, at least on the outside, from a panel of impartial judges. But, I always felt like Cinderella's ugly stepsister trying to force my foot in the glass slipper."

He smiled, a thin shaft of sunlight making his hair gleam. "Trust me, you are not the ugly stepsister in this story."

"I felt like one on the inside. You helped me see beyond my selfish little circle in the world. Suddenly finding the right pageant dress wasn't as important as making sure you were okay. I wanted to make you happy."

He looked to the treetops and muttered something unintelligible before looking her in the eye again. "Get over here."

Only a few feet separated them. The command in his voice and eyes were more than she could deny. She stood and the boat tipped, pitching her into him. He swept her up and positioned her across his lap, her feet hanging over the side and brushing the water.

"You didn't date me to piss your mother off?" he asked.

"That was just a side benefit." She forced a tease into her voice. Considering their most recent encounters, her mother still had not forgiven nor forgotten. Dating Sawyer had turned their mostly cordial mother-daughter relationship into a battlefield. And his betrayal had given her mother the victory.

She had disguised constant carping as constructive criticism. She still did, as a matter of fact. It had been Sawyer and his faith in her that had given her the strength to stand up for herself. With him gone, she'd lost the will to fight and settled back in Cottonbloom, her dreams smaller and her heart protected.

"Things have never been easy for us, have they?" she asked.

"Life is hard, Regan. Have you not figured that out yet? If you want something, you work for it."

His lecturing tone put her on the defensive, tensing her. "I understand hard work, thank you very much. But don't you wonder if maybe we were doomed from the beginning? I mean, Shakespeare knew how Romeo and Juliet would end before he started, right?"

"Predestination is a cop-out."

"What do you mean?" She slid her hands from around his neck to his chest, the resistance in her body growing.

"We both screwed up. You broke up with me—"

"It was a—"

"It wasn't a break, it was a breakup. Don't justify it. You hurt me so bad I wasn't sure I would survive." The pain in his voice mirrored her own. "You want to know what happened that night?"

Did she? Not like this. Not in his arms and on the river. The place that held only the best memories of him. When she squirmed to put distance between them, he only held her tighter.

"Nothing happened," he said shortly.

She froze, still pushing against his chest, but no longer fighting. "What?"

"My friends dragged me out that night to cheer me up. I drank myself into a blackout. I don't remember anything until you barged in that morning."

"I wasn't delusional. I know what I saw." A decade-old hurt reared up.

"I didn't have sex with that girl. I was physically incapable."

"How do you know that? You said yourself you didn't remember anything."

"Aside from the fact that alcohol makes it difficult for a man to get it up, I tracked her down later and asked her. If I had been awake I wouldn't have let her in my room, much less my bed, I can promise you that."

"Why not?" She wanted to believe him with a desperation that took her by surprise.

He loosened his hold, but she stayed put, her hands sliding to the edges of his shoulders. Gently, he brushed her hair back and tucked an errant piece behind her ear. "You were my first. It was special and sacred and I wouldn't have thrown that away on a one-night stand."

"Even though I . . . broke up with you? Broke your heart?" For the first time she took ownership of the part she'd played in their demise.

"Even so. Didn't mean I stopped loving you overnight."

"Why didn't you—?" She swallowed a lump of tears down. "You tried to tell me."

"So many times. Between your mama blocking me and you not taking my calls . . . And then you told me you didn't love me. That you were with someone else. I was furious. Everything I thought we had together meant nothing to you. You cut me out of your heart with such ease that—"

"I lied."

"What?"

"I wasn't with someone else. I didn't even date for a really, *really* long time."

He rolled his head back and closed his eyes.

Immaturity had doomed them, not the fates.

"I almost flunked out of Ole Miss." Her humorless laugh drew his attention back to her face. "I was heartsick. Monroe was beside herself. Even Mother seemed to be genuinely concerned. I came close to having to move back home and go to Cottonbloom College."

"Is that why you didn't get your degree in political science and move to Washington?"

"Partly."

"What was the other part?"

"When I didn't have you anymore . . . my dreams seemed silly. Too big."

"Was that your mama getting in your head again?"

"She didn't understand, but neither did Monroe. She'd always planned on coming back to Cottonbloom from the time she left. Her ties were unbreakable, and she was fine with that."

"But you always wanted away."

"Thinking that you'd cheated on me —" He made a protesting noise, but she continued. "It was my reality whether it was the truth or not. My confidence was shaken, and I was afraid to take chances. I ended up doing something that was comfortable. Something Mother approved of."

"Decorating?"

"Interior design, if you please. I'm really good at my job, and it made me happy again. I got a minor in political science."

"You would have been really good as a Washington bigwig too. Does being mayor make you happy?"

"It's not the UN, but I'm making a difference."

He chuckled. "I'd say some of the characters around here are more challenging than anything the UN deals with."

"I love Cottonbloom. I haven't regretted it." It was true. She loved knowing her neighbors, having lifelong friends to call when she needed help, and seeing the tangible differences she was making.

A silence fell, but much of the tension had dissipated. She rested her head on his shoulder and let her toes touch the cool water. He took her hand, their fingers playing.

She owed him something else. "I'm sorry, Sawyer."

"For what?"

"For cutting you out of my life. For not giving you another chance."

"I'm sorry I didn't try harder to make it up to you. We were both young and kind of dumb."

"Yeah." She smiled. "You were dumber than me though."

"Oh, really?" He weaved their fingers and tickled her waist with his other hand. She squealed and bucked in his lap. He shifted her back to the other seat in the boat. "All right, enough messing around. We have a saboteur to find."

A grin threatened but she kept it confined to a small smile. He cranked the motor and maneuvered them into the middle of the river, pointing them back upstream. The wind made a conversation impossible. Their relationship had shifted. A path forward had been cleared of the ballast from their pasts. How and what it meant was still unclear.

He slowed the boat on the approach to the bank. The sense of déjà vu paralleling the feelings of a new start unbalanced her. They didn't speak again until they were under the oak tree.

"You got plans for tonight?"

Was he asking her out on a date? "No plans. Nope. Nothing." How desperate did she sound?

"I've got an idea where we might look for our mystery man."

"Gotcha. Sure thing." No date then. A mission.

"Wear something casual. I'll pick you up around nine."

"Boat or truck?"

A mischievous smile played around his mouth. "We'll start with the truck."

She backed from the shadows of the tree into the bright sunlight, the change like the flash of a camera, blinding her.

"Until tonight." His lips brushed over her cheek and then he was gone. Would the promise she heard in his voice be fulfilled?

She watched him hop down the bank and stared as he rounded the first bend in the river, the past both close and a lifetime away.

Chapter Seventeen

"This is not a good idea," she said.

"Not in those shoes it's not. I told you to dress casual." Sawyer's voice teased as the truck bounced and rocked through the ruts.

"I have shorts on." Her voice rose defensively. She'd ended up driving to his farmhouse and leaving her car there. Otherwise, she would have changed on his burst of laughter when he'd greeted her.

"You paired them with heels and a silk shirt. Not my definition of casual."

"I don't own hiking boots." She braced the pointy end of her shoe against the edge of the floorboard. "I did not think casual meant a bonfire and a keg in the middle of the marshes. I'm not outdoorsy." She'd chosen the heels with him in mind and hadn't been disappointed in the way his gaze heated and flickered down the length of her legs.

"That's not what I remember. You used to come out on my boat every chance you got."

She harrumphed, but there was no heat behind it. "I wasn't on your boat because I enjoyed getting eaten alive by bugs and splashed with mucky river water. I was there because you were there, dummy."

"I love it when you're all sweet with a bite of tart with me, Regan." He covered the hand she had braced on the center console with his own. The steering wheel jerked to the right, sending them toward a bank of trees before he corrected.

Light flickered through the trees. Her stomach's flip-flopping grew more pronounced even as the rough track smoothed into a field. It would be mostly Louisiana people gathered. She couldn't imagine her ladies' Sunday School group or the Junior League of Cottonbloom, Mississippi, drinking beer from red plastic cups out in the boonies. Would she know anyone?

He parked next to a jacked-up four-by-four and opened his door. She grabbed his arm. "What's our story going to be?"

He turned toward her with one foot on the running board. "What do you mean?"

"You know, if someone asks what we're doing here together."

His smile faltered and his brows drew in. "What do you want to tell people?"

"We certainly can't say we're looking for the man who vandalized my shop and tried to kill my mother's tomatoes and possibly cut up your parish's crayfish baskets. I guess we can go with the ubiquitous 'we're hanging out.'"

"Sure. Hanging out. Sounds fine." He was there to offer a hand as she slid onto the running board. A very polite hand.

Maybe that's all they really were doing. Hanging out. "Because we are old friends, right? Not so crazy that we would hang out." She checked his expression, but it was bland. Her nerves took control of her mouth. "My best friend and your brother are practically living together. Not so far-fetched our lives would intersect. Plus, the festivals."

He stopped with them still hidden between two truck beds. "Are you nervous or something?"

"Maybe." At least, the hard-packed ground made her heels manageable. "I look ridiculous."

"Please. You'll be the prettiest thing out here." The compliment rolled off his tongue with unsettling ease. They stood close enough for her to feel his body's heat. He was in jeans and a plain black T-shirt. With his longer hair and stubble, he looked rough and tough. No one would mess with her with him at her side.

"You won't go off and leave me to fend for myself, right?"

"No one is going to bite. Cade's bringing Monroe and Uncle Delmar will be around. I'm sure you'll know plenty of people." He stepped into the wavery light of the bon-fire, took her hand, and didn't let go. "Do you think you'd recognize the man you saw outside your mama's garden if you ran into him again?"

The mission. She needed to focus on the mission and not on how good his big hand felt or the way his arm brushed hers as they stepped in tandem. "I didn't see his face. Maybe if I saw him moving, it would trigger something. Nothing that would hold up in a court of law though."

"No. But enough I could put some feelers out. Keep a lookout, all right?"

She nodded. The line of people standing at the edge of the field parted to let them through to the keg. Sawyer received good-natured pats on the shoulder and dropped her hand to dole out handshakes. She plastered a smile on her face. Most people either gave her a polite nod or ignored her altogether.

In their wake, she could hear the whispers. Maybe they were discussing the dry spell, maybe they were discussing the constellations, but Regan was pretty sure she and Sawyer were the subject of the buzzing.

Sawyer's uncle Delmar sat on a wooden stool a dozen feet away, strumming on a guitar. Sawyer stuffed a twenty into a mason jar filled with money, pumped the keg, and filled two cups with beer. He handed one over, and she drank half in one go. The cold beer offered a small amount of liquid courage.

He guided her away from the bonfire with a big hand on her lower back. Delmar and Sawyer exchanged a half-hug as Regan rocked on her feet. She'd not exchanged more than two words with his uncle since she'd hired him to finish the pavilion, primarily to poke Sawyer into a snit. It had worked rather spectacularly, but her guilt about leveraging Delmar had grown.

"Hi there, Miss Mayor." He accompanied his greeting with a strumming chord. "You're looking mighty pretty this evening."

Nothing in his eyes or demeanor fed her guilt, yet she took a step forward and laid a hand on his arm. "Delmar, I'm sorry about the thing with the pavilion back in June. I shouldn't have hired you just to gig Sawyer."

He chuckled, his eyes twinkling with the same good humor that had passed to his nephew. "Well now, you're going to force me to apologize for dropping those rabbits in your mama's backyard, aren't you?"

She burst into laughter. "I guess we're even then."

"You couldn't convince Ms. Leora to come out with you?" Sawyer's voice was teasing.

"Nah. Leora's too refined for these shenanigans. This is her bridge night anyway." He strummed a chord. "I miss her though." The random chords took on a rhythm and turned into a haunting melody in a minor key.

She took a step back and bumped into Sawyer's chest. He circled his arms around her, anchoring her. She closed her eyes and turned her face into his neck. Linear time ceased to exist. The music unraveled her insides and left her yearning for something she couldn't name, but she wondered if it wasn't wrapped up in the man whose arms were wrapped around her.

"There you two are." Monroe's voice startled Regan's eyes open. She squirmed and Sawyer released her to talk to Cade while Monroe pulled her a little away from Delmar and the men.

"I'm glad you're here," Regan said. "I was afraid you and Cade were going to get all distracted and leave me hanging."

"Wouldn't miss the biggest social upheaval in the history of either side of the river."

"What are you talking about?"

"People are agog."

"Agog?"

"Cade and I already knew about you and Sawyer, but seeing you getting all cozy in his arms is still a shock." Monroe waggled her eyebrows.

Regan wiped a prickling sweat from her forehead and killed the rest of her beer. "I don't know that anything is going on. He made it sound like tonight was more about finding the man I saw in Mother's garden, not a date."

"Puh-lease. You two are meant for each other. Like Romeo and Juliet."

"They both died at the end. It was not a love story."

"Okay, bad example. How about *Pretty Woman* . . . except she was a hooker. *The Notebook*? Wait, she lost her mind in the end, didn't she? Never mind, you'll write your own story. Like me and Cade."

"You and Cade were never star-crossed lovers; you were fated lovers. You two are pathetically adorable."

Monroe looked toward the Fournette brothers. "I won't argue."

Regan stared into the bonfire, the licking flames hypnotic. Part of her wanted to spill everything Sawyer had confessed on the river to Monroe. But a bigger part of her wanted to keep their afternoon for herself to pick over and analyze in the dark of night. "Let's say something is going on between me and Sawyer. What if I'm setting myself up for more disappointment?"

"Why do you assume it will end badly? Or end at all for that matter?"

"Just a feeling I suppose. One of inevitability."

"Give him a chance. Instead of searching for excuses to not trust him, look for reasons to trust him." Monroe shifted around until they were both staring into the fire. "Are you worried about what your mother might say?"

"Not really." A weak denial. She had spent a good portion of her youth toeing her mother's line. Meeting Sawyer had weakened her mother's hold, but not broken it.

Monroe narrowed her eyes and tilted her head as if Regan's insecurities were playing out like a drive-in movie. "You should follow your heart. Don't look to your mother or to me or the town for approval." She squeezed Regan's hand. "But I have your back no matter what happens. Chicks before you-know-whats."

Regan hip-bumped her, and they both laughed. They walked over to Sawyer and Cade. As if it was the most natural thing in the world, Sawyer slipped his arm around her waist while Cade laid his over Monroe's shoulders, not pausing in their conversation about bolt suppliers.

"Don't you two get enough shop talk in at the garage?" Monroe elbowed Cade in the side.

"Sorry about that. Actually, I need to talk to Uncle Del real quick about his engine." Cade graced Monroe with a sheepish smile before walking away. Monroe trailed behind him, tossing a wink over her shoulder.

Sawyer moved behind Regan, put an arm over her chest and put his mouth close to her ear. Shivers tingled through her and she leaned her head against his shoulder and closed her eyes.

"It's time to scope out the crowd." His whisper jolted her. She kept her head tilted back, but turned her face toward his and gazed up. Conversations and laughter rose and ebbed, drowning out Delmar's quiet strumming. "I want you to look over all the men. I know you didn't see his face, but you knew Jeremy wasn't him based on the way he moved."

"An informal lineup?"

"Exactly." He weaved their fingers and led her to the outskirts, where the orange light of the fire bled into inky darkness. They made their way around the perimeter. Clumps of men and women conversed. Long, movable shadows from the bonfire made it difficult. "See anyone familiar?"

"I can't point a finger. Sorry."

"It's okay. It was a long shot." Even though his words absolved, disappointment colored his voice, and the disappointment cut deeper than it should have.

"It's too dark and no one's moving. And, like you said, I never saw his face."

"Regan, it's fine. I didn't really expect to find him. Do you want another beer?"

"Not really."

His eyebrows were drawn down, leaving his eyes a mystery as he studied her for a moment. "I'll be right back, okay?"

He didn't wait for her answer, but walked off, lost in the crowd of people by the keg. She chafed her arms, not cold but uncomfortable. A man sauntered toward her from the parked trucks and SUVs on her left.

Heath Parsons. She'd wavered between dislike and fear of him in school. He'd made fun of her hair and freckles and sticklike legs until she'd popped him on the nose on the school bus in fourth grade. Tears had shined in his eyes as they'd stared at each other, both in shock, in the aftermath.

He'd shoved her hard against the window, his eyes promising retribution. Not long after, Nash had moved from Louisiana to Mississippi to live with his aunt and started in their school. He had been the poster child for the bullied nerd, and easy prey for kids like Heath. Selfishly, she'd been happy someone else had become the focus of his ire.

She shuffled toward the group of people and craned her neck. No sign of Cade or Monroe or Sawyer. Only six feet away now, Heath flinched slightly when he saw her and veered in her direction.

Her lips curled in a smile in spite of the swirling negative memories of him. Their paths had rarely crossed since high school graduation in spite of living in the same town.

"Regan Lovell? What in tarnation are you doing here?"

"I'm here with a friend."

"Monroe and Cade Fournette have been thick lately. They around?"

"Somewhere. How have you been?" An ingrained habit of making small talk came to her rescue.

"Had a streak of bad luck. Got laid off back in the spring."

"Sorry to hear that." No evidence remained from the beating he'd gotten from Nash a couple of weeks earlier. Although, she'd guess his ego was still bruised.

"Yeah, I bet you are." He spit a stream of tobacco to their right.

An awkward silence stretched, yet he didn't move on.

"Nice to see you after so long. Maybe we'll run across each other again soon." She all but shooed him away with her hands.

"Heard your shop got messed up. Police have any idea who broke in?"

Her polite smile froze, the nerves on her neck tingling a warning. "I'm not sure. They've dusted for fingerprints."

"Bet they won't find any."

"Why do you say that?"

"Doubt he was dumb enough not to wear gloves." He pushed at the tobacco pooching his bottom lip with his tongue.

The idea that flashed would qualify her for the FBI. She watched him from beneath her lashes, the fib rolling off with the ease of a seasoned investigator. "I don't know, he misspelled a message he left for me, so my guess is he's pretty stupid."

"What?" More defensiveness than was warranted cut the word short. She didn't recognize the tense set to his shoulders until they relaxed with his chuff and he stepped off, walking backward a few steps. "Whatever. Hope they find him."

"Yeah, I bet you do." She mimicked his earlier ironic tone, but softly and to his back.

While she couldn't definitively say he had been the man outside her mother's garden, his size and walk put him on the short list.

Sawyer jogged out of the crowd, a smile on his face. This time she didn't have to work for the smile on hers. The worry and tension Heath had instilled melted under the heat of Sawyer's gaze as it trailed down her body.

"You ready to head out?"

"Sounds good." And it did. Maybe someday she would be comfortable hanging out at a bonfire with him, but a tentativeness to their interactions still existed. Even though she knew many things about him, they had both changed and a new dynamic pushed and pulled between them looking for balance.

He kept hold of her hand and led her past the line of trucks and SUVs and into the woods. The farther they went, the softer the ground became, and her pointy heels sank.

"My shoes . . ." She braced herself against a nearby pine and slipped them off. "If I step on another pinecone, you'll have to carry me back."

"How about I carry you right now?" He swung her into a cradle hold. She yelped and grabbed around his neck as he laughed. "Anyway, we're not going back."

She pushed away from his shoulders, but the darkness was too deep to see his expression. "Hold up. I'm not skinny-dipping with that crowd just through the trees."

He stopped short. "Would you skinny-dip if we were alone?"

She huffed out a few "huhs" and "I means" before settling on "Maybe."

He started walking again, shifting her to avoid trees, and murmured, "Well, now, I'll have to keep that in mind."

"You're going to hurt yourself."

He made a scoffing sound. "You weigh next to nothing."

Although she wasn't petite, she appreciated the compliment. "I meant carrying me through the woods in the dark. You're liable to walk us into a tree or straight in the river."

"I can see, remember. Anyway, I could close my eyes and find the river."

"Based on what? The sound of the water?" She strained, but all she could hear was laughter and noise drifting from the bonfire and the softer sounds of the wind through the trees.

"That and a feeling I get." The reluctance in his voice intrigued her.

"A feeling?"

"Don't laugh, but the river's always been my constant.

It's . . . alive." The streak of sentimentalism in his voice didn't surprise her. After all, this was the man who'd planted a row of flowers for his dead mother.

Everything in her chest seemed to be playing musical chairs. With her heart in her throat, she kissed his cheek and tightened her arms around his neck.

"Here we are."

The sound of water lapping softened the calls of cicadas and muted the crowd. She could barely see, but sure-footed, he descended into a washed-out gully. She grabbed him tighter.

"Don't look so worried. You trust me, don't you?" he asked.

The advantage he had over her in the dark meant she had no idea beyond the testing tone of his voice what he was thinking. The question loomed larger than the context of letting him carry her into the dark woods. Did she trust him?

The truth was . . . she wasn't sure. But everything he'd said to her that afternoon rang true. She wanted to believe him. Anyway, she no longer was a naïve love-blinded teenager. This time she would keep her eyes wide open and her defensives at the ready.

She nodded, and he continued up a hill. The sound of the river gurgled louder and moonlight sliced through the break in the trees, reflecting off the water. The scene was magical.

He put her down but when she turned to him, he shushed her and whispered, "An owl roosts on the far bank. If we're quiet enough, we might see him."

She leaned into the nearest tree trunk. A pine by the feel of the bark and the smell. He was focused outward, toward the water, while she stared at him. In the meager light, his face appeared solemn and thoughtful. The part he played around town was the friendly jokester with the ready smile.

She knew differently. While she was sure now that he hadn't told her everything, he'd told her more than anyone else knew about his life after his parents' death. The struggles, the sadness, the pressure to succeed. And the responsibility of holding his two darker siblings together when everything threatened to fracture.

She'd had a part of him that no one else had been privileged to see. And she'd thrown it away because she hadn't been brave enough. Tears stung the backs of her eyes.

"Look." He pointed toward the water, and she tore her gaze off him in time to see a huge white bird coast a few feet over the water, its wings silent. It rose with a beauty and grace that brought a different sort of tears to her eyes and settled on a tree branch. Its hoot startled her after the silence of its flight.

"How did you know?" She kept her voice low and gestured.

"Sometimes when I can't sleep, I'll come out on the river."

"To hunt?"

The owl hooted again. In the aftermath, he whispered, "To hunt peace, I suppose."

Maybe he was feeling as confused and anxious and hopeful about their confessions that afternoon as she was. She curled her hand around his neck, wanting to soothe the rawness she sensed in him.

Her eyes drifted shut. She didn't need light to find his lips. He'd been her constant for enough years that she could find her way to him even in the darkest night. Their kiss was simple and sweet with a twinge of sadness.

Against her lips, he said, "Will you come home with me?"

The question struck sparks in her body and burned away the melancholy of the moment. "Yes, please."

"You've become such a lady." He wound his fingers in her hair. "I remember a girl who wasn't afraid to get a little wild in the back of a pickup or a boat."

"I'm not messing around with you out in the sticks with half of Cottonbloom, Louisiana, a stone's throw away." She tried to sound priggish, but a small laugh snuck out.

He skimmed his lips across her jaw and bit her neck. His warm breath at her ear sent shivers through. "For once, I'm in complete agreement. I want all night and a big bed. What do you say?"

They'd never had either together. "Yes, *please*."

His laugh was throaty, and she squealed when he scooped her back up. Instead of heading back toward the bonfire and his truck, he picked his way closer to the water and set her down. Cool metal was under her feet. He'd put her in a boat.

"Is this yours?"

"I wouldn't steal someone's boat, Regan." He tutted, but with ill-concealed humor, and stepped in. The boat rocked and she dropped her shoes and grabbed his forearms. "Cade and Monroe came by boat from the shop. They're going to take my truck."

He guided her backward until she hit the horizontal metal seat with the backs of her calves. She sat, slipped her shoes back on, and found handholds on the edges of the boat. He stepped back and shoved them off, hopping back on and passing her to get to the stern.

Night cast a dark veil for her, but his movements were smooth and sure. He cranked the engine, a quiet murmur, and the wind tossed her hair. The trees thinned and she could make out the high banks and the wide section of river they travelled.

He veered them to the left, up a different branch, this

one narrower, the water flowing faster and splashing up on her hands. A dock came into view, the white clapboard of his house glowing in the moonlight. He drove the boat straight up onto the land instead of the dock.

"Sit tight for a minute."

He bypassed her and tugged the boat farther up on the bank, tying it off to a tree. When he returned, she stood and he swept her up again. She could hear him splashing through the shallows before hitting the dirt-packed bank. Only a couple of weeks had passed since her impetuous accusations of tomato treachery on this very bank.

Now the man she thought she hated was carrying her to his house, and if she hadn't misread his signals, he planned to leave her very satisfied. Nerves jumped. With the exception of their quick, dirty sex against her wall, this would be their first time together in a very long time.

What did it mean, if anything?

Chapter Eighteen

Regan was a welcome weight in his arms, keeping him grounded. Sawyer rubbed his chin against her temple. Her natural sexy scent weaved with the earthy smell of the bonfire. He hadn't been sure if she'd agree to head off into the darkened woods with him, much less up the river.

Cade and Monroe would drop his truck off later and had strict instructions not to interrupt if Regan's car was still out front. Nerves and anticipation battled, much as they had when he was a teenager with her. It seems some things hadn't changed.

But some things had. They were adults, and instead of snatching time in the back of a truck or on a blanket under a tree or in his boat, he had a king-sized bed upstairs and all night long.

He set her down once they reached the patio where the footing was less precarious. The back door was unlocked. He waved her inside first, unlacing and toeing off his muddy boots. The hall light provided dim illumination. Tension ratcheted higher. He ran his hands down the back of his jeans.

"Do you want a drink or something?" He stepped forward, opened a cabinet, and pulled down a bottle. "I've got some of that Jack you like."

"A little would be welcome." She shifted on her heels. His gaze travelled all the way down her lean legs.

"You've got the most amazing legs. Always have." The thought bypassed his filter to his mouth. When her shoulders relaxed and a small smile flashed over her face, he was glad he had spoken without thinking. It had been one of her rare, real smiles. While her big, white pageant grins might win voters, they hid her real emotions. Her real smile quirked only one corner of her mouth up, dimpled her cheek, and made him feel like they were sharing a private joke.

"I guess you have my mother to thank."

"Next time I run into her, I'll do just that."

Her smile fell. "You wouldn't really."

What had she meant by that? Did she want to keep things on the down-low like they had as kids? He hesitated before handing over a tumbler with a little whiskey. "Cheers."

They tapped glasses, and she took a sip. Her gaze cast upward toward him, unintentionally flirty. Or maybe intentionally flirty. She hummed and darted her tongue across her upper lip. He choked on his own sip.

"My vandal has good taste. It's the only thing he stole."

"What are you talking about?"

"The whiskey I kept in my filing cabinet. It's the only thing that was actually missing."

He threw back the rest of his drink, set the tumbler down, and leaned back against the countertop. "That's odd."

She traced the edge of the glass with a finger. "When you left me at the party, I ran into Heath Parsons."

Sawyer's hands tightened around the edge of the

counter. The mere mention of Heath Parsons set him on edge. After the drama between Heath and Tally and Nash, he wished the man would disappear.

"Did he bother you?"

"Not really. But, I'm wondering if he's the man."

"The man?"

"The one from Mother's garden and maybe the one who broke into my shop. If so, he's probably the one who set the pavilion on fire and cut the baskets."

"He's an asshole, no doubt, but is he that dumb?"

"Desperation trumps dumb. Is he desperate?"

"I have no clue." He stared into her eyes. "What would he have to gain?"

She shrugged and tipped the glass back, emptying it. He took the glass with one hand and wrapped the other around her wrist. He didn't want Heath Parsons or the festivals or anything else to put a pall over the evening.

"You know what?" He shuffled his legs farther apart and pulled until their hips met. He moved his hands to her waist, and she braced her elbows against his chest, her hands curled over his shoulders.

"What?" she asked softly, her gaze somewhere around his throat. She looked young and unsure, and he shot back to their first time. The sweet innocence of her touch and the intoxicating welcome of her body.

"I don't want to focus on anything or anyone but you. Let's leave all the rest for the morning."

Her throat worked as her gaze swept up. "The morning?"

"Yep. I want you in my bed all night. You got any objections, mayor?"

Something flared in her eyes. He hoped it was excitement and arousal, but the tentativeness of the shake of her head made him wonder if a fair amount of the emotion was fear.

"I'm going to take real good care of you. You don't need

to worry about a thing." He levered himself forward, walking her backward, their bodies still locked together, their feet shuffling in tandem.

They reached the door to the hall and he turned her, his hands on her shoulders guiding her to the darkened stairs at the end. He kept their bodies close, taking each step slowly, afraid if he let her go, she might bolt for freedom.

She paused when they made it to the top. "I've never been up here."

The statement startled him. Of course, she hadn't. He'd bought the farmhouse well after college graduation. The first time he'd stepped foot in the house, he'd heard the echoes of memories. He'd envisioned his own children running through the halls and out to play on the river or in the woods. None of that had come to pass, but it was still his dream. He just hadn't found the right woman. Yet.

While she'd never tread across the wood planking to his bedroom, she'd haunted this house through his dreams. Too many times she'd come uninvited to torment him in delightful ways at night. He'd awoken frustrated and angry more mornings than he could count. Angry she was only a figment of his imagination, angry at himself for his inability to move on.

"The bedroom is at the end of the hall." He tightened his arm around her waist, thankful she was real. Flesh and blood and fire.

She took a small step, and then another. He followed, his heart and lungs cramping. With the toe of her high heels she pushed the door open, and they stood in the threshold. The drapes were open and moonlight softened the stark lines of his furniture. A wave of self-consciousness had words tripping out.

"Not as sophisticated as your room."

"No." She cast a teasing smile up at him, shifting to tuck herself under his shoulder, her arm around his waist. "But it suits you. No frills. Although, how do you survive without some cute throw pillows?"

She stepped from under his arm farther into the room. He propped a shoulder in the doorway, watching her wander his domain with a sense of possession and satisfaction that disturbed him. She turned on a small lamp on his dresser. Soft light permeated the room.

A single picture sat next to the lamp. An old one of his family before everything went to hell. She leaned closer to touch his face in the photo.

"Look how cute you were." The smile she tossed him was sweet, and he had the urge to hug her close and bury his face in the waves of her hair.

His past was like a once-complete, unbroken picture, now fragmented into regrets and sadness. Some memories, like his parents' death, would stay forever shattered. But some, like his breakup with Regan, seemed to be knitting themselves back together. The broken, unfinished place inside of him mending the more time they spent together. Yet it was fragile.

"Do you mind if I clean up?" she asked.

"'Course not. The bathroom's back out in the hall."

Her teasing smile had turned tentative. He wouldn't be surprised if the next thing he heard was the gravel spinning from under her wheels. She walked into the bathroom and closed the door.

What now? Did he strip and wait in bed for her or was that too presumptuous? He blew a slow breath out and rubbed his hands down the legs of his jeans. Jesus, he was nervous. At the very least, she would be comparing him to his younger self. How would he measure up?

From the bottom drawer, he pulled out two candles he kept for when the power went out, lit them, and turned off the lamp in the corner. He also verified he had condoms in the top drawer in case she insisted he use one. He hoped she didn't. The feeling of burying himself inside of her bare had been amazing.

He straightened his bedcovers and fluffed his utilitarian pillows. After pacing the room once, he sat, ran his hands through his hair, weaved his fingers around his nape, and stared at an etched scar in the flooring. She was taking forever. Was she having second thoughts?

A small gasp from the doorway sent him up so fast he rocked the straight-backed wooden chair against the wall. She shifted on her heels, fingered the collar of her shirt, her gaze pinging from the bed to the candles to him, and back again.

He held out a hand and said nothing. She stepped forward and slipped hers into his. The slight tremble roused a warm protective feeling. Keeping hold of her hand, he pulled her into him, slipped his arm around her waist, and swayed them.

Her soft laughter vibrated her body and sent a thrill through his. "There's no music, Sawyer."

"A shame. I should have been better prepared. We never got to dance together, did we?"

"No, I don't guess we did." She relaxed in his arms and nuzzled her lips against his jaw.

"I wanted to take you to prom so bad."

She pulled back so their eyes met. "I thought you were fine not coming?"

"I wanted to hire a limo and pick you up at your mama's house with a big corsage, dance all night, and then get a hotel room. Somewhere we could be alone with a bed for once."

Her eyes were sad but understanding. "You didn't have that kind of money. I know you didn't."

Even though it was the truth, it still hurt. "Were you

being nice or was it your mama or would you have been embarrassed to show up with me in a rented tux in Cade's old truck?"

"I wouldn't have cared about the truck or a corsage or a limo or even a hotel room, but Mother didn't want me going with you, and knowing your situation, it was easier all around if we didn't go together." She smoothed a hand over his heart and dropped her eyes to the motion. "I wish I'd gone with you anyway. I was a coward."

He stopped their sway and covered her hand with his. "What are you now?"

"All I know is you make me feel brave. Make me want to take chances. Doesn't mean I'm not scared."

He understood because the same feelings were battering his heart. "Me too."

The fact they were finally in the same boat on the same river calmed him. Maybe she felt the same. Tension left her body, and she smiled her little half-smile. Talk of the future would ruin the moment. Anyway, the present was very, very good, and he wanted to savor it.

He leaned in to kiss her and backed her toward the bed. Her legs hit the mattress, throwing her balance off. She fell to her back with a burst of giggles. He crawled over her, propped his elbows on either side of her, and smoothed her hair back. Her face was alight with the same joy that warmed him from the inside out.

Her soft body under his became a welcome distraction. Everything felt new yet familiar. In the light of day, he would broach questions of the future, but tonight he wanted to explore a new magic.

The gamut of emotions stampeding through her made it difficult to think clearly. The part of her that had spent years protecting her foolish, vulnerable heart urged her to step away, apply brakes to the careening train of emotions.

Her body's needs overruled emotions and logic. She arched under his weight pressing her into the soft mattress. Tomorrow. Tomorrow she could examine every nuance of tone and word. Tonight she would succumb to the hunger of lust and longing streaking through her body. Would he be the playful, gentle lover she remembered, or would he take her with same intensity he'd shown when he'd rocked her world against the wall? She was desperate to discover.

He stood at the edge of the bed, the loss of his weight setting her adrift in her own insecurity. Taking her hands in his, he kissed the back of each and pulled her to sitting. He transferred his attention to her face, brushing his lips over her forehead, her fluttering eyelids, her cheeks.

"Take off your clothes." The confidence in his voice was new and exciting and frankly terrifying.

A shiver passed down her body, branching out to every extremity, making her tingle. Her experience since him had been limited, and she had no idea what he expected of her. But she was unable to deny him and fumbled the buttons of her blouse open. He pushed the soft silk over her shoulders, the rougher pads of his fingers a welcome contrast to the soft fabric. He slipped the bra straps over the curve of her shoulders, his thumbs staying to feather along her collarbones.

"Now the bra."

Her white lace bra was pretty, but suddenly felt too girlish with the pink ribbon in the middle and where the straps met the cups. Two tries later, painfully aware of his eyes on her, she slipped it off. A deep sigh escaped from him, but he didn't touch her.

Even though her hair wasn't long enough to cover her nakedness, she shook the waves forward using them to camouflage her no-doubt splotchy cheeks. Her shorts were next, and she stood, her ankles shaky in her heels. He took a step back, and she could almost feel his gaze like a physical touch. Her nipples peaked without being touched. Moving faster now, she undid her shorts and pushed them and her panties to the floor.

"Leave your heels on and lay down."

The husky rumble in his voice settled her unease. He wasn't unaffected. She swept her gaze down his body. The definite bulge in his pants lent her a sense of confidence, and she scooted back on the mattress. Confidence or not, she kept her knees pressed together as she lay back on the pillows.

He gazed on her, not moving. The moment drew out for too long. Cool air from the ceiling fan caressed her body. The sense of overexposure and vulnerability morphed into a strange awareness. Every nerve ending joined in the call for his touch.

Her need was growing uncontrollable. Did he want her to beg? His eyes narrowed on her with a searing heat the same time a teasing smile turned his lips. A naughty playfulness had her arching on the bed and running her hands from her hips up to her breasts.

"Are you trying to drive me insane?"

He stripped off his T-shirt and tossed it aside. His jeans were off in record time, and she didn't have time to process or enjoy the sight of him in his underwear before he was running his hands up her legs from ankles to knees and back again.

"You in these shoes . . ." He lifted one leg and laid a kiss on her calf.

"What about them?"

"When you strutted up to me all sassy and pissed off after the town meeting, you incited all sorts of dirty thoughts."

She remembered having a few dirty thoughts herself. "I wanted you to press me up against the wall that night. So. Bad."

"Did you really?" His hands trekked farther north until he gripped her thighs. "I've been having dirty dreams about you for years, but things reached DEFCON 5 levels this summer."

Her thighs tightened against the outward press of his hands, and she covered one of his hands with hers. "Sawyer, I . . ."

"I'll be gentle, baby, I promise, but I want to make you scream my name. Trust me."

His hazel eyes bored into hers. In that moment she would have given him anything. Everything. She dropped her hand and relaxed her legs. He pushed her thighs apart as his hands slipped under her backside. His shoulders wedged her legs apart.

When he put his mouth on her, she squirmed. He hummed and petted her leg, and under his care, the tangled swirl of emotions and physical need unspooled into only one thread. A thread she grasped and held onto until she climaxed.

The burst of pleasure was simple and satisfying. Maybe she had wanted to scream, just a little, but she confined the burst of emotion to a long, low moan. In pleasure's wake was the realization she hadn't entrusted herself to any man since him. As simple as the physical pleasure had been, the complications were immense.

He didn't give her a chance to dwell on the complicated. "I'm sorry Regan."

His hips had replaced his shoulders between her legs, his chest hair rubbing her sensitive nipples in a pleasure-pain. "For what?"

"I'll take my time with you later. I need you now. You understand?"

He was bare and hot against her, his underwear gone. Maybe disintegrated in the chaos of her orgasm. Rational thought ceased. He pushed inside of her, slow and steady, yet he didn't chase his own climax as promised. Instead, he stayed propped up on his elbows, watching her.

Could he see all of the scary emotions vying for dominance inside of her? Could he see how close he was to battering down the walls she'd spent a decade building? Could he see how unprotected she was against him, how easily he could destroy her?

She didn't look away. And suddenly it didn't matter if her heart were splayed open for his dissection. He moved, his strokes gaining in ferocity with each twist of his hips. She clutched at his shoulders and arms, the muscles thicker and more solid than she remembered, and pressed her heels against his backside, trying to impart her growing need.

He heeded her unspoken plea, shortening his thrusts, but driving into her harder and faster. The impossible happened. She climaxed again. A moaning scream tore from her throat, as she bucked and arched and pulled his body closer.

Once her body calmed, he kneeled between her legs, big and hard and still inside of her. She'd never seen the expression on his face. It was almost scary in its primal, blinded need.

He wrapped a hand around each of her ankles and pushed her legs up and out. He went wild on her, but her body was primed and welcoming. She raised her hands and pushed against the headboard, wanting to feel everything. On his last thrust, a low growl reverberated around the room, his head back, the tendons in his neck taut, the hands around her ankles squeezing.

The boy she'd given her virginity and heart to so many years ago had turned into a man in every sense. His body glowed in the soft light, his chest heavily muscled, rising and falling as if he'd sprinted across a finish line.

The fair skin of her thighs was in contrast to the naturally darker tone of his hips. He was unblemished and tanned across his shoulders and chest. She'd seen his bare chest earlier that summer, but now she could touch him.

With his eyes closed, she pushed up to an elbow and ran her hand down one side of his body from shoulder to waist and back up to cover his heart. It thumped along. He dropped an ankle and covered her hand with his, but didn't open his eyes.

Even in his strength, his body trembled. A womanly satisfaction she hadn't felt since their first time together had her blowing out a long, slow breath to control the well of emotions.

He opened his eyes into hers. Neither of them moved. Neither of them spoke. Their impetuous sex against her wall had been a physical release valve against the pressure that had built all summer. This seemed different.

He was the first to move, flipping her shoes to the floor one at a time. His gaze never left hers. The connection beyond the physical stayed intact even as he withdrew from her body and stretched out beside her. She turned her head so they could maintain eye contact. He propped his head on one hand while he tangled the other in her hair. The electricity in the air faded, leaving her surprisingly comfortable, even though they were naked on top of the covers.

"Do you have any idea how many times I've pictured you laid out on my bed, your hair spread out on my pillows?"

A residual power, bolstered by his confession, coursed through her. "Since I tackled you in the dark with your marauding bunnies?"

He hummed, not answering her directly. "Could you feel this thing growing between us that night?"

She dropped her hand to between his thighs, her fingers brushing over him. "I could feel it all right."

His smile made his eyes twinkle, yet a seriousness lurked somewhere in his expression. "You were smoking hot all self-righteous about your mama's tomatoes."

"You were trying to ruin my festival."

He made a scoffing sound. "The loss of your mama's tomatoes wouldn't have put a dent in your local supply."

"Then why did you go after her tomatoes?"

"Because she never thought I was good enough for you. I wanted to hurt her."

"Even after all this time?"

He avoided answering by dropping kisses along the side of her breast, moving toward the nipple. How her body could crave more, she didn't know, but her back arched. He took her nipple at the same time he tightened his hand in her hair and tugged, the prickles at her scalp somehow intensifying her pleasure.

"Oh my goodness." Her breathless exclamation made him smile around her breast.

"I'd forgotten how responsive you are with me." A shadow stole his smile, his insecurity a surprise.

She threaded a hand in his hair and tugged his face to hers. "I'd forgotten too."

He took her mouth in a drugging, fierce kiss that left her reeling. The veering from playfulness to intensity was brand-new even if her unbridled reaction to his touch wasn't. Childish feelings had no place between them.

"You're not tired, are you?" His lips moved against hers, and she felt the words more than heard them.

He made love to her again. This time he pulled her on top to ride him and let her set the rhythm until she took her pleasure, then he guided her, his hands strong on her hips, in a harder, faster ride until he climaxed.

Still breathing hard, her body sated and lax, he tucked her under the covers, cuddling her into his body. She faced away from him, her eyes closed, her body boneless and sore and satisfied. His fingers traced patterns over her shoulders like he was playing connect the dots.

"I remember every single one of your freckles." He laid kisses along her shoulder blade.

"I always hated them. Mother called them blemishes and said they ruined my chances at Miss Mississippi. She used to rub lemon juice on them."

"Your mama is a . . . she's something else." The dripping irony wasn't a shock.

"I know she can be a bit much, but she loves me. I think."

"Maybe too much. She didn't want to let you go. To me or to the world."

She shifted around so she could see him. "What do you mean?"

"No man would have been good enough for you. But I was her worst nightmare." He brushed her hair back. "And based on her reaction the other morning, not much has changed."

"Do you want it to change?" She wasn't sure what she was asking, but she tensed.

He rolled to his back and tucked his hands behind his head. "I think you should quit toeing her line and do what makes you happy. What would make you happy?"

You. She didn't say the one word that would probably send him running into the swamps, buck naked. "I'm proud of what I've accomplished in Cottonbloom. I've thought a lot about the state of Mississippi in general. The poverty, the illiteracy rates, the domestic abuse."

His head lifted off the pillow. "You want to run for state office."

She hadn't told anyone. Not even Monroe. The papers to file for a run at the state house of representatives was tucked away in her office. How had he guessed so easily? "You don't think I'm crazy?"

"Crazy? Baby, I think you're insane for wanting to deal with those wahoos up in Jackson, but Mississippi would be lucky to have you. If what you've done in Cottonbloom is any indicator, you might just catch Mississippi up with Louisiana."

Behind the tease in his voice was true admiration. He believed in her. He always had. "But Mother—"

"Don't tell her. Or tell her, but understand she'll try to talk you out of it. You can do it, Regan."

She pillowed her head on his arm and snaked an arm and a leg over his body. His assurance shouldn't mean so much, but it did. Anything felt possible. Even the rekindling of something she'd thought had burned into ash. But the ember they had lit would need to be nurtured. Would he welcome questions about what they were doing and where they were going?

He pulled her close, his sigh relaxing him. Time would reveal his intentions. Until then she would hold him close. When they'd been together as kids, she'd never thought it would end. Their last time had been a hurried hook-up in his brother's truck. Fun and lighthearted before heading to their respective colleges. Their schedules had kept them apart for weeks, allowing her mother to fertilize the seeds of doubt she'd been assiduously planting.

If she'd known it would be their last time, would she have held on tighter? Would she have extracted promises and made promises of her own? Or was it best not to know when the end was coming?

She tightened her arms around him and hoped the trickling tear that managed to escape onto his shoulder went unnoticed. Even after his breathing settled into a steady rate, she forced herself to stay awake, savoring the feel of his body next to hers and the welcome she'd found in his arms, even if it was only for a night.

Chapter Nineteen

He awoke to gentle snuffling and the awareness of a sweet softness pressed into his side. Before opening his eyes, he took a deep breath, plagued by a vague sense of melancholy. Some things had changed, but not her scent. Her scent had captivated him from their first date. Innocence and seduction weaved into something uniquely Regan.

He cursed the light leaking through his curtains. If the pleasure he'd found with her hadn't been so all-consuming, he would have stayed awake longer, teased her into another round. His body's call for rest had trumped his desire.

Images from his dreams reentered his consciousness. They had been populated by Regan, but not of the erotic variety he battled most nights. Instead, they were echoes of the kind he'd had after they'd broken up. Heart-wrenching loneliness even as she slept in his arms.

What if he refused to let her leave until she agreed that whatever this was between them wasn't the final chapter to their old relationship, but a new beginning. Would he scare her? It smacked of desperation.

He pulled the sheet down, exposing one perfect breast. The nipple pebbled as if sensing his appreciation.

If he examined the last few years of his life, he wondered how much of his drive to succeed—climbing to plant manager and becoming parish commissioner—was to prove himself to Regan, to her mama, to his family, and to himself.

His parents' death had hit him as hard as Cade and Tally, but he was the optimistic one, the one who was expected to smile through it all. While Cade was sacrificing everything for the family, he'd expected Sawyer to continue on with his life. School, studying, sports. The pressure to not let Cade down and the need to contribute something to the family had been suffocating.

Sawyer was the one who insisted they eat together. Insisted they talk and play games. He was the glue. The one Tally talked to when she was hurting over Cade's defection. The one who'd dragged Cade back home when he needed family but was too proud to ask.

With Regan he had been able to drop the smiles, share the troubles he hadn't wanted to burden his already-fragile family with. She'd given him hugs and smiles and kisses. She'd cried for him and laughed with him.

Through it all though, a crushing sense of not being good enough dogged him. He was tired of smiling and pretending and sick of wondering if he was finally good enough. But how could he ask her without revealing his heart, his intentions?

Neither of them was ready for that. But, that didn't mean he couldn't try to convince her in other ways how well they fit together. He could show her, even if he couldn't tell her. His body was primed from the feel and sight of her body. He shifted to face her, tucking his leg between hers. Although her eyes were closed, she arched into him, the tips of her breasts brushing his chest.

Any question as to her state of wakefulness vanished when her hand circled him and guided him to her entrance.

He pushed inside an inch, and her eyes fluttered open with a gasp he couldn't classify as pleasure or pain.

"Are you sore?" He'd taken her twice the night before—hard. Maybe now he could make up for his frantic need.

"A little, but I want you."

Memories of their first time dredged through the mire of need in his brain. He pushed fully inside of her, and they both released a pent-up sigh. He brushed her tousled hair off her forehead. He didn't want to move, didn't want whatever was growing between them to vanish like it had when they were young.

Banging sounded downstairs. They froze. The cocoon of their night was ripped apart.

"Sawyer?" Tally's voice rang through the house. He and his sister would have a long talk about boundaries. "Where the heck are you?" Footsteps sounded on the steps, but stopped prematurely.

Regan pulled away as if she'd been hit by a taser and scrambled for her clothes, a litany of "Oh Gods" falling from her lips. Even though the presence of his sister and the possibility of getting caught with his pants down cooled his ardor, he wanted to take Regan into his arms and tell her to calm down. So what if Tally knew about them? Wouldn't everyone soon?

Unless, there was no "them." Unless Regan was ashamed and didn't want anyone to know they were hooking up. He rose and pulled on his jeans sans underwear more slowly, attempting to gauge her reaction.

Panic seemed to be the predominant emotion. When she came closer to scoop up her shoes, he grabbed her arm. "Why are you having a fit? It's Tally."

"Exactly."

"Can I see you again?"

Behind her panic, other emotions brewed, but as always, she was a mystery. "Sure, let's meet up or something." Her tone held a bait, but he wasn't sure what she was fishing for. He dissected her words for hidden meanings. Did she mean she was up for a booty call? Or a date? Or did she have the damn festivals on her mind?

From the stairs, his sister's throat-clear echoed. "Oh Lordy, I'll just be . . ."

Regan twisted out of his grip and made a run for his door, fumbling with the doorknob before slipping out. He followed, barefoot and bare-chested. He didn't give a crap what his sister thought, but Regan sure did.

Sawyer watched her retreat from the front porch, the day already heating. He muttered a curse at fate, at himself, at Tally's timing. Her unexpected drop-ins had never been a problem in the past as he'd never brought a woman back to his place. Easier and less messy if his getaway was clear. Now Regan was the one making a getaway.

He slammed the door on his way back to the kitchen. Tally had the good sense to look chagrined. "Whoops. Sorry about that, stud. Thought you two were just trying to work out the mystery of the festival saboteur."

"Big word there. Looks like Nash is rubbing off on you."

Anger wiped any apology off her face, leaving a bitterness that reminded him too much of Cade before he'd come home and found Monroe. Before Sawyer could launch into his own apology, she said, "Somehow I don't think you're going to discover his identity during sex with the enemy. And for your information, I have started one-on-one tutoring for my dyslexia. I was never illiterate, you butthead."

Even though her arms were crossed and her face promised bodily harm, he threw an arm around her shoulders and brought her in for a half-hug. "Sorry, Tally. I took my frustration and confusion out on you. Although your timing could have been better."

She pushed him away with a finger. "Gross. Go put on a shirt. I didn't realize you two were getting involved again. When I saw her car out front, I thought you might need backup." She shrugged, her face soft and slightly apologetic again.

"I'm not sure we are involved."

"But you're having sex. That has nothing to do with the festivals."

"We're having fun is all." As the words came out of his mouth he recognized them to be a lie. What the hell *were* he and Regan doing? It had been fun. But it had been more than "Sure, let's meet up again" sex. It had been "I want you in my bed every night" sex. At least it had been for him.

"O-kay." She drew the word out mockingly. "If she makes you happy, then you should go for it."

Sawyer wished it wasn't too early to drink something mind numbing. He made coffee instead, grabbed a shirt while it brewed, and took a seat across from her at their old table. "Your magnanimous response to Regan is surprising. I thought you detested her."

"I don't."

Sawyer shot an ironic eye-roll in her direction.

"I used to harbor ill feelings toward her, true, but Nash's stories have changed my mind. If you decided to get serious with her, I'd support you."

"I'm shocked."

She leaned over the table and jabbed a finger in his direction. "But if she hurts you again, I'll tie raw meat around her neck, drag her into the swamps by her perfect hair, and leave her for the gators." Smiling sweetly, she pushed up and poured herself a cup of coffee.

"Geez, I'm glad you're on my side."

Tally returned with two steaming mugs. The smell alone was enough to galvanize him.

"Are you two actually dating? Or was this a one-time thing to relive the past?"

He averted his face from her piercing green gaze. Was Regan riddled with regret over their night together? "I don't know what *she* wants, but I hope it's not a one-time thing."

"You'll figure it out. You've got an engineering degree for goodness' sake."

"If only she came with an instruction manual."

They shared a moment of silence. Regan was a puzzle that wouldn't be solved over a cup of coffee with his sister. However, there was something else Tally might be able to help him with.

"So you and Heath had a volatile relationship." He poked at the old wound as gently as possible.

Although she didn't move, tension flowed from her and colored her voice. "You could say that. Why?"

"He doesn't seem like the most reliable, upstanding guy."

"Agreed."

"In fact, I wouldn't be surprised if he got in trouble with the law eventually."

"Are you trying to make me feel like an idiot for dating him or are you going to get to your point?"

"Sorry, sis. The thing is . . ." Sawyer spun the coffee cup in his hands.

"Ohmigoodness, spit it out."

He raised his gaze to hers, wanting to gauge her reaction. "Could Heath be behind all the trouble we're having with the festivals?"

Her eyes flared and her mouth dropped. She blinked a few times. "I mean, is he capable? Certainly. But why?" Surprise trumped her exasperation.

"I've been turning that very question over in my head.

Regan thinks Heath might be the man she saw out at her mama's a couple of weeks ago."

"I didn't think she saw whoever it was."

"She didn't see his face, but she gave chase. Knows his build, the way he moves. Apparently, her pageant experience made her an expert on the way people carry themselves."

Tally tapped her fingers on the tabletop, betraying her agitation. "Heath can be a scary dude. Intimidating. But what does he have to gain? Unless someone is paying him to wreck things."

Sawyer opened and closed his mouth. Was Heath the muscle and someone else the mastermind? Come to think of it, he couldn't imagine Heath sitting around cutting and gluing letters into a vague threat.

Tally glanced toward the clock and rose. "I've got to go. You need to talk about anything else?"

He followed her out the kitchen door. "You don't know where Heath is living, do you?"

"Nope. I cut that cancer out of my life. Banned him from the gym and threatened him with a restraining order."

Sawyer hid his shock. While he was aware things had gotten hairy between Tally and Heath, he hadn't understood the extent. "He hasn't hassled you since?"

"He wouldn't dare," she said darkly, almost as if she wanted him to try. "His mom and dad might know where he's holed up. Or his buddy Bryce."

Sawyer waved her off and retreated to change clothes. He had two choices, go find Heath or go find Regan. The way she hightailed it out of his bed that morning might have set a world land-speed record.

Figuring out whether Heath had been involved would give him an excuse to seek her out later. Maybe then he'd know what to do or say. He pulled out his phone and texted Cade. He was pulling up to Monroe's Craftsman-style house less than twenty minutes later. Cade opened the front door before he had the chance to knock. The smell of pancakes and bacon drew him in like a siren's song.

"Grab a plate, I'm making extra." Cade walked back around the counter and flipped the golden circles. Monroe was nowhere to be seen.

Feeling like a kid again, he stood next to Cade, holding an empty plate. He let Cade spatula every single one onto his plate. The sly smile on Cade's face didn't escape his notice, but he didn't care. His brother added two strips of bacon cooked just the way he liked it.

Sawyer took a seat at the bar, covered the pancakes in syrup, and took a bite. A blast of memories spun in his head—all good. First, waking to the smell of pancakes on a Sunday morning and emerging from his bedroom to find his mama in a robe in the kitchen. Then, Cade continuing the tradition after they'd moved to the crappy trailer. His brother coming off a third shift, him and Tally waking in the back bedroom they shared to the smell of frying bacon. The laughter and stories they all shared over the scarred table that had sat in his childhood home, the trailer, and now his house.

"You always made the best pancakes. What's your secret?"

"Love." Cade winked and an unexpected burn of tears crawled up Sawyer's throat. It had been the answer their mama had always given too.

Sawyer dropped his head and shoved a piece of bacon into his mouth to camouflage the sudden tumble of emotions. He hadn't cried on Cade's shoulder since he was a kid.

Monroe emerged from the hall, dressed in shorts and a T-shirt, barefooted and with damp hair. She graced him with one of her easy, sunny smiles, the opposite to Cade. Although his brother had gained a sense of lightness and tease since returning to Cottonbloom and falling in love with Monroe.

"Hey, Sawyer."

"Sorry to steal Cade so early on a Sunday."

Monroe took three pancakes and settled onto the bar stool next to him. "No worries. I had plans to help Regan with something anyway." She craned her neck to try to catch his eyes, but he ignored her.

A shot of unease tensed him. What would Regan tell Monroe about their night together? A more unsettling thought pinged. Would Regan ask Monroe for advice? Or did Regan even care enough to ask? Maybe last night was a one-time thing for her. Except yesterday had changed everything for him.

A lie. Everything had changed the night she had tackled him in the dark.

He had never suffered from the kind of crippling insecurity Regan seemed to inspire. He'd never stressed about school or work or women. Why were things so different with her now? A sense of urgency had his blood thrumming. The festivals were less than two weeks away, and Sawyer had a sense he needed to have a hold on his feelings by then, but he wasn't sure why.

He cleaned his plate, but the pancakes lost the magic they'd held earlier. He mumbled a good-bye as Monroe kissed Cade on the cheek and left.

"Jesus, what's wrong with you?" Cade shot him a half-smile as he washed up.

"What do you mean?"

Cade shook his head. "Please. One mention of Regan Lovell, and you acted like a firing squad was in your near future. I assume last night either went spectacularly well or was an utter failure. Which was it?"

Sawyer pushed the plate toward Cade, who slipped it into the dishwasher. When had his brother become so astute in matters of the heart? He supposed he had Monroe to thank for that too.

"I thought it was A. But, the way she ran out this morning, I suspect it's more B. Of course, the typical morning-after awkwardness was magnified by Tally's sudden appearance."

Cade pulled his bottom lip between his teeth, but laughter threatened to break free.

"Go ahead. I know you want to."

A rich, booming laugh filled the kitchen, reminding Sawyer of their father and Uncle Del. "Dang, I'm sorry. Did she catch you in the act?" Cade wiped down the counters and tossed the dishrag into the sink.

"Not exactly. But Regan got dressed so fast and ran, her blouse was buttoned wrong and she was barefoot. Felt like strangling our dear sister."

"Can't say that I blame you, but it's your fault for giving her a key."

"I'm getting it back ASAP. Anyway, I'm sure Regan is going to fill Monroe's ear, and she might tell you some stuff if you ask." Sawyer raised his eyebrows.

"Let me get this straight. You want me to pump Monroe for information about things her best friend has told her in confidence and pass these little nuggets along to you."

Sawyer wagged a finger. "Exactly. Trust me, I need all the help I can get with Regan."

"That I believe, but I doubt Monroe will spill her best friend's secrets." Cade poured a cup of coffee and joined him on the chair Monroe had vacated. "What do you want to do about Heath?"

Sawyer gave him a rundown of what Tally had said. "We can talk to his parents, then Bryce if we hit a dead end. Find Heath and apply some pressure. We can play good cop, bad cop."

Cade killed his coffee. "Let's hit it. You drive."

Once they were on the road, Cade broke the silence. "Obviously, I'm bad cop."

"Why obviously? Maybe I want to be bad cop. You're here for backup."

Cade scoffed. "Sorry, bro. You are not bad cop material. You're too All-American and nice. It's why you're a good politician, while I, on the other hand, have made a fortune by being a tough asshole."

"Charming. But, I'm not sure you're as bad as you think you are anymore."

Cade shifted his back against the passenger door, half-facing him. "What do you mean by that?"

"You don't even know how whipped you are." Sawyer barked a laugh and fluttered his eyes at Cade, and said in a singsong voice, "Oh I can't go. I need to make pancakes for Monroe and rub her feet and draw her a bath and make all her dreams come true."

Cade flipped him the bird. "Like you're in any better shape." His voice turned mocking. "Could you ask Monroe to ask Regan whether she really likes me or not? Please?"

Sawyer knuckle-punched Cade in the arm. They grappled for a moment until Sawyer curbed a tire and let go of Cade's wrist to grip the steering wheel with both hands. He wasn't angry or perturbed with Cade. In truth, he enjoyed the brotherly tease. It reminded him of better times, easier times.

"Fine. You're bad cop." Sawyer turned down the street where Heath's parents lived.

Cade barked a laugh but was otherwise silent, maybe getting into character.

Heath's parents lived in an aging neighborhood, but

the houses were well maintained. Brick ranches interspersed with two-story wood-shingled more-stately homes.

Sawyer checked the address on his phone and pulled up to stop in front of a modest two-story brick-faced house with an immaculately manicured lawn. A foreign-made, decade-old sedan was in the driveway.

He and Cade exchanged a glance before hopping out and ringing the doorbell. A middle-aged woman with her black hair up and in a Sunday dress answered with a polite smile. "Hello, gentlemen. Can I help you?"

She hadn't opened the screen door, so Sawyer couldn't offer a hand, but he did offer a friendly smile. "Mrs. Parsons? My name is Sawyer Fournette. I'm the Cottonbloom Parish commissioner, and this is my brother Cade. So sorry to bother you on a Sunday morning, but we were looking for Heath. I don't suppose he's here."

The woman's smile had fallen at the mention of her son. Wrinkles deepened in the corners of her eyes and around her mouth, aging her a decade in a few seconds. "Harry, these gentlemen are looking for Heath."

A man who was the salt to his wife's pepper appeared, a hand smoothing white hair back from his forehead. In contrast to his wife's initial politeness, he carried himself with a defensiveness reminiscent of his son.

"What do you want with Heath? Is he in trouble?"

"Not that I know of. We needed to talk to him is all." Sawyer kept his smile in place.

"Has this got something to do with your sister?" Mrs. Parsons asked.

"Absolutely nothing." Cade rumbled over his shoulder.

Mr. and Mrs. Parsons exchanged a look, but both of them had relaxed slightly. "You might as well come in." Mr. Parsons didn't sound welcoming, but Sawyer stepped over the threshold with a smile in place, Cade on his heels.

They settled side by side on a couch, and Sawyer waved off an offer of tea or coffee. "Looks like you're ready for church. We don't want to delay you. Is Heath living here? Could we come by later, perhaps?"

"He's not." Mr. Parsons bit the words out while Mrs. Parsons gazed off to the side.

"Do you happen to know where he's staying?" Cade asked.

"Don't know and don't care." Mr. Parsons's voice was cold.

Mrs. Parsons made a small sound of distress. "That's not true. We do care, but things got bad. We're trying tough love with him."

"What happened?" Sawyer set his elbows on his knees and leaned toward Mrs. Parsons, holding her gaze.

Her chin quivered. "He stole some money from us. Not sure if he's into gambling or drugs or what."

Mr. Parsons piped up. "Had problems managing his anger. Felt like his life hadn't turned out like he'd expected. Although the boy never wanted to work for anything. Expected things to fall into his lap. I guess for a time things did. Until they didn't."

"You might ask Bryce. They've always been thick as thieves. Don't know who else he'd turn to. Will you help him?" Mrs. Parsons's eyes pleaded with him. To her, Heath would always be her little boy, the one who'd always need the protection of a mother. Sawyer wanted to pat her shoulder and make promises he'd be unable to keep.

"They're not here to help Heath. Why would they help him?" Mr. Parsons muttered a curse and stormed out of the room.

Mrs. Parsons rose, her cheeks pink. "I apologize for my husband, gentlemen. He's upset about Heath. We're at a loss how to get through to him and steer him back to God's path. I pray about him all the time."

Sawyer took her hand, not in a shake but in a comforting squeeze. "Sometimes that's all you can do. Thank you for your time."

Sawyer stepped out of the house and took a deep breath. Once back in the truck, Cade said, "That was depressing as hell."

"Tell me about it. Makes me want to find Heath and drag him home by the ear to apologize to his poor mama."

Cade typed on his smartphone. "Bryce lives over in Country Aire on our side."

Country Aire was a trailer park on a gravel loop off the main parish road. The gentrified spelling of "Aire" had always hit Sawyer with a shot of sad irony. He pulled onto the gravel lane. Any identifying trailer numbers had long been worn away or covered by grime.

"There's Heath's truck," Cade said darkly.

"How'd you know what he drives?"

"Made it my business to know once I heard he was harassing Tally."

"Why didn't I know sooner?" Sawyer and Tally had always been close, and he wouldn't lie and say his feelings weren't a little hurt.

"Don't get your shorts in a wad. Tally would rather die than depend on me or you or anyone for that matter. Monroe mentioned it."

"See, she does tell you things." Sawyer pulled to a stop in front of the trailer, blocking Heath's truck.

"Let's do this." Cade hopped out before Sawyer even had the engine off.

Sawyer stepped up behind Cade as the trailer door squeaked open. Heath stood in the narrow space, a pit of darkness behind him, the faint scent of marijuana drifting out. The dark stubble on his face emphasized pale skin and dark circles under his bloodshot eyes.

"I ain't talked to Tally in weeks." His voice rumbled with equal amounts of trepidation and defiance.

"We're not here about our sister."

"Why then?" He didn't seem inclined to invite them inside.

"We're here about the festivals."

Heath's eyes widened before he laughed softly. His hand emerged from behind the door with a hand-rolled joint, and he took a drag. It took several seconds for the smoke to emerge out of his smiling mouth, giving him an odd Cheshire Cat vibe. "You boys looking for volunteers?"

"Not hardly." Disdain and impatience cut Cade's words. "You been messing with the festivals? Cutting traps? Arson? B&E? That kind of stuff isn't child's play. We could have the sheriff down here with a call."

Heath made a show of looking over their shoulders. "Why ain't he with you, then? You don't have any proof, am I right?"

Cade's upper lip twitched, an old tell that he was ready to lose it.

Sawyer shuffled forward, an answering smile on his face. "We don't want to nail you. We want to know who's been paying you."

"Don't know what you're talking about." He took another drag, but his smile had fallen along with his gaze. Sawyer and Cade exchanged a glance.

"You got yourself some money troubles? Have you been working?"

Color flushed into Heath's cheeks. "No, I ain't been working. Got fired from working the harvest and your bitch of a sister banned me from her gym, so my MMA career is on the skids."

Cade was up the two concrete steps faster than Sawyer could react. He grabbed Heath's dingy T-shirt and slammed him into the doorjamb. "What'd you say about my sister, bub?"

"N-Nothing. Sorry."

Sawyer didn't intervene. It was time to let bad cop be bad.

"Who is paying you and telling you what to do, 'cuz we all know you're not smart enough to come up with shit on your own."

"Ms. Martha." The name came on two short breaths. Cade eased back and let him go. The mangled remnants of the joint were on the ratty welcome mat. Heath massaged his neck and picked it up. He took another drag, the joint shaking between his fingers.

"You expect us to believe Ms. Martha, owner of the Quilting Bee, has been paying you to sabotage the festivals?" Cade asked.

"I don't care whether you believe it or not. It's the truth. She and my mama are in a prayer circle together. I guess Mama's been praying for my soul. That's how Ms. Martha knew I needed money."

Cade muttered a curse word and walked away.

"If you call the sheriff on me, I'll deny everything."

Sawyer got in Heath's face, the bitterness and resentment plain to see in the other man's eyes. "You think Ms. Martha is going to cover for you? What are you to her except some meathead she hired to do her dirty work?"

"Soon as she pays me the last of what she owes me, I'm heading to Naw'leans to find a gym. I'm going to be a star in the UFC, you wait and see."

Maybe with his family's support, Heath Parsons could have turned things around. Cleaned up, found a good woman, worked an honest job, lived an honest life. The summer had stolen that chance. New Orleans would feed his vices and then devour him.

"You're going to be nothing, Heath." Sawyer backed away and joined Cade in the truck.

The rising dust from his tires on the way out of Country Aire swallowed Heath's reflection in the doorway of the trailer in his rearview mirror.

"Ms. Martha's probably at church unless lightning struck her down," Cade said.

Even though none of it had been a surprise, a gloom overcame Sawyer. The desperation of a mother to save her son led to his final corruption. Yet Ms. Martha was a decent woman, driven by her own desperate desire to save her business. An unwelcome guilt settled on his shoulders. The festival competition had been the spark that set everything ablaze.

Sawyer drove past the Cottonbloom Parish sheriff's office and headed to the bridge over the river.

Cade straightened. "Aren't you handing this over to law enforcement?"

"Not yet. I need to talk things over with Regan."

"The state of your relationship has nothing to do with this."

"Not as . . . lovers." The word rolled off his tongue with the awkwardness of an elephant performing ballet. He cleared his throat. "But as parish commissioner to mayor. Do you want to see Ms. Martha in jail?"

"I want her to get what she deserves."

Sawyer glanced at his brother who was staring out the windshield, a haunted expression on his face. "What if Chief Thomason had given you what you deserved instead of a second chance?"

They were silent the rest of the way to Monroe's. Cade had been gone too long. He had deliberately cut his ties to Cottonbloom, but Sawyer understood the symbiotic relationship between the two sides and between the citizens.

Cade had the door open as soon as Sawyer pulled to the curb. He turned back with one foot in and one out. "Look, I get that turning Ms. Martha over to the law is hard, but it's the right thing to do. She hurt innocent people. Our crayfish harvesters deserve to be reimbursed at the very least."

Sawyer tightened his hands on the steering wheel. "The Quilting Bee will die."

"Then it dies." Cade rubbed over his jaw, the green of his eyes reminding Sawyer of their mother. "People change. Something has to end for something new to take its place. Maybe something better."

Sawyer blinked. Cade's eyebrows went up, the corner of his mouth quirked, and Sawyer had the distinct feeling they weren't discussing the Quilting Bee anymore. "Maybe the something new, something better will die too."

"Maybe it will. Life is about risk and reward. You won't reap the reward without risking everything. It's what I did when I left here and what I did when I came back. I hold no regrets."

Cade stepped back and closed the door. Behind him, Monroe stepped onto the porch and waved, the smile on her face brilliant. His brother swept Monroe into a hug as if they'd been separated for weeks instead of hours.

Everything in Sawyer's chest ached. He drove by Regan's house, but her car wasn't in the driveway. He continued on, past her mama's house. Mrs. Lovell was in the front yard with gardening gloves and a floppy hat, pruning her roses.

Without considering it, he pulled to a stop and walked over to her. She was short and curvy where Regan was lean, but their strawberry blonde hair was the same. They also shared the same complicated brown eyes. Eyes that were staring at him with unvarnished hatred.

"Mrs. Lovell." Sawyer tipped his head.

"Mr. Fournette. Or should I say Commissioner Fournette. You've made quite a name for yourself over in Louisiana."

"Why do you hate me?" The question that popped out shocked them both into a temporary silence.

Her jaw worked before she turned back to her roses, cutting off a bloom that appeared to still be in its prime. Hot pink fell in the middle of a pile of browning blossoms. "It's unchristian to hate."

"You've done everything you can to keep me and Regan apart. I want to know why."

She clipped off a dying bloom. "You were a phase. Something I had to suffer through. The two of you weren't meant to last. I saw you for what you were. A poor boy who wanted to prove something by dating a pretty girl from Mississippi."

A nugget of truth lay in her words. He had loved Regan, but a tiny part of himself was ashamed to acknowledge he had been validated by her love. "I'm going to date your daughter whether you want me to or not."

The woman laughed and clipped off a browning rose. "What you and my daughter are doing is not dating. You are something she needs to get out of her system before she can move on."

"What are you talking about?" In spite of the heat, a numb wave stilled his heart.

Mrs. Lovell turned and pointed the sharp tip of the clippers at his chest. The first time she'd given him her full attention. "Please. Things ended abruptly years ago. She needs closure. If that consists of sneaking around and reliving some of her wilder moments with you . . . ? Well then, I'll keep my mouth shut. For now. But don't for one second think she wants to date you in front of all of Cottonbloom. That's laughable."

Why was he standing in this woman's yard? Had he expected to receive her blessing? She was petty and cruel, and he was terrified she spoke the truth. He wanted to build something new with Regan. Was all she was doing was reliving their past?

"It's been a pleasure, Mrs. Lovell." His bitter, dry tone drew her narrowed gaze, her brown eyes as flat as Regan's were deep.

He was almost to his truck when she called out. "I believe my daughter is at a festival meeting, Mr. Fournette. Our festival will make anything you put together look pathetic."

The questions reeling through his head dinged his already fragile confidence where Regan was concerned. Nevertheless, he pointed his truck toward Church Street.

Chapter Twenty

Regan took a cookie off the doily-covered tray and sipped her glass of lemonade. The festival committee was finalizing plans. While the festival was her baby, she'd enlisted the help of several denizens of Cottonbloom society to spearhead certain functions.

The Home and Garden tour was in the capable hands of Ms. Beatrice, her seventh-grade English teacher. The farmers' market, where fresh tomatoes and tomato concoctions like salsa and chutney would be displayed and sold, was headed up by Mr. Holcomb, whose tomatoes rivaled her mother's. Regan was in charge of entertainment, food, and the general set-up, but kept her fingers in all the pies. It was frankly exhausting to make sure no one went off the rails.

"I heard-tell someone tried to kill all your dear mother's tomato plants. Is that true?" Ms. Beatrice's needle-sharp voice pierced her reverie. Her mind wasn't on the festival at all but back in Sawyer's bed. Her face heated as if everyone could read her thoughts.

"We caught someone lurking around."

"If he came around my garden, I'd put a round of

buckshot in his butt." Mr. Holcomb's voice reverberated in the meeting room typically used for Bible study.

The tittering of the ladies alternated between outrage and outright laughter. "This is a house of God, Mr. Holcomb." Ms. Beatrice adjusted the reading glasses on her nose, looking like the disapproving teacher she'd been before retiring. She still intimidated Regan.

"Didn't the Lord himself tell David to chop off all the foreskins from the heathen tribes? That's a sight worse than a little buckshot, if you ask me."

This time the room erupted while Mr. Holcomb sat back with a smile on his face. Regan tried not to laugh. Rising and clapping her hands, she said, "The festival is a little over a week away. Does anyone have any receipts or last-minute issues we need to discuss?"

Mr. Holcomb raised a hand. "I got an idea. Selling tomatoes is one thing, but we'll have hungry people out there. Old Rufus is going to be on the other side selling barbeque and crayfish po'boys."

"We'll be selling cotton candy and fritters and such."

He made a scoffing sound. "That's all well and good for the kiddies, but I promise when people get a whiff of what Rufus'll be cooking up, they'll hightail it over the river. We'll be looking pretty pitiful to those *Heart of Dixie* boys if that happens."

"You have a suggestion?"

"Got a cousin who is a crayfish harvester down in Macon Parish. How about we offer up some jambalaya? Good use of any overripe or bruised tomatoes that come in too."

If Mr. Holcomb had come to her with the suggestion two months ago, she would have given him a high five. Not only was she bound by her pinky promise to Sawyer, but serving up crayfish jambalaya would hurt his festival and his feelings. She couldn't do either. Not now.

Several members of the committee spoke up in favor

of the idea. Sweat prickled her forehead. "We don't have the space or manpower to pull it off."

"I'll put my boys in charge of it. We have plenty of propane stoves and pots. All I'd need is some money for the crayfish, but my cousin'll give us a good deal. My granny passed down a mean jambalaya recipe." He rubbed the mound of the belly that hung over his pants and hummed.

Mr. Holcomb was only trying to be helpful, but that didn't stop Regan from wanting to gag him with one of his suspenders. "I'm not sure we have the budget, but let me review our plans, and I'll get back to you." She only had to put him off another few days before it would be too late. "Don't forget we have the pizzeria right off River Street."

Any remaining issues the committee discussed were minor. As long as the weather held, the festival had the potential to be a home run. She made notes in her phone as the meeting broke up. Ms. Beatrice cleared her throat in such an obvious way that Regan glanced up.

Sawyer filled the doorway, staring at her. A tingling awareness of what he'd done to her with his mouth and hands and—she glanced down—other parts of his body had her core tightening.

"Why Commissioner Fournette, here to spy, are you?" Ms. Beatrice held her notebook against the roll of her bosom and favored Sawyer with a glance that would wither most men. "I can assure you, the Cottonbloom tomato festivities will rival any state festival. We will win the *Heart of Dixie* competition. Mark my words."

"I'm sure your festival will be spectacular, ma'am." Sawyer inclined his head and prowled farther into the room, his gaze never leaving Regan. His intensity was part sexual and part something she couldn't identify, but that set her knees trembling.

Guilt over nonexistent crayfish jambalaya had her shuffling backward a few steps until the backs of her legs hit a folding chair. The legs squeaked across the shiny, waxed floor, drawing eyes and silencing conversations.

After the awkwardness of the morning, she couldn't imagine why he had tracked her down to the church meeting hall in front of everyone. She had never been more embarrassed in her life than when she'd heard Tally in his house. The magic of the night had been shattered.

Tallulah Fournette did not like her. She didn't like Regan for who she was and what she had done. Rightly so. Regan was still reeling from their confessions of the day before and the intimacy of their night together. The fracturing of their relationship so many years ago had been as much her fault as his. Maybe even more so. She could blame her mother, but she was the one who had let her mother's opinions guide her life instead of making her own decisions.

While she and Sawyer had resolved the truth of the past—if she chose to trust him—they hadn't discussed the future or whether a future was even possible. The sex had been phenomenal, but was it more than that to him? All these questions and more battered around in her head.

Mr. Holcomb took her forearm. "Would you like me to stay, Regan?" He sounded as if he'd enjoy unleashing buckshot into Sawyer right now.

Regan tried on a smile and patted his hand. "I'll be fine. I'm sure Mr. Fournette has festival business to discuss, isn't that right?"

Everything about Sawyer tensed. "Sure. Festival business, Miss Lovell." Was she imagining the snarky, resigned tone?

Everyone filed out, and she intercepted several curious glances. Silence descended. He ran a hand through his hair as he continued to stare at her. She followed his hand's progress, watching the strands fall through his fingers. Those hands had touched her everywhere last night. He'd been over, under, inside of her. She'd wanted him again . . . and again. What would have happened if Tally hadn't interrupted them?

She massaged the lump in her throat. What should she say? "Do you want a cookie?"

"No."

"Lemonade?"

"No."

"Was there something about the festivals you wanted to talk about?"

"So that's what we're doing?" He propped his hands low on his hips and stepped forward.

She tried to take a step back, but lost her balance and plopped into the chair. He loomed over her, a thunderous expression on his face. Unable to tolerate the unintentional dominance, she rose. Old habits were hard to break, and he was acting like the old, contentious Sawyer.

"I don't know what we're doing," she finally said, his attitude unsettling.

"I'm here because"—he threw up his hands and again she followed their arc through the air—"Cade and I found your man."

She opened her mouth and closed it. His statement was unexpected. She had expected them to hash out their relationship, or lack of relationship. She was more confused than ever. Did his avoidance mean their one night was just that—a one-night thing?

Give her a city to run or a council meeting to guide, and she would take charge. Force her to confront an old-new lover, and she was at a loss as to what to say and do.

"Who is it?"

"You were right about Heath Parsons. Ms. Martha is the one who hired him."

"No," she whispered and regained her seat, covering her mouth. Even though she'd wondered and suspected, hearing the truth made her stomach feel like a pincushion. Ms. Martha was well-liked and respected and, although they'd had their differences, Regan didn't want to see her behind bars. "Things must be dire with the Quilting Bee. What should we do?"

"Heath swears he'll deny everything if the police ask, although I'm sure we could find some evidence to pin on him. I think we should go talk to Ms. Martha."

Her mind circled the problem. Something niggled at her. "I showed Ms. Leora and Ms. Effie the letters."

"And?"

"And they were shocked but not surprised, if that makes any sense."

"You think they're involved too?"

"I don't know. If not involved, then maybe they had an inkling something was going on." She chewed on her bottom lip. "I think we should talk to Ms. Leora first."

Sawyer closed his eyes and ran a hand over his jaw. "What am I going to tell Uncle Del if she is involved? He's finally happy."

Between his frown and his downtrodden tone, he looked defeated. She stood, wanting to hug him, but not sure how he would react. She settled for a brief touch of his arm. "Don't jump to conclusions just yet. She might be able to help us."

"Fine. Shall we, Miss Lovell?" The formalness of his tone even though no one was around only increased her confusion.

"Sawyer . . ."

He didn't acknowledge the plea in her voice nor her outstretched hand as he trudged out the door. She caught up with him in the parking lot. "What is your problem?"

"I don't have a problem." The way he said it insinuated that she was the one with the problem.

"Well, I don't either." The bald-faced lie sounded like

one. She had a crap-ton of problems, including the festival, her mother, and him.

"I'll meet you at Ms. Leora's." He stalked toward his truck and revved the engine before she even made it behind the wheel of her Bug.

On the drive over, Regan's head spun around the problems of Ms. Martha and Sawyer. She couldn't concentrate on either long enough to draw a logical conclusion.

Nash's truck wasn't there, but Delmar Fournette's was, along with a second gray tanklike sedan that seemed to be standard among the ladies of a certain age. She and Sawyer exchanged a glance on their climb to the porch.

Sawyer rang the doorbell. Before the first tone had faded, the door swung open. His uncle chucked his chin up and pushed the screen door open. "Have a feeling I know why you're here. We were just discussing it ourselves. Come on back to the parlor."

Sawyer's worry was palpable, but a distance existed between them that had been absent the night before, and he didn't reach for her hand or touch her in any way when he gestured for her to precede him down the dim hallway.

Delmar perched on the arm of the chair Ms. Leora occupied, and Mrs. Vera Carson sat catty-corner from them on the formal-style sofa. Regan had helped Ms. Leora pick out the upholstery the year before and the pillows the month before. She took a seat next to Mrs. Carson.

"The pillows look fabulous," she said for something to say.

"Yes. You have a good eye, Regan." Ms. Leora and Mrs. Carson exchanged a glance. "You're here about Martha, aren't you?"

Sawyer, who was pacing in the background, came to rest with his hand on the fireplace mantel. "She's behind the trouble we've been having with the festivals."

Mrs. Carson smoothed a perfectly plucked eyebrow. "But she couldn't have ransacked poor Regan's shop."

"Not her." Sawyer and his uncle held gazes. "She hired Heath Parsons to do the grunt work. She sent Regan the threatening letters, though, and maybe burned the pavilion down by herself."

Ms. Leora reached for Delmar's hand but kept her gaze directed toward Regan. "Vera and I were afraid something was going on. And, when you showed me those terrible letters . . ."

Mrs. Carson took up the thread. "We knew then she was up to her eyeballs in trouble. The shop has been barely breaking even and last year she had some medical issues and then with the tax increases . . . her desperation came to a head and I suppose the festivals were her breaking point."

"Up to now, no one has been physically harmed, but between my shop and the baskets and the pavilion, several thousand dollars in property damage has been accrued. Even so, I don't want to see her arrested. What do you say, Sawyer?" She glanced over at him.

"I agree. Not exactly the publicity we want a week before a huge magazine rolls into town to cover the festivities." He left the mantel to take a wingback chair opposite Ms. Leora. "I have the feeling you ladies and my uncle have been cooking up ideas on how to get everyone out of this mess while saving face, am I right?"

"Told you, Leora-darlin'. Sharp as a fishing hook and about the biggest heart this side of the Mississippi." Delmar grinned in his direction. "Leora was afraid you would want to throw the book at Martha."

"Look, what she did was wrong and hurtful, but I understand desperation." He shot Regan a glance she couldn't interpret.

Mrs. Carson folded her hands in her lap and sat up straighter. "I'm going to buy the Quilting Bee."

Leora gasped. "But Vera—"

"No. It's already in motion. The Quilting Bee has been my haven for more years than I can count. Without the ladies there . . ." She shook her head and looked toward the window. "Seeing Cottonbloom ripped apart by the actions of our fathers and husbands and brothers could have broken us all apart, but we kept the faith and the peace and have tried to mend this town stitch by stitch."

"There are plenty on the Mississippi side who'll never see me as more than a Louisiana swamp rat." The antipathy in Sawyer's voice surprised Regan. She stared at him, willing him to look at her, but he was focused on Mrs. Carson.

"No, but there are plenty who see you just as your uncle does." Mrs. Carson cast a look toward Regan. "Isn't that right, dear?"

Sawyer cut his hazel eyes toward her, but his face stayed blank. After a bumbling affirmative hum, she said, "Plenty of people. Everybody . . . loves you." Her face heated. Why had she said that?

Sawyer's eyes narrowed before he turned to his uncle. "How do we keep the harvesters from pressing charges?"

"They'll be paid out of the profit Martha will be making on the sale," Mrs. Carson said.

"Even so, they might not be of the forgive-and-forget mentality," Sawyer added.

"You leave them to me." Delmar tucked his chin to his chest and crossed his arms. "I might not have much influence over the banks and highfalutin society types over here, but I know those boys on my side. They'll take the money and keep their mouths shut."

"Obviously, we can count on your discretion, Regan?" Mrs. Carson patted her hand.

"Of course. But, we haven't discussed whether Ms. Martha will even sell. She might dig in and refuse. Go down with the ship." Regan looked back and forth at the two ladies.

"Don't worry about Martha. You let Vera and me handle her." Ms. Leora's voice was full of the steel that had always intimidated Regan. She reached over to touch the back of Sawyer's hand, her voice softening. "I appreciate you being so understanding, Commissioner Fournette. My relationship with your family hasn't been the smoothest. Delmar told me you'd understand though."

"Call me Sawyer, please." He rose, and Regan took her cue from him, following him to the door.

When he didn't seem inclined to stop and talk to her, she caught up with him as he reached his truck and grabbed his sleeve. "Hang on a minute."

"What?" He propped a hip against the fender in his typical stance, facing her with his arms across his chest. Where was the man who had held her on his lap, rehashed the past with her, and gave her hope? Where was the man who'd made love to her the night before and made her believe they were building something new?

Although things with Ms. Martha weren't concluded and the festivals hung over their heads, she couldn't wait for the perfect time to clear the air between them. Things would always be complicated, but maybe complicated wasn't bad, maybe it was interesting.

"Listen. Things were weird this morning with your sister . . . and stuff." Her courage faltered. She'd never asked a man out on a date. What if their night together had been a one-time thing for him? What if he turned her down and humiliated her? Didn't she have to try anyway? "Do you want to maybe see each other again? Or something?"

The longer the silence stretched, the hotter her face became until it rivaled the surface of the sun. His face was serious, no mocking laughter threatened at least. Her tongue bumbled around. "Look, if last night was just . . . I mean, if you don't want to get together, I—"

"Get together? You mean hook up?"

Answering her question with a question only tipped her further off-balance. "Sure, if that's what you want." After they grabbed dinner, she wouldn't protest if they went back to her place. Not if it was anything like last night. "As long as no one busts in on us again." She smiled at her weak attempt at a joke, but no answering tease cracked the seriousness of his expression.

"Yeah, getting seen would probably ruin your rep."

"What?" The embarrassment factor had nothing to do with her reputation.

"How about tonight? I'll pick you up at seven." His gaze skimmed down her body. "Wear a skirt."

She nodded, relief streaking through her body like a cool blast of air. He had said yes. Seven was late for dinner on a Sunday, but maybe they would go to the country club if he wanted her to dress nice. Even though a strangeness still permeated the air between them, an actual date would be the next step to creating something new.

"I'll see you tonight." Her smile came easier as she moved to her car. He hadn't moved from the shadow of his truck, his brow scrunched low. She waved and drove off, her body already thrumming with the knowledge she would see him again and soon.

Sawyer slammed his back door open. A clawing pain was ripped at his heart. *Mr. Fournette,* she'd called him in front of the social leaders of Cottonbloom. The air of guilt around her had been unmistakable, but she didn't feel guilty enough to not want to sneak around with him. It shouldn't have hurt, but a crippling ache rushed into his hollowed-out stomach.

He flipped the shower on and stepped straight into the lukewarm water. Regan's mama was right. He scrubbed himself as if the feeling of not being good enough to touch the likes of Regan Lovell could be washed away.

The flare of hope when she'd suggested getting together was crushed when she'd agreed to a hook-up. What he really wanted was to take her out, talk over dinner, maybe cuddle on the couch and watch a movie. He wanted to god-damn cuddle, and she only wanted to get laid somewhere no one could catch his dirty hands on her.

Last night he'd made her scream his name. And he'd do it again tonight. Make her beg. One more time. Then he'd be done with her and her mama and all of Cottonbloom, Mississippi. He'd work his ass off for Cade and ignore the feeling that something was missing from his life.

The hours crept by. He pulled on a pair of broken-in jeans and a T-shirt. As he was driving over the bridge, he tapped the brakes. Why had she agreed that he pick her up? More discreet if she met him somewhere for their booty call. Rolling down her street, doubts wormed their way into his self-righteous resentment.

No, this was their thing. Creeping around on the river or the back roads. They'd never flaunted their relationship in high school. She'd seemed fine with the fact he hadn't had the money to take her anywhere fancy. It was clearly more than charity on her part. She hadn't wanted to parade him around to her family and friends in Mississippi. He understood that now.

He parked at the curb, barely refrained from flipping a bird toward her mama's house, stomped through the grass to her front door, and banged with his fist.

The door opened. His anger felt out of place confronted

with her tentative, sweet smile that made her eyes dance. In her swishy skirt, high heels, and V-neck sleeveless sweater, she looked ready for a church social, not a hook-up in his truck.

Her smile slipped as she took him in, and slivers of uncertainty sent a tingle up his neck. His plan was set. "You ready?"

"Let me set the alarm." She disappeared back inside. He turned on his heel and headed toward his truck. Hesitating, he glanced over his shoulder, his gaze tracing the long line of her legs. Her heels were ridiculous. Instead of forcing her to climb into his truck by herself, he opened the passenger door and waited. There were limits to his assholery.

Her legs were more ridiculous than her heels. The skirt swished a few inches above her knee, exposing seductive glimpses of her thighs. Thighs that had clenched him tight the night before. Her sweater clung to the curves of her breasts, the white lace of her bra peeking from the deep neckline.

She took his hand and stepped onto the running board, finding her seat but not releasing him. Her fingers brushed up his forearm a few inches. Goose bumps rose in the wake of her touch. "Thanks," she murmured.

When he joined her and cranked the truck, his internal organs seemed to have started a bar fight. "Thought we could head out on a back road. For old times' sake. What do you think?"

He waited. Her answer would determine which direction he took.

"Sure. I guess." Her agreement lilted into an almost-question, sounding another alarm in his head.

He swallowed and pointed them back toward the Louisiana line. They were silent all the way down the rumbling pavement to a field in front of the river. He parked, rolled the windows down, and turned the radio up. He raised the console between them, turning the front into a bench seat.

"So all that stuff with Ms. Martha was pretty crazy, huh?" Her hands played in the folds of her skirt.

"Lots of crazy in Cottonbloom."

"Which side?" She laughed softly, the sound prodding his heart to beat faster.

He didn't want to talk anymore. Everything she said and did confused him. They were only good at one thing. He wrapped a hand around her nape and drew her closer. He felt her resistance right before their lips met and stilled, holding her in place but not forcing her forward.

The sun was low in the sky, and fingerlike shadows danced over her face. The longer he looked in her eyes, the more confused he became. He didn't want to hurt her. It would be like slicing his own heart open. He would allow himself these last moments with her before putting her in the past forever.

He took her lips and moved his hand into the artfully tousled waves of her hair. One kiss followed another, each one more frantic and passionate. She slipped her arms around his shoulders, her fingernails leaving erotic trails of sensation through the thin cotton.

He circled her waist and brought her to his lap, her back against his front. She tried to turn, but he pressed a hand against her ribs. He couldn't risk getting lost in her eyes. "This is how I want you."

She arched her back and her head fell onto his shoulder. He nuzzled her neck the same time his hands cupped her breasts. She breathed his name. The realization that this was the last time he would touch her ripped at his soul.

He slipped his hands under her sweater and covered the soft, lace-covered skin. Her nipples were hard against his palms. She loved his touch. Why couldn't she love all of him?

"Do you want me?" He rasped the words in her ear. Her intake of breath and the spreading of her legs was answer enough.

With one hand staying to toy with her breasts, he hooked his feet around her ankles, drawing her legs even farther apart, and lifted her skirt with the other hand. She writhed on his lap. He was harder than he'd ever been.

The petty part of him wanted to take her then and there. Sate himself inside of her. He grazed his knuckles over her damp underwear. The white lace matched her bra. He slipped a finger underneath. She felt amazing. Soft and smooth and wanting.

"Do you like this?"

"You know I do." She circled her hips, driving him crazy. He bucked into her with a low moan.

"You like my rough, dirty hands on you, don't you?"

She hummed and searched for his mouth. He drove his tongue next to hers, but retreated.

"Say my name."

"Sawyer, please." He recognized the tinny, plaintive note in her voice.

"Tell me how much you want me."

"I want you so bad. I've wanted you for so long." The thread of longing tugged at something similar that unspooled from his heart. He paused in his ministrations, but she wouldn't allow it.

It was too easy. She was too responsive. He wanted it to last forever, but she wasn't allowing forever. She covered his hand with hers and drove his finger deep. She shattered, and he practiced some deep breathing exercises to keep from following her.

She went limp against him and weaved her fingers with

his, still touching her intimately. The sound of their breathing overlay the soft country song playing and the escalating noise as dusk approached. She twisted enough to nuzzle her lips against his throat.

God, he loved her. Again. Or had he ever stopped? Was she the reason he'd never gotten serious with another woman? How could he admit his feelings after so many years of animosity? So many years of believing lies and building distrust. How could they build something that lasted on such shaky ground?

With the willpower of a saint, he uncoupled their hands and shifted her off his lap. He missed the weight of her, the feel of her against him already. At first she didn't move, her skirt bunched around her upper thighs and her breasts exposed.

He looked out the front windshield, adjusted the seat, and gripped the steering wheel. The rustle of clothes signaled she'd gotten the hint. Leather creaked and she laid a hand on his forearm. His muscle jumped.

"Do you want me to . . ." Her voice tread through the dimming cab.

Of course he wanted nothing more than to have her touch him in any way she wanted. "I'm taking you home."

"Home? I thought we were going someplace nice for dinner?"

He swiveled his head toward her, surprise jamming his brain. "Dinner?"

"You told me to wear a skirt."

His mouth dropped open but he was at a loss. The silence didn't last long.

"Ohmigod. I am an idiot. You wanted sex. Easy access. That's it." She scooted farther away and stared out the passenger window, her hand over her mouth.

His moral high ground grew shaky. "You indicated you were good to go for a hook-up."

"Excuse me for not being clear. I was asking you out on a date since it didn't seem like you were going to make a move. Yes, I wanted to hook up, because . . . well, the other night was pretty spectacular. At least for me. Obviously, you were just scratching an old itch or something. Take me home."

"You ran out on me so fast I nearly got whiplash."

"Your sister—who doesn't particularly like me if you haven't noticed—walked into your house while you were freaking *inside* of me. What did you expect me to do? Invite her in for the show? I was mortified."

"You were ashamed."

"Of course I wasn't ashamed. I'm a grown woman, Sawyer. This isn't *The Scarlet Letter*. Take. Me. Home."

When he didn't move, she leaned over and turned the keys. The engine roared on. Not knowing what else to do, he shifted into drive and got them moving. The headlights cut through the gloaming, bugs flying in every direction. She kept her window down and her face averted.

"You didn't seem too happy to see me this afternoon at your festival gathering." He lobbed his last potshot, hearing the defensiveness in his voice.

"I was acting as Cottonbloom mayor. You are a colleague. Did you expect me to drop to my knees and give you a blow job?"

If he'd heard tears in her voice he might have pressed harder, but anger ripped through her words, smashing the last of his logic. But he knew one thing. He'd royally screwed everything up. He pulled up to her house and grabbed her wrist before she could escape.

"What?" she clipped out.

He would have welcomed the anger that marked their recent relationship over the chill that blasted from her now. "Look, tonight was a misunderstanding—"

"Same as in college, huh? That seems to happen a lot

with us, doesn't it? Good luck with your festival." She hopped out and slammed the door, rocking the truck. Before he could formulate a reply, she was gone.

The poverty and hunger and loneliness of his youth had left wounds that had festered. He'd always been the one to put on a smile for everyone else. Just like Regan did.

She had been the one he talked to. Once she cut him out of her life, he hadn't realized how much he'd missed her until he had a grasp on her again. A fleeting grasp as it turned out.

Chapter Twenty-one

Regan sat behind the counter of her shop and made phone calls confirming details about the festival and checking things off her list. With less than a week to go, her neck was sore, her head hurt, and she didn't even want to consider the state of her heart.

The bell tinkled as the front door opened. Tallulah Fournette stepped over the threshold and looked around as if exploring an alien planet.

"Let me call you right back, okay?" She disconnected without waiting for a response and slid off the stool, but kept the counter between them. Tally was dressed in spandex, and with her toned arms and legs would take Regan down within seconds in a girl fight.

"Can I help you with something?" Regan asked.

Tally fingered the fringe along one of the new pillows in her display. "You can't even tell your shop was vandalized. Looks good."

"It was mostly pillow stuffing. Looked worse than it really was. Are you thinking about redecorating?"

"Maybe once Nash gets our cabin built you could help us?" Tally flipped her long, dark braid over her shoulder and side-eyed Regan with a smile.

She'd known Nash and Tally were dating but hadn't re-alized they had gotten serious so fast. "Of course. Nash is a great guy."

"He really is."

Regan wasn't sure she'd ever seen Tally smile. Not a smile like this anyway. It reminded her of Sawyer. Her heart did something funny. She probably should have skipped the extra cup of coffee that morning, but after a restless night, she'd needed something to get her moving.

"Did you want to look at some color swatches?" Regan came around the counter and fanned out a color wheel.

"Maybe later. "

"O-kay," she drew the word out and waited, tense and expectant. Was she going to bring up the other morning?

"About the other morning—"

A brittle laugh emerged from Regan's throat. "That was very weird. Forget about it. Please."

Tally's brows drew in. "Yeah. That's kind of why I'm here. You know, to apologize."

"Look, I know how you feel about me. Nothing is going on between me and Sawyer. Not anymore."

An awkwardness descended. Tally rubbed her nape and glanced to the door. "I haven't been a hundred percent fair to you. Nash told me you were really nice to him in school. I appreciate that. I do. We were sort of each other's protectors. Until we weren't."

"He used to let me cheat off him." Regan tittered an-other laugh that sounded fake, because it was. She had no idea where this conversation was going.

"He used to let me cheat off him too."

Tally smiled again and radiated such warmth and love that a shot of jealousy speared Regan's gut. The unexpect-edness of the feeling amplified her own heartbreak. Dam-nable tears pricked her eyes, and she grabbed the color wheel and studied it, hoping she hadn't exposed a weakness for the other woman to exploit.

Tally's hand, her fingernails painted a dark purple, covered hers for only a second, but the squeeze was unmistakable. "My brother is moping around like someone shot his favorite dog."

"He's never owned a dog." Regan sniffed the tears back.

Tally muffled a laugh. "Metaphorically speaking. He won't tell me what happened, but I can't help but worry I'm the cause."

"You're not the cause. At least not in my eyes. I'm not sure how to tell you this, but . . . your brother is an idiot."

"Aren't all men at one time or another?"

They shared a laugh, this one coming easier for them both and settling a layer of ease over the awkwardness. The bell tinkled again, and Regan was glad for the interruption. Tally was a Fournette and not her friend, yet she'd come dangerously close to spilling her problems.

Regan slapped on a smile, but as she stepped away, Tally laid a hand on her arm. "Wanted you to know that I'm all for you two if it makes Sawyer happy."

Regan watched her disappear out the door and turn toward the river.

"What do you think, Regan? Does it match?" Her customer held a swatch against one of the pillows, and Regan tried to redirect her brain.

The rest of the afternoon passed in fits of working on the festival and helping customers. She made several design appointments for September, not sure if she was looking forward to the festival being over or dreading not having something to distract her. If she had never read that magazine article about the festival competition, she would have never been tossed together with Sawyer again. Despite her hurt feelings and confusion, she was glad for it.

It was almost as if she had been biding her time in Cotton-bloom until fate had veered them on a collision course.

The bell over her door tinkled, and all thoughts of Sawyer were shoved away. Ms. Martha stood on the threshold, and by the shell-shocked look in her eyes, Mrs. Carson and Ms. Leora had laid out the facts. The lines and creases had deepened since their last conversation less than a week earlier.

She and Regan held eyes for a few beats longer than was comfortable. When it became obvious Ms. Martha wasn't going to initiate a conversation, Regan said, "I take it you've met with the ladies?"

"Leora thinks I wanted to get caught." She moved farther into the shop, fingering the same pillow fringe that had drawn Tally. "Maybe I did." Her whisper barely registered.

"Why do you say that?"

"The Quilting Bee was my mother's passion. Not mine. Never mine."

Regan recalled her admission that she didn't even quilt. "Then why keep it going all this time?"

"Because I didn't have anything else. I grew up wanting to please my mother. I did what she expected of me and didn't protest. And after she died, I wasn't strong enough to let it all go. I felt trapped. Can you understand that at all?"

Were she and Ms. Martha so different? Hadn't Regan toed her mother's line and smiled for the sake of everyone else? Sawyer had been the one who had made her feel brave and able to follow her passions. When he'd guessed her dream of running for state office, he hadn't laughed. He hadn't scoffed and spouted some platitude while patting her head. He'd told her the state would be lucky to have her. With Sawyer, anything felt possible. But she also knew how hard things had been without him. How easily her mother had stolen her confidence.

"Actually, I can understand your position, Ms. Martha, even if I don't understand why you took such drastic actions."

Her gaze darted around the floor, her jaw working. "I sent the letter thinking it would be enough."

"No offense, Ms. Martha, but it was a little campy. I thought a teenager had done it."

Ms. Martha shook her head. "You saw the gas can, didn't you?"

"I did."

"That's when you started to suspect, wasn't it?"

"Around then, yes."

"It got out of hand. I told Heath to paint graffiti on the pavilion, not burn it down. The baskets were his idea. It seemed like he was settling his own scores along the way."

"I suppose he was the one who broke into my shop as well?"

"Yes," she said in a small voice. "I've felt like you've wanted me gone since you became mayor. You want some trendy little boutique to take my place. Or maybe you want my space for your own shop."

"I didn't want either of those things to happen, Ms. Martha. I truly want the best for Cottonbloom and that does not include forcing you out of business."

The woman's lips trembled. "Vera bought me out. We signed the papers this morning."

"I'm sorry." No anger came, only pity.

A smile flashed across Ms. Martha's face. "Don't be. I'm not. I'm embarrassed, sad, ashamed, but not sorry."

"What are you going to do?"

"I'm going to do something that Mother always thought was foolish. She couldn't understand anyone wanting to leave Cottonbloom. I'm going to Florida. I have a cousin there who's been after me to move for years."

"I hope you're happy there, Ms. Martha. You will be here for the festivals, won't you?"

"I don't think so, dear. The sooner I'm gone the better, to my way of thinking. But I wish you luck with them. And I hope you win the money for your plans. Truly, I do."

Ms. Martha moved to the door and Regan followed. They exchanged tight smiles. After she stepped outside, Regan flipped the dead bolt on the door. An interior design emergency was unlikely.

Once home, she kicked off her heels and wandered the quiet of her house, mind and body restless and unsettled. Instead of consoling herself with the tub of butter pecan ice cream calling from inside the freezer, she headed to the river. The wind had stiffened since that morning and gray clouds to match her mood loomed on the horizon.

Her feelings for the river were entwined with her feelings for Sawyer. At one time she'd loved the river, found solace there. Sneaking down to the water to wait for Sawyer when they were teenagers had filled her with exhilaration. When her heart had shattered, the river had become her nemesis. She'd hated the river instead of herself. Hated the river instead of her mother. Hated Sawyer. It had been easier that way.

She settled with her back against the water oak and gazed over the river into the field of snowy cotton bolls. Her phone rang, and she startled. It was Monroe.

"What's up?" Regan twirled a fallen leaf, sunbeams limning its yellowed, curled edges.

"You're not going to believe this." Monroe's voice held a note of euphoria.

"You and Cade are engaged."

Silence. "What? Of course not. Good grief." Her protest seemed half-hearted at best. "Why would you even think that? He's only been back a couple of months."

"Could be the cow-eyes you send in his direction pretty much all the time." Even with her own love life in turmoil, Regan would be ecstatic for Monroe. She and Cade were meant for each other. It was a matter of time until the man put a ring on it. He wasn't as dense as his brother.

"This is not about Cade. Well, in a roundabout way, it's because of him. Sam Landry is getting extradited back to Georgia. The private investigator Cade contracted back in June tied Sam to an embezzlement of funds from the insurance agency he worked for."

"What about your case against him? Surely you want some retribution?"

Sam had tried to take advantage of one of the young girls in Monroe's girls-at-risk group. Monroe confronted him and egged him into hitting her. As soon as he had, she'd broken his nose and a couple of ribs before filing charges against him.

"Assault and battery is chump change compared to criminal embezzlement. The lawyer says I can testify as a character witness for the prosecution though. He'll be behind bars far longer with this new charge, and I'll do my best to keep him there."

"In that case, that is fabulous news."

"What's wrong?"

"Nothing."

"Better check your pants. I can smell the smoke from here."

"Ha-ha. Very funny." Regan picked up a flat rock and tried to skip it across the river, but it plopped and sank with the first hit.

"What did Sawyer do? Or not do? Your car was still there the other night when we dropped off his truck, but you didn't say anything the other morning." Monroe's voice lilted up. Regan could either answer or not. Monroe wouldn't press her any further.

"We spent the night together. All night. And, it was amazing."

"Amazing enough to forgive him?"

Regan outlined his confession to her.

Monroe whistled low. "Wow. Of course I always wondered, but considering how many secrets I kept back then, I was hardly one to force you to tell me."

"I told Mother I'd found him in bed with another girl, which was a huge mistake. She never liked Sawyer and once she had something tangible to hang onto, she put up roadblocks on any path back to together. But, I thought we were finally moving forward." Regan rubbed the middle of her forehead. "Until last night."

"What did he do?"

"I asked him out on what I thought was a date."

"Impressive and unusual. What happened? I can't imagine he shot you down?"

It had been the single most humiliating event of her life. Worse than having to stand on a stage while someone else won Miss Mississippi. Worse than Tally nearly walking in on them. Worse than catching a naked woman in Sawyer's bed. Now that she knew the truth at least.

"He thought I was asking for sex. And that's it. Told me to wear a skirt. He took me out on some back road. I thought we were going for dinner, maybe a movie." The last words emerged from a throat strangled with tears. She'd cried more the last month than she had since they'd broken up. Her splotchy face was all his fault.

A crackling silence stretched before Monroe muttered a string of words that would have half the church congregation fainting. "What did you do?"

"Made him take me home. What else could I do?"

"Drop by one of my classes and I'll give you some ideas." A hint of humor crackled over the phone. "That's where you left things?"

"Yep. Any advice?"

"Do you love him?"

The question had her flopping back in the grass and closing her eyes, pinpricks of sunlight moving like stars on her eyelids. "Of course I do. I always have."

"Can I tell you something I've learned about the Fournettes?" Monroe didn't wait for an answer. "They are smart and amazing and loyal and proud. But underneath their thick hide of pride are little kids who still hurt from their parents' deaths, their struggle to survive in the aftermath, and the feelings of shame all of that produced."

Everything, from the moment she ran out of his house to their disastrous "date" scrolled through her mind, including his defensiveness. "Sawyer thinks I'm ashamed of him."

"Cade thought the same thing until I set him straight."

"At the fund-raiser."

"Exactly. These Fournette boys are surprisingly sensitive."

"I should go talk to him?" Capable of making decisions that affected thousands of citizens, clear-eyed and logical, she wandered around blindfolded when it came to her own life and Sawyer.

"You two have made a habit of not talking things out." She heaved a sigh. "Look, I can you tell you two things. One, Sawyer is a great guy. Two, he has been carrying a torch for you since forever. He was really worried about you after the pavilion burned down even though you accused him of doing it. He cares about you. A lot."

Regan disconnected after promising to let Monroe know how everything went.

On the drive to Fournette Designs, words garbled in her head, and she parked next to his truck without any clearer idea what she planned to say. Maybe for once she would come straight out with a truth he couldn't misinterpret. Three potent little words would work.

A BMW and a motorcycle were parked in front as well. She slipped out and stretched her neck and shoulders as if preparing for a physical confrontation.

She pushed open the shop door a few inches and stuck her head inside. No one was around. Stepping in, she smoothed her skirt down. Movement shadowed behind the window of the break room. She walked on her toes to keep the clacking of her shoes from echoing in the cavernous space.

A few feet from the break room, Sawyer's laugh rumbled, and she bit the inside of her cheek. Moving closer, she opened her mouth to call a greeting, but froze.

The same gorgeous woman he'd had dinner with a few weeks earlier stood in front of him touching his chest with a perfectly manicured hand. He was leaning against the counter, his pose relaxed, his feet and arms crossed, smiling down at her.

She wasn't sure how long she stood there. Seconds, minutes, hours lost in a spiraling black hole watching the woman touch him and watching him smile and laugh. A flashback of walking into his dorm room and seeing a naked woman pressed against him in the narrow twin bed, his roommates laughing behind her made heat flush through her.

No matter how much she loved him, she couldn't trust him. Couldn't expose herself to more of the same from him. Maybe her mother had been right. Was Sawyer Fournette using her to settle a score?

She pressed herself against the wall. The cement bricks seeped a welcome coolness through the heat of her humiliation. She pressed the heels of her hands against her eyes, but all she could see were past and present colliding. A sick feeling oozed up from her stomach.

She ran-walked to the door, not caring this time whether she made noise or not. Gulps of warm air settled her stomach back where it belonged even though it tied itself into painful knots. Back in her car, she fumbled the key into the ignition. Away. She needed to get away.

She drove too fast down the narrow drive back to the main road. Cade's old truck met her around the last bend. She stomped both feet on the brake pedal. Two wheels skidded off the road into gravel, but she muscled her car around Cade's truck and didn't look back.

She didn't stop until she was back on her side of the river. Her phone stared at her from the passenger seat. A sense of betrayal had her scrolling through her contacts. The phone rang twice before Mr. Holcomb answered.

"I've thought more about your plan. Let's do it."

"Are you sure?"

She wasn't sure about anything anymore. "I'll get you a check tomorrow."

He whooped on the other end.

Regan hit the end button and rested her forehead on the steering wheel. What had she done?

Sawyer left Terry Lowe in the break room reviewing the finalized contracts and escaped to his engine. The woman wanted in his pants. While her flirting made him uncomfortable, he had to admire her tenacity, considering he'd turned her down once already. He needed to borrow some of her gumption and go confront Regan. Get everything out in the open.

Cade rounded the corner, drying his hands on a work towel. "What'd Regan want?"

Sawyer straightened. "Did she call?"

Cade tilted his head, his brow crunching. "She nearly ran me off the road on her way out of here. Surprised she didn't bust a tire."

"I didn't even see her."

"Were you out back or something?"

He pointed toward the break room. "No, I was . . . hellfire. I was attempting to discuss the contract with Terry, but she was more interested in discussing other things."

"Like getting you naked?"

"Not in so many words, but yes. I'm trying not to out-right offend her until the deal is set in stone."

"You are just too damn charming and nice." The disgust in Cade's voice tugged a smile from Sawyer in spite of the situation. "Let me handle Terry from here on out."

"I don't know. Terry might set her sights on you next. Monroe's turned you into a smiling, whipped wimp."

"Monroe might look all sweet and demure but the woman could take Terry down with one punch if she tried to put the moves on me." Cade waggled his eyebrows, only confirming Sawyer's opinion.

"I feel like I'm having a flashback. What do I do? Explain to Regan that nothing happened?"

"She needs to learn to trust you. I'd make her come to you."

Sawyer groaned. "It's more complicated than that." He gave Cade an encapsulated version of events.

"Dude, really?" Cade threw his hands up. "Only one thing matters. Do you love her?"

"I'm not sure I've ever stopped loving her."

Understanding flared in Cade's eyes. While Cade could be tough and closed-off, something of their father resided in his eyes and voice and attitude. "Then you have to go get her, don't you?"

If Cade wouldn't think he was losing his mind, he would give his brother a long, hard hug. God, he'd missed him the years he'd been gone. Missed his no-nonsense advice and steadying force.

"I would run by the hardware store for knee pads

though." The hint of dark humor was all Cade. "You're going to need to grovel your way out of this one. Take the rest of the afternoon off and handle your shit."

Cade walked off, shaking his head and muttering to himself.

Was his brother right? Of course, he was. Sawyer washed up in the shop sink and headed out. Cade was in the break room. Their eyes met for a second. Cade tipped his chin and transferred his attention back to Terry, smiling and murmuring something Sawyer couldn't hear.

He drove over the steel-girded bridge and spotted her at the gazebo talking to Nash Hawthorne. He parked next to Nash's Defender and took a few seconds for a silent pep talk. He could do this. It was only his heart and future happiness on the line.

Regan and Nash watched him approach, her face unreadable. He would have preferred hurt or anger over coldness. It reminded him too much of the months after their breakup. She had told him she'd been as broken as he had been during that time even if it hadn't showed. Maybe she was feeling the same now.

"I need to talk to you." He hoped he didn't sound as desperate as he felt.

"I guess you heard. It's going to happen. No use in talking me out of it. Nash thinks it's a great idea, don't you?'

Nash sidestepped away and looked at his bare wrist. "Wow, look at the time. I need a drink, so I'll let you two discuss things and stuff."

Regan huffed at his back as he jogged toward the walking bridge, probably headed for Tally's gym.

"What idea does Nash think is great, and I'm supposed to know about?"

"The jambalaya."

"What jambalaya?"

"The crayfish jambalaya Cottonbloom, Mississippi, will be selling during the Tomato Festival." Her chin rose and her eyes flashed.

"What the hell, Regan! Where are you getting the crayfish?"

"Mr. Holcomb's cousin down in Macon. It's going to be delicious. Way better than some pathetic po'boys."

She was probably right. Ripe tomatoes and fresh-caught crayfish made for the best jambalaya. She'd reneged on their agreement for the same reasons she'd cut him out of her life for so many years. She was hurt and she cared about him. At least the years had left him with that small amount of wisdom.

As maddening and frustrating as she could be, he loved her. "Cade told me you stopped by the shop."

She crossed her arms and shrugged, looking somewhere over his shoulder.

"I'm not sure what you think you saw or why you high-tailed it off, but Terry Lowe is a customer."

"You're working on a reputation for excellent customer service." Her eyes flitted to his for a second. He recognized the pain. "She's very pretty."

"Not as pretty as you are." The compliment landed with the weight of an anvil. "You have to trust me, Regan."

"Why? We aren't in a relationship. You made it perfectly clear you only wanted to have sex with me. Maybe that's what you want with her too?"

He ran a hand through his hair and sent his gaze skyward.

"Don't you roll your eyes at me." She shoved his shoulder. "Why should I trust you when all you do is betray it?"

He clenched his teeth together. Anger finally won out. "I didn't sleep with that girl in college, and I won't ever sleep with Terry Lowe. I feel like an ass for treating you like I did the other night. Your mother—" He bit off his words. No use in blaming the woman. He'd been the one to screw up. "You should trust me because I love you. I loved you then and I love you now and I've never stopped. Think about that and come find me if you think you might love me and can trust me. If you can't then don't bother."

He stormed back to his truck and took off back over the bridge. Only one thing would soothe him. The river.

Chapter Twenty-two

Sawyer drove off leaving her ripped apart and vulnerable. He loved her. Had always loved her. Even spoken in anger, she sensed the truth behind his words. Or maybe because they had been spoken in anger, she believed him. She had broken her promise to him, yet he still loved her.

Something else he said niggled at her. Her mother. What about her mother?

She tore through town and pulled into her parents' driveway behind her mother's high-end Mercedes. Not bothering with the bell, she opened the door to Donny and Marie yipping and jumping around her legs.

They trailed her into the sunroom where her mother was lazing on a couch, flipping through a glossy fashion magazine. "Did you say something to Sawyer?"

Her mother looked up while turning another page. "He stopped by on Sunday while I was deadheading roses. Is that what you mean?"

"What did you say to him, Mother?"

"Only the truth."

The truth as her mother saw it, no doubt. "What exactly did you say?"

"That you were reliving your wild past with him. Isn't that about right?"

"It's nowhere near right. We are—were—*are* trying to build something new. I love him, Mother. He's a good man. I'm sorry if he's not what you envisioned for me, but he's what I want. What I've always wanted."

Her mother slapped the magazine shut and swung her legs off the couch. "What about Andrew Tarwater?"

"What about him?"

"You two went on a date recently. Did it not go well?"

"It wasn't a date; it was a business dinner to discuss refurbishing the Tarwater offices."

Her mother huffed a sigh and smiled a smile that sent the hairs on the back of her neck up. "Regan-honey, you could have Andrew Tarwater eating out of your hand and a ring on your finger by New Year's if you put your mind to it. You and he would make a fine match."

"Ohmigod, will you listen to yourself? You don't even care what I want. What's best for me. All you care about is yourself. You poisoned me against Sawyer because of your prejudices. And then you tried to do the same to him." Thunder rumbled in the distance. A purple stain was spreading across the sky to the west.

She headed toward the door, her mother and the dogs behind her. Her mother grabbed her arm, the perfectly manicured French tips in contrast to the veined tendons of her hand. Even her mother couldn't fight the march of time.

"Don't go. Wait until the storm passes through. It looks bad." Her mother sounded truly worried. But Regan couldn't be sure it wasn't another one of her mother's manipulation tactics.

She stared at the gathering storm and muttered, "I wasted too much time already."

She turned her car toward the state line. Too many

wasted years between then and now. Too many years where she'd been treading water. If only she'd been stronger then and stood up to her mother. If only she'd given Sawyer a chance to explain.

He loved her. The tingly warmth started somewhere in her chest and spread outward. He had always loved her. She believed him. Trusted him. Would he believe her? Could *he* trust *her* not to turn her back again?

She turned down his long driveway, her little car shimmying with crosscurrents of air. The sky had darkened further, turning an eerie purple-black. The bright sunshine of the morning was engulfed, giving the impression of twilight even though it was only late afternoon.

His truck was out front. The wind tore the car door out of her hands and bounced it open. Pine needles and leaves whipped around her legs with enough force to sting her bare skin. She kicked off her heels and ran around the side of the house to pound on the door. No answer.

She made for the metal shed, the sides shaking from the force of the wind. Empty. She ran back outside and looked up. The storm was approaching too furiously, the color and darkness ominous portents. It didn't feel like a normal thunderstorm. Real fear wobbled her knees.

The wind gusted around her with renewed vigor, the drop in air pressure making her feel like she was running through a void. Tornadoes were the boogeymen of her youth. The stories and drills they practiced in school were embedded in her mind. It had been two decades since one had hit either side of Cottonbloom.

Where was Sawyer? Was he safe? Please God, let him be safe. Panic turned her movements clumsy. She stumbled and stubbed her big toe against a root on her run back to the house. She felt like Dorothy from *The Wizard of Oz*. The back door was unlocked. She called his name, even though she sensed the emptiness.

The creaking of the old house didn't settle her nerves. She'd seen pictures of houses strewn like matchsticks in the wake of a tornado. She stopped and considered her options. Driving home wasn't one of them. Being caught in any car in a tornado was bad. In her Bug, it could prove disastrous. No ground-floor door revealed steps that might lead to a basement.

She ran back outside and looked around, not sure exactly what she was even looking for. In the brief minutes she had been inside, the atmosphere outside had grown worse. Rain bursts pelted her, and she pushed her hair out of her eyes feeling like a deer caught in a hunter's spotlight.

A ground-floor closet was her best option. Time to make a decision was slipping away. What if she'd waited too long? What if something terrible happened before she had the chance to tell him?

She ran back inside. Two steps into the kitchen, and a loud crack made her jump. Various parts of her body stung. Wind whipped her hair around her face, the noise growing louder. Seconds ticked off before her brain lined up the facts. The branch of a crepe myrtle, a few tenacious pink blossoms dangling from the end, was in Sawyer's kitchen. The small window over the sink was broken and tiny cuts from flying glass stung her arms and legs.

She wiped her cheek, and her trembling fingers were red with blood. Terror froze her, barefoot and with glass over the floor.

From a great distance, she heard her name. Sawyer

Then before she could move or call his name, the back door banged open and he was there.

"What the hell are you doing here? Don't you know tornadoes have been spotted?"

A sense of calm came over her in the swirling chaos. Only one thing mattered in that moment. "I had to tell you . . . I love you. I love you, Sawyer Fournette."

His eyes flashed. "We are cursed with crappy timing—have you noticed?" He tucked a piece of hair behind her ear, but the wind negated his efforts. He rubbed a thumb across her stinging cheek and looked around. "Let us try to stay in one piece, shall we?"

He lifted her into a cradle hold and carried her outside. A flying piece of debris hit her temple, and she ducked her head into his neck. He muttered a curse and bypassed the shed. She peeked over his shoulder, blinking against the rain. The metal of the shed seemed to waver with the force of the wind.

Sawyer tried to run, but between her weight and the wind, he moved like he was swimming through thick honey.

"Put me down. I can walk now."

He set her down, grabbed her wrist, and pulled her toward a copse of pines at the edge of what used to be a cotton field. Adrenaline kicked her into a higher gear, but she wasn't afraid anymore. Not with him.

Double doors sat a few feet higher and nearly parallel to the ground. A storm cellar. He grabbed both handles and pulled. Nothing happened. He kicked at the hinges and applied himself to opening one side. With a squeal of rusted hinges, the door lifted. The wind caught it like a sail and slammed it open. A musty, moldy smell poofed out, and she covered her nose and mouth.

The situation took on an unreal, dreamlike quality. While Sawyer descended a few steps into the black hole, she looked around. Debris floated in the air as if gravity was no longer in effect. In the distance, white birds flew in the storm, flitting and diving.

He took her hand and pulled her backward.

She pointed. "What are those birds doing?"

The birds seemed to move closer, the noise increasing with each second that passed. He went from still to frantic. "That's siding off houses, not birds. Get your sweet ass down here. Now."

He pushed her past him into the blackness. The steps were rough. Splinters cut at her feet, the pain a reminder of their current reality. A cobweb wrapped around her calves. She was too scared to scream. She kept her gaze up. Debris was spinning over them now as Sawyer wrestled with the door, finally winning.

The darkness was complete. Her knees were watery, her body shaky, and imagining what lay beyond wasn't helping her state of mind. Her foot touched solid ground. The distance seemed immense as she descended, but it was only ten feet or so in reality. Sawyer clamored down with less hesitancy. A rain of dust had her blinking and finally closing her eyes.

Her toes scrunched in dirt. The air was cooler, and her rain-dampened clothes chilled her. The door bucked, but she kept her eyes closed. She wished she hadn't watched that movie *Twister* a dozen times when she was a kid.

Sawyer's arms came around her, and she burrowed her face into his neck, grabbing him tight around his waist. "I'm scared," she murmured.

"Me too." White noise from the storm filled the silence. His hands roamed her body and as if they had actual healing power, her various stings receded. "How badly are you hurt?"

"Some cuts. Nothing serious." His hands skimmed over her backside and stayed to knead it. Her twinge of laughter bordered on hysteria. "My ass is fine."

"No arguments here." How they could find humor in their predicament was beyond her comprehension.

"Your face is cut," he said softly.

"Is it bad? Will you still love me if I'm hideous and scarred?"

"I will. I'll even love you when you turn gray and lose all your marbles."

She rubbed her cheek against his but pulled back when his words sank in. "Wait. You mean 'if' not 'when,' right?"

His laughter tumbled through her but faded quickly. "Did you mean it?"

"Mean what?"

"Do you love me?"

With the fear of the storm and their lives hanging in the balance, the truth came with ease. "Of course I love you. I loved you even when I hated you." In the darkness, her lips found his for a brief touch. "I talked to Mother. She got to you, didn't she?"

He rested his forehead against hers and twined their fingers together. "She did. I knew what she was capable of and yet she still injected doubts. That night in the truck . . . I was hurt and stupid and thought you were just after a hook-up for old times' sake."

"This summer hasn't been about closure or reliving the past for me. It's been about the future."

He sighed. "That's what I thought too, but then your mother said—"

"How about we cut that phrase out of our lives? It doesn't matter what my mother said. Not anymore. I know that what happened between us so many years ago was fundamentally my fault, but you scared me."

"I scared you?"

"You were so handsome and mature and confident. We were young, and I didn't trust my feelings, I suppose. Mother only amplified what was already bothering me. When I found you with that girl, my worst fears were realized."

"I wasn't as mature as you thought I was, obviously, or I wouldn't have gotten so blitzed that I blacked out. I should have tried harder to get through to you, but . . ."

"But what?"

"I never felt good enough for you, but the way you treated me afterward drove that point home like a stake through my heart."

She leaned away and slid her hands over him until she cupped his cheeks. She couldn't see him, but maybe he could see her just a little with his Fournette sight. "I was the flighty, pageant girl who never felt good enough for you. Everything you went through and dealt with made me love you even more. I was never ashamed of being your girl, Sawyer Fournette."

He grabbed her wrist and laid a kiss on her palm. The world might be going to hell above them. He didn't care though with her in his arms, her words filling the voids in his heart. "Maybe being good enough doesn't matter when you're perfect together."

"I love you and want to be with you, and if you want me to organize a parade to announce it to all of Cottonbloom, I will."

He thought about taking her up on the offer for the amusement factor alone. "I don't think that will be necessary, but I'd be honored to take you to the Cottonbloom Country Club for dinner tonight."

"That would be—" She gasped. "If it's still standing."

Anxiety pierced the cocoon of their existence. Uncertainty existed outside of the darkened storm cellar, and Sawyer was loathe to face it. "I don't hear anything, do you?"

The wind had stopped battering at the doors, and the trainlike noise had faded into a pattering rain.

He tried to pull out of her arms, but she wrapped her hands around his nape and jerked him in for a kiss. It was quick and confined to a press of their lips together. But he understood. It sealed their commitment to each other no matter what they faced.

His steps on the ladder reverberated. It took a long heart-stopping minute of imagining them dying in each other's arms in the dank pit before he managed to wrench the door open.

Dark clouds raced across the sky, but the unnatural purpling was gone. From the adrenaline-fueled race up the river to outrun the storm to the shock at Regan's appearance to the bone-deep relief at finally settling things after a decade apart, his emotions were all over the place. And now this.

"Dear Lord," she whispered beside him.

A soft rain fell on the destruction. Shingles and siding and broken planks lay around them. The roof of the metal shed had been peeled back like a tin can and tilted like a cartoon house. The farmhouse had taken the brunt of the damage. It looked like a giant had smashed a fist into one side. His kitchen was exposed and covered in debris.

He pulled out his phone, punched buttons, and stared at the "call failed" message. "Cell service is out. That means at least one tower is down."

Fear for his family layered his anxiety, stymieing him. Cade. Where would Cade have been? The shop probably. He was out of his mind with worry for Monroe. And Tally? Had the downtown and her gym escaped damage?

"What do you want to do? Save things from your house or go driving?" Regan asked.

He strode toward the house. Anything of value was in a safe tucked into a hall closet, but there was one item, not worth anything beyond kindling, that he had to salvage. He heaved himself into the kitchen and knelt down next to the kitchen table. It was tipped onto its side, but miraculously seemed intact. He ran a hand over the scarred top before heaving it to all fours. A new chip marred one side, but it had survived with another tale to tell.

He picked his way across the kitchen and into the hall. The wood floor made a cracking sound, and he stopped. Everything seemed ready to collapse like a rickety house of cards. He stayed close to the wall and shuffled to the closet to grab a tarp.

The blue canvas would protect it from the worst of the rain. Regan was barefoot and picked her way over to where the back door used to be. The screen portion was fifteen feet away on a crepe myrtle tree that had tipped over like a passed-out sailor on leave, its roots dangling.

"I need to find Cade and Tally." Bone-deep fear grew, the kind he hadn't felt since right after his parents died and he'd overheard Cade and Uncle Del's whispers about the state separating them.

He jogged to the front of the house. The willow tree had fallen on Regan's car. His truck had been spared minus a few scratches, the ends of the braches blocking the passenger side.

"I guess we should take your truck," she said.

"Sorry about your car."

She climbed through the driver's door and over the console. "If we're going to be together, I need to get something you're comfortable riding in anyway. Because I don't think you're going to be doing all the driving."

He grabbed her hand in a tight hold and pressed it against his mouth unable to thank her for being her—pragmatic and funny and fierce. As he swung inside, the sound of a vehicle coming closer had him out and running around the fallen willow to the edge of his drive. The rain had slowed to a few plinking drops, the sun edging into the dark clouds on the western horizon.

Cade. It was Cade in their daddy's old truck, swerving around fallen branches. Sawyer ran up the last few feet to meet him and grabbed his brother up in a tight hug on his first step out of the truck. Tears pricked his eyes. He didn't even care if Cade saw them and called him a wuss.

Cade's arms were just as tight around his back, and when they finally broke apart, his eyes were as misty as Sawyer's. They turned to face the caved-in farmhouse at the same time, neither one speaking for a long moment.

"Sorry about your house." Cade's voice was rough. "But, damn I'm glad to see you in one piece. Where'd you ride it out?"

"Old storm cellar out back. It was touch and go whether I was going to get the doors open. Did you get in touch with Monroe? I don't have cell service."

"Called from the shop—which made it through fine besides some downed trees—she's fine and so are Tally and Nash."

Regan picked her way toward them. Shingles and siding, not all of it from his house, littered the field. "Thank goodness, Cade. How's Monroe?"

While Cade filled Regan in, Sawyer hauled her close and nuzzled his chin at her temple. He'd learned life was fragile years ago with his parents' deaths. The tornado had been a refresher course.

"You two got everything worked out, then?" Cade smiled one of his rare smiles.

He opened his mouth to answer, but Regan beat him. "We do. I love your brother very much, Cade. I hope you'll give us your blessing."

Cade rubbed a hand over his jaw, his voice growing even rougher. "You don't need my blessing. I know we've had our differences in the past, but let's leave them there. The two of you were obviously meant for each other."

Sawyer bumped Cade's shoulder with a fist. "Thanks, bro."

"What do you say we head to town?"

"Did Monroe say anything about damage?"

Cade shook his head. "We didn't have long to talk. There was a line of people to use the landline."

They sat three across in Cade's truck. He swung them out into the field to turn them around. Trees were down all along the county road. They met a handful of trucks out doing the same thing.

The going was agonizingly slow. The rain had stopped and rays of sun crept over the sky by the time the steel-beamed bridge came into view. Regan scooched to the edge of the seat, one hand on the dashboard, the other blindly reaching for him.

The Louisiana side of Cottonbloom had escaped relatively unscathed. Buildings stood, although debris was scattered over the road. Even his mama's flowers had weathered the storm with remarkable resiliency.

The Mississippi side had borne the brunt of the storm. The last two shops, including the Quilting Bee were obscured by a downed oak tree that also blocked the main road. Tumbled bricks trailed from green leaves into the street. A half-dozen people milled around the still-standing gazebo, hugging or talking or pointing.

It was the way of tornadoes. The winds could flatten one house, skip over the next, and take the next three as sacrifices. There was no rhyme or reason to the destruction. The river rushed through the divide, close to spilling over its banks.

Cade turned down the Louisiana side and parked near the footbridge.

Regan turned to him, her eyes wide, her hair tousled and windblown. "Sawyer . . . I need to check on my parents. And what about the Quilting Bee ladies? Were they in the shop?"

Chapter Twenty-three

As soon as Sawyer hopped out of the truck, Regan shot by him and ran over the footbridge to the edge of the street where the uppermost branches swayed in the light breeze, leaves dancing. The massive oak had tipped over from behind the shop, blanketing it in green.

"Where's the fire department or the police?" She asked as Sawyer came up beside her.

"Don't know. Cade's gone up to Tally's to call. They might be digging themselves out too. Let's head around back. See if we can get in from there."

They picked their way around to the alley. The massive root system of the tree was exposed, ripping up the asphalt and tumbling the bricks of the stone wall along the edge. The sidewalk and road would need reconstruction, but what worried her now was whether anyone had been trapped inside either business.

From the back, it was obvious the hardware store had taken the brunt of the force from the fall.

"Stay here." Sawyer stepped closer to the back door of the Quilting Bee.

Regan ignored his command and picked her way through, branches leaving new scratches on her legs. It didn't matter. A thick limb obscured her view of the door, but there seemed to be room behind it. "I think I can squeeze through."

He cast her an exasperated glance. "No way. You're barefoot and won't be able to see anything if you even get in. I'll try. You go back around front and rally some help."

"Will do." Before he ducked under the next branch, she grabbed the back of his shirt and hauled him around for a hard kiss. "Be careful. Love you."

"Love you too." He wrapped an arm around her waist and kissed her again, deeper and slower and with more than a hint of promise. "Can't wait to get you alone tonight."

He let her go and disappeared. The night seemed a long way off. She chafed her arms, her clothes drying but still damp. When he didn't immediately emerge, she assumed he managed to get in and picked her way around to the front.

A black truck backing down River Street stopped when branches brushed the tailgate. Two more pickups pulled in behind it. A brawny fortyish-year-old man in full camo, including a baseball cap, climbed out of the driver's side. Delmar Fournette slid out of the other side.

The driver spit a stream of tobacco and hauled a chain saw from the truck bed. Two more men walked up, one with a second chain saw and one pulling on leather work gloves. All three were strangers to her.

Sudden tears flooded her eyes at their kindness. Delmar put an arm around her shoulders and squeezed her tight. "Glad to see you in one piece, Miss Mayor. Where's my nephew?"

"Sawyer's fine. He squeezed into the Quilting Bee around back." Her voice was tight. "Are the ladies in there?"

"Sure are. No one was in the hardware store, thank

goodness. The boys and I will have a path cleared lickety-split."

"Thanks for helping, Del."

"My girl's in there." The look he sent the building was serious, before he caught her eye with a smile. "Anyway, we're all neighbors."

Three more men came jogging over the footbridge, Cade included. "All these are Louisiana men?" she asked.

"Most of them. Darryl over there is a Mississippi boy."

She wasn't sure which one was Darryl, but she was grateful for them all. Both chain saws fired up and conversation because impossible. She backed away. While the men cut away branches, the others loaded the beds of the trucks. When those were filled, they dragged the cut limbs into the common area.

She took five minutes to survey damage through the rest of downtown. Another tree tipped at an odd angle on her street, the roots crumbling the cement of the sidewalk and street. The pizza place had sustained some roof damage, and the owner and his two sons were on the roof securing a tarp. Her shop appeared untouched. She grabbed a pair of flip-flops she had stashed in her drawer and ran back.

By the time she returned, space had opened up and revealed the edges of the door. She bounced on her toes. Sawyer cleared the leaves with Vera Carson perched in his arms holding her pocketbook with both hands, her legs crossed at her ankles as if sitting in a church pew.

A laugh borne of relief burst out, and she rushed forward. Sawyer set Mrs. Carson down and the lady brushed her skirt down and patted dust out of her hair. Regan couldn't help from touching Sawyer. He appeared fine except for a coating of reddish dust. "Was everyone alright inside?"

"Fine. The side wall caved in, but the ladies had taken refuge behind the counter. I need to get Ms. Effie and Ms. Leora out." He winked and ducked back into the opening.

"I'm so glad everyone is safe, but I'm sorry about the Bee, Mrs. Carson. You only just signed the papers this morning."

The lady turned to look, her expression more pensive than upset. "They say God works in mysterious ways." Before she could say more, her daughter rushed up, put her arms around her, and led her away.

Ms. Effie came out holding Sawyer's arm, and as soon as she was deposited with her son, he ducked back in. The tree groaned and the men let out a shout and scattered backward. More of the buildings sagged underneath the weight, bricks tumbling into the street.

She stepped forward but Cade grabbed her arm. He was sweaty and scratched up from his work pulling branches out of the way. "Hang on. Let everything settle down."

Everything quieted. The men clumped around one of the trucks, arms hanging over the edge of its bed talking. Delmar paced, staring at the door. No Sawyer.

"Where is he?" Regan walked up to join Delmar.

"I'll go. You two stay here." Cade strode by them.

She stayed on Cade's heels. The door's frame had been warped from the weight, and Cade strained to open it. She slipped by Cade and stepped inside. Dust hung in the air, and she waved her hand in front of her face and coughed.

"Sawyer? Ms. Leora?"

"Back here." Ms. Leora's voice was wavery.

Bricks and bolts of fabric were scattered over the left side of the store while the right appeared untouched except for the layer of dust. The interior was dim, and Regan picked her way through the destruction.

Sawyer was sitting on the ground behind the counter, his hand pressed to his opposite arm, and she squatted next to him, unable to see him clearly. "Are you hurt?"

He removed his hand. A gash in his bicep trickled blood, the smell adding to her churning nausea.

"That'll need stiches. What happened?" Cade leaned over her shoulder.

"We were almost to the door when the wall completely gave way. A nail on one of the support joists caught me."

"Tetanus shot and stitches, coming right up." Cade helped Sawyer to his feet.

Regan tucked herself against him. "You help Ms. Leora. I got Sawyer."

Cade didn't argue. He swept Ms. Leora up and headed toward the door.

"I don't want to get you all bloody." Sawyer gingerly put an arm over her shoulder.

"I'm already bloody. Anyway, I don't mind." She wrapped her arms around him. "I'm just glad you're safe."

They helped each other to the door and emerged into bright sunshine. She blinked, blinded. Although the peaked roof was missing slates, the gazebo weathered the storm, and she guided him toward it.

Ms. Leora and Delmar sat side by side on one seat, his arm around her, and Regan and Sawyer joined them on the seat catty-corner. Mr. Holcomb and Ms. Beatrice, her two festival lieutenants, bustled over.

Ms. Beatrice preformed classic hand-wringing while Mr. Holcomb accompanied her with a solemn headshake. "This is a disaster, Regan. The festival is only three days away. We'll have to cancel." Ms. Beatrice's voice pitched high.

"My first priority is to make sure everyone on both sides of the river is safe." The festival hadn't crossed her mind.

"Even if this tree gets cleared, the buildings aren't safe. And have you seen the tree over in front of your shop? It will need to be taken out before it falls." Mr. Holcomb kept up a constant headshake.

"Then I guess we cancel." Regan shrugged. The festival didn't seem as important anymore.

"You don't have to cancel," Sawyer said. Everyone looked at him. "Our side came through undamaged."

"Are you saying what I think you're saying?" Regan shifted to take his hand. Dried blood trailed down his forearm.

"Let's combine. We've got barbeque and po'boys. Jambalaya would go along with that great. We can set all the food up along River Street. The gazebo made it through. So did the footbridge. We can have the music over here in the grassy area. We'll make room for everything you had planned over on our side."

"But what about the competition?" Ms. Beatrice asked with a huff.

"It doesn't matter anymore. Look around." Regan gestured toward the men working on clearing the tree. "When it comes down to it, we're all neighbors. I think combining the festivals is a great idea."

A truck horn sounded. Cade waited on the main road. "There's my ride." He stood, and she stepped in tandem with him out of the gazebo and into the grass. He stopped. "Hold up. You need to stay here."

"No. I'm coming with you."

He circled a hand around her nape and put his forehead against hers. "I'll be fine. You need to make a whole bunch more lists so you can win us this competition."

"But, Sawyer—"

He kissed her. "Stay here and be mayor for both sides. I'll be back as soon as I can."

She watched him walk away, every part of her wanting to go with him. But he was right. She had taken an oath. Cottonbloom needed her.

The instability of the trees forced her to set up operations across the river. Rufus offered his restaurant, along with free food and drinks for all the volunteers working on clearing the street on the Mississippi side.

Chief Thomason and Sheriff Berry both stopped by to give her reports. Her parents were both fine as were most houses minus some missing shingles and siding. On the Louisiana side, besides Sawyer's house, the only damage besides downed trees was reported at the Country Aire trailer park. The worst damage seemed confined to the Mississippi side of downtown Cottonbloom. Thankfully, no lives were lost and no life-threatening injuries had been reported.

Sawyer returned, and she gave him a brief hug and made an examination of the row of stitches along his biceps. "Does it hurt?"

"Little sore, but I'll live."

His glib pronouncement splayed her heart open, a cry of distress escaping her tear-tightened throat. She fell into him and wrapped her arms around his waist, finding the pulse point on his neck with her lips. He returned her hug with equal ferocity.

Alive. They were alive and the future was spread out in front of them. Their story had a chance at a happy ending instead of a tragic one.

His tight hold eased, one of his hands stroking her hair. "Cade's waiting for me. We need to check on the trailer park and the isolated houses. Make sure no one's hurt or trapped. Wait for me here, okay?"

"I'll wait. Promise."

The kiss they shared was brief yet fierce. Once he disappeared from sight, she shook herself and got back to business. She and Monroe shared barbeque and sweet teas as dusk fell and the men working on clearing the trees from downtown packed up their equipment. Monroe headed home, and the milling crowd shrank by the minute. Regan waited next to Sawyer's flowers.

Chapter Twenty-four

Sawyer turned down River Street. Full darkness was almost upon them. Had she gotten a ride from Monroe or her mother? The survey of the damage had taken longer than he'd anticipated, and he hadn't even had the chance to sift through what was left of his own place. He'd only had time and light enough to pack up the family pictures and load their old kitchen table in the truck bed. The second floor was too dangerous to navigate.

A figure popped up at the edge of the flowers. The tight fist around his heart eased. She had waited for him. Even though he'd been late, she'd trusted him to come. Seemingly insignificant, it didn't feel that way. He stopped at the curb, slipped out, and grabbed her close.

"I wasn't sure if you'd still be here," he whispered into her hair.

"I promised to wait."

Emotions twisted and brought a lump to his throat. He could count on her. "Come on, let's go home."

"I assume you mean my place?"

He hadn't considered what the destruction of his house would mean long-term, but one thing he did know. "Baby, wherever you are is home."

Her simple smile washed away the stress and anxiety of the day. She climbed into his truck, lifted the center console and settled in next to him, her head on his shoulder.

"I grabbed a change of clothes from the shop, but otherwise I have nothing. The second floor of the farmhouse could go any minute."

"I still have the toothbrush you used. We can buy you new clothes tomorrow." Her voice was calm and no-nonsense. "I'll make a list in the morning."

He chuckled, slipped an arm around her shoulders, and drove toward her house, dodging the numerous braches in the streets. "What about the festival? Can we pull it off?"

"A reporter from Jackson came down, and I assured her the festival was on, so we'd better be able to do it. The way everyone pulled together was really wonderful. No matter what happens, Cottonbloom will be better off."

"Agreed." He heaved a sigh and shook her shoulders. "Your mama is waiting on your doorstep."

She straightened and checked her appearance in the rearview mirror. "Lord help us."

He pulled in beside her old work truck and turned the engine off. "How do you want to play this?"

She stopped fussing with her hair and turned toward him. "How about we go with the truth?"

He nodded, helped her out of the truck, and grabbed his duffle from the back.

"Hello, Mother." Regan exchanged a stiff hug with her mother.

"Why didn't you call us? We've been worried sick."

"Chief Thomason let me know you were safe. He told you I was dealing with the situation downtown, didn't he?"

"Well, yes." She glanced over Regan's shoulder as Sawyer joined them on the front porch. "I expected a little more sympathy. My trellis was blown over and several tomato plants will need to be rerooted."

Regan reached behind her, and he knitted their fingers together. "Sawyer lost his house today, Mother. Several people in Country Aire lost their trailers. Their homes. A tree fell on the Quilting Bee and the hardware store. The pizza place's roof was torn off. Now if you'll excuse us, we're exhausted."

"Kind of you to offer Mr. Fournette a place to stay for the night." Mrs. Lovell stared him down.

Before he could answer, Regan squeezed his hand and said, "He's moving in, Mother. I love him and he loves me and we're going to live together. So you probably want to knock before you barge in from now on." She unlocked the door and pulled him in after her. Her declaration grew his heart three sizes and the look of shocked confusion on her mama's face brought an unchristian smile to his.

"I'm sure we'll be seeing a lot of each other around the neighborhood, Mrs. Lovell," Sawyer managed to say before Regan shut the door in her mother's face.

She dropped his hand, disarmed the security system, and smiled over her shoulder. "That was inexcusably rude, and I'll have to apologize tomorrow, but dang, it felt awesome."

"I'll admit, I enjoyed it more than I should have." He followed her into her bedroom. "How about we get cleaned up?"

Her bathroom had been updated with amazing tile work and a huge shower with dual heads. They kissed in the middle of the warm water, the feeling decadent and something he could get used to quick.

The soft touches and kisses took on a frantic edge. How close had they come to losing each other? He spun her around, her back to his front. As if they were performing a dance they knew by heart, she propped her hands on the wall and arched her back. He entered her with an insincere gentleness.

Her throaty, desperate moan drove him to drop any pretense. He took her fast and hard. An affirmation they were alive and together. They dried each other off in the steamy bathroom, both of them unable to stop touching the other. He pulled on underwear, and she pulled on a tank top and panties.

"Let's get in bed." She pulled him backward, holding both his hands.

His gaze trailed down her body. The cuts along her legs stood in stark relief against her pale skin. "You need some ointment on all your cuts. You have some?"

"In the medicine cabinet."

He retrieved the tube while she de-pillowed the bed and lay down. Trailing his hand up her calf, he dabbed on antiseptic as he went. Her legs were a mess of cuts and scratches, but they would heal. If he hadn't seen her car and run inside looking for her, what could have happened? The possibilities made him lightheaded.

"You didn't tell your mama I'm moving in just to get a rise out of her, did you?'

"Of course not. We've wasted enough time, don't you think?" She wrapped a hand a few inches under his stitches.

"If I'm moving in, there's one thing that has to change."

Her hand tightened. The gash on his arm throbbed. "What?"

"I can't handle living with all these pillows. I'm pretty sure they're spawning."

A heartbeat of silence followed. Then, her laughter peeled. She pulled him up the bed to lie beside her. "I'll compromise on that, but you have to do something for me too."

He propped himself on his elbow, suddenly tense. "What's that?"

"You have to regrow that sexy beard. I never got to experience it and I haven't been able to stop thinking about what it would feel like in certain . . . places."

He tickled her, and she squirmed against him, giggling. "What kind of places?"

"*All* the places."

It was comforting to know he'd been driving her as mad as she'd been driving him over the summer. He worked them under the covers and pulled her close. "I think I can accommodate you. Give me a couple of weeks."

More wanted to spill out of him, but the realization there would be a tomorrow and a next day and a next week to share with her settled a patience in his heart. He had the rest of his life to share everything with her.

The next days were sure to be as exhausting and stressful as this day had been. Still they whispered words of love and laughter and remembrance until sleep stole them away, safe in each other's arms.

The third and last day of the festival was winding down. The turnout had been better than either Regan or he had expected. The tornado had brought them news coverage and the melding of the festivals had turned into the feelgood story of the week.

They had even made it into nationally syndicated AP news. Sawyer grabbed a seat next to one of the *Heart of Dixie* reporters. His high-end camera was on the table next to one of Rufus's pork barbeque plates. The crayfish po'boys and jambalaya had sold out at lunch.

"Did you have a good weekend, Kyle?" Sawyer and the man had hit it off immediately and had already made fishing plans for the fall.

"I'll have to say for a first-time festival, y'all did good. Real good." He wiped his mouth with a paper napkin. "My only complaint is the ten pounds I've put on in three days. Dadgum, but you people know how to cook."

"That's the best part of any festival, isn't it?"

"True that. I enjoyed the fight last night too. Can't say that I've ever seen anything quite like that."

Sawyer grinned. He couldn't take a bit of credit for it. Tally had outdone herself. Between Monroe's self-defense exhibition, the kickboxing demonstration, and the MMA-style fight, they had drawn huge crowds. The night finished with homemade pies from the Ladies Church Auxiliary and music courtesy of his uncle.

"I've got to ask you though. If you folks should win, which project will you fund?" Kyle scooped up another spoonful of baked beans and glanced over at him.

"Obviously, the project on the Mississippi side. They're the ones impacted by the tornadoes." Sawyer gestured across the river. Regan was wearing a buttercup yellow sundress and standing by the gazebo as pretty as one of his mama's flowers. Somehow she sensed his regard and turned her head, giving him a little wave.

"Funny, but Regan said it was obvious the Louisiana side should get the grant money."

"Why would she say that?" He was honestly shocked. After all the trials and tribulations of the summer, after the damage her side had sustained, after all the work she'd poured into combining the two festivals, she deserved to win the money.

"She said something about how some things don't die, they just go dormant, waiting for a chance to live again. She thinks the park should live again."

Sawyer looked to the river to hide the onslaught of emotions. He wished everyone would get gone, so he could whisk her home and finally have her to himself for the next fifty years or so.

"You've been all over the south, Kyle. Do we even have a shot at honorable mention?"

"From what I've seen, I'd say you have more than a fair shot at winning the whole shebang." He sat back and laced his hands over his stomach, the center button of his short-sleeved blue oxford straining to hold. "Not to be insensitive. But the tornado probably boosted you into contention. The editors are going to lose their damn minds over how warm and fuzzy the story is. Not to mention, we're already getting national play out of it. Way better than two festivals duking it out."

Sawyer laughed and shook his head.

Hours later, after the out-of-towners had headed home to face the workweek, and most locals were home watching football, Regan and Sawyer met at the center of the footbridge. She stood at the rail, and he wrapped his arm around her from behind. The setting sun sparked off her hair and made the water dance.

"You told Kyle Louisiana should win the money if it comes down to it. Why did you do that? The weekend was only a success because of you. Mississippi should get the money." He rubbed his stubbly chin against her temple.

She covered his hands with hers. "It's been a long time since the two sides of Cottonbloom came together for anything. I don't want things to go back to the way they were tomorrow. Cottonbloom Park can be our common ground for the future. You can reinstitute the intermural baseball league and invite businesses and organizations from the Mississippi side to take part. We can host joint picnics and block parties. This festival can be the beginning of healing the rift between the swamp rats and the 'Sips."

"But—"

"Quit trying to be a gentleman, Sawyer Fournette, and take the money if we win it." She twisted around in his arms and linked her hands behind his neck.

He didn't voice Kyle's prediction that the tornado had

wrapped up the competition for them. Instead, he ran his hands down her back to tap her backside. "How about I stop being a gentleman altogether and haul you home."

"I suppose everything will keep until tomorrow." She arched her brows and smiled.

One thing wouldn't keep for another second. "I love you, Regan Lovell. Remember the promise I etched in wood?"

Her smile turned tremulous, and she nodded, her chin wobbling. "Love you too."

He swooped in for a kiss. They made it home . . . eventually.

Epilogue

The crack of the bat was followed by an eruption of cheers when the ball sailed over the left-field fence. Regan jumped up and down and hollered as loud as anyone even though she was the opposing team's coach.

Sawyer jogged around the bases and locked eyes with her as he rounded second. She tucked her hair behind her ear and adjusted her ball cap. Instead of heading straight to home, he made a detour in her direction, wrapping an arm around her waist and pulling her close.

"Sawyer Fournette, you're liable to get disqualified." Her smile negated the warning in her voice.

"It'll be worth it. Just like the time I was carted off the football field." He laid a sweet kiss on her lips, knocking her baseball cap to the ground.

Whoops and wolf whistles sounded around them, reminding her they were in the middle of the newly dedicated, renovated Cottonbloom Park surrounded by citizens of both sides of the river.

He pulled away, gave her bottom a pat, and jogged over home plate while holding his hands over his head in a sign of victory. She shook her head, still smiling, and turned to the dugout filled with Cottonbloom, Mississippi, city employees. The first inaugural intermural game was between their two towns. The rivalry was intense, but underneath the good-natured ribbing was a sense of community that had been missing since the town split across the river.

The heated festival competition and the tornado had done more good than harm. The damaged buildings on the Mississippi side had been rebuilt. Under Vera Carson's direction, with Ms. Effie and Ms. Leora acting as her assistants, the Quilting Bee had transformed into something more than a fabric store.

While the ladies still met to quilt and gossip in one corner, the shop sold tea cakes supplied daily by the Cottonbloom Bakery and a steady flow of sweet iced tea and coffee. Mrs. Carson also displayed several of Regan's home décor pieces on consignment as well as works by local artists. It was a win-win for all the business owners downtown. Stepping inside was a feast for the senses, and on pretty days, the door was propped open, the buzz of lively conversations and the smell of tea cakes inviting everyone to step inside.

Next up to bat was Cade. Sawyer had stretched the rules of city employees to recruit his brother. Another home run cracked off Cade's bat. When all was said and done, Cottonbloom, Louisiana, won the game with ease, but much laughter accompanied the handshakes between the teams at the end.

She slipped back to watch Sawyer laugh and greet people from both sides of the river. She loved him so much her heart felt near to bursting.

Monroe hip-bumped her. "Fun game. Too bad Deputy Preston had to leave for that call. He was your only hope."

"I know. But recruiting Cade to the Louisiana team was pretty shady."

"Yep, but he couldn't resist. You should have seen

him trying the uniform on." Monroe shook her head, but a smile hovered as she looked in his direction. He was shoulder to shoulder with Sawyer, shaking hands and talking. "He never really got to have that experience in high school. He could have been great."

"Things worked out just the way they were supposed to, Mrs. Fournette." Regan side-eyed her friend who flushed and played with the ends of her hair. The wedding had taken place two weeks prior at the edge of the river. The small list of guests had enjoyed lemonade and cake inside the great room of the house Cade and Monroe built within shouting distance of Fournette Designs' complex.

Cade had wanted to elope and whisk Monroe to Seattle for their honeymoon. Monroe insisted on a wedding but compromised by keeping it intimate. Regan had whipped up plans in less than a week, and everything had gone off without a hitch.

"How's married life, anyway? Different?"

"Mostly the same, except for getting used to a new name." Monroe cast a smile and raised brows in her direction. "You'll be finding out soon enough."

This time it was Regan's turn to blush, knowing she didn't do it as gracefully as Monroe. She twisted the diamond engagement ring in a circle. "I'm nervous. Not the marriage part. I can't wait to make it legal. The part where I agreed to the huge church wedding. Mother has been in a tizzy."

"I told you to keep your mother out of it. She's likely to stand up when the preacher asks for objections."

After her mother's manipulations over the summer, Regan had been ready to cut her completely out of her life. Shockingly, it was Sawyer who had talked her into trying to mend their fractured relationship. His parents were gone forever, and he didn't want Regan to have regrets. So she'd cracked the door open by allowing her mother a small role in the wedding planning. It had been like releasing a wild, starving monkey on a bunch of bananas.

"Now that we're living down the street, Sawyer and Mother have run across each other more and more. He actually tolerates her demon dogs, which has gone a long way to endearing him in her book. And, you know he has a way with plants—flowers especially—they've bonded over gardening. Sometimes I wonder if I've stepped into *The Twilight Zone*."

"The day I see your mother and Sawyer walking down the street arm in arm walking her dogs will be the first sign of the apocalypse." Monroe burst out laughing. "Are you going to stay in your house or rebuild or what?"

The damage to Sawyer's farmhouse from the tornado had been extensive, and he'd made the difficult decision to level it. "We sort of have to stay in Mississippi."

"Why?"

Regan couldn't contain her smile. "I'll be making an official announcement after the wedding, but I filed to run for state representative yesterday in Jackson. I'll be on the ballot in November."

Monroe squawked something between shock and congratulations and grabbed Regan for a hug. "I had no idea you were even considering a run."

"I've had the papers in my desk forever. Sawyer gave me the confidence to just do it. But it means we have to live in Mississippi."

"And he was okay with that?"

Tears pricked her eyes, and she leaned her head back, but the bright sunshine only made it worse. "He wants me to pursue my dreams and be happy. Said he'd even move to Jackson if I wanted to run for governor."

"Wow. Governor?"

"Who knows? Someday, maybe. I could do it." The

words came out with a surety that surprised even Regan. She didn't need to convince anyone, not her friends, not her mother, not herself. She *could* do it. As long as Sawyer had her back. And, he would always have her back. She trusted in that. She trusted him.

"I may technically be a swamp rat now, but you can count on me to cross over and campaign for you," Monroe said.

"How's it going?" Tally stood behind them, her hands behind her back as if she were afraid she was intruding, but a small smile making her look hopeful.

Monroe shifted, put an arm around Tally's shoulders, and pulled her in between them. "What'd you think of the game?"

"I hope it becomes a regular thing. It's nice seeing everyone mingling and having fun. I mean, look at Ms. Leora," Tally said.

Ms. Leora had her hand tucked in Delmar Fournette's elbow and was talking with a group of his fishing and hunting buddies, a smile crinkling her face.

"Do you think Delmar will make an honest woman out of her and move to Mississippi? I can't imagine her living in his place." Regan had thought their pairing was odd at first, but once Ms. Leora had let go of her anger and regrets, what had been left was love. Regan thanked the heavens she and Sawyer hadn't waited forty years to put the past behind them. A decade had been ten years too long.

"It's the only thing they argue about. No way is Uncle Delmar living in Mississippi, and no way is Ms. Leora moving to his place. Can you imagine her playing hostess is his little ramshackle house?" Tally laughed softly.

"They could build something like Cade and I did and you and Nash are doing," Monroe said. "When is your place going to be done, by the way?"

Tally groaned. "Not until summer at this rate. You know how Nash is. He's wanted to learn everything about everything and do some of the work himself. But his classes are taking up most of his days, and his book is going through edits in preparation for publication . . . He's busy."

"That's so exciting. Where is Nash?" Monroe looked around.

Tally pointed across the field to the far bleachers. "The Quilting Bee ladies grabbed him as soon as we walked in."

Regan squinted. Sure enough, Nash was sitting two rows up surrounded by a semicircle of old ladies. He gave the impression of giving a lecture. "They sure do love them some Nash Hawthorne."

"Well, I do too, so it's hard to complain." Tally's voice was unusually soft, the smile on her face lighting her from the inside out.

"When is Nash going to put a ring on it?" Regan elbowed Tally. It was only recently that Regan and Tally had reached the point they could tease each other like friends.

A flush raced up Tally's throat and into her face. Regan shifted toward her. Had she ever seen Tally Fournette blush?

"We're married."

"What?" Regan and Monroe popped out with the same exclamation.

Tally covered her face with both hands, but a smile peeked through. "We went to the courthouse a few weeks ago. Nash didn't care, and I'm not exactly the white-gown, everyone-staring-at-you kind of girl."

"When are you going to tell your brothers?"

"Tonight at dinner. We're all still getting together at your place, right Monroe?"

"Yep. Already picked up the barbeque from Rufus."

"Thought maybe you two should know in case I need backup."

"Please. We all love Nash. He's the nicest, sweetest guy

in Cottonbloom." Regan snaked an arm around Tally's shoulders and squeezed.

"He totally is. Not sure what I did to deserve him, but he's mine now. Forever." Tears shimmered in her eyes despite her huge grin. "I'd better rescue him from the pack of little old ladies. I'll see you guys in a bit."

Regan and Monroe were silent as Tally walked across the field. Nash excused himself from the ladies and met her near the dugout, hauling her in close for a kiss.

"Well then," Regan said.

"Indeed." They crossed glances and burst into laughter.

As their giggles faded, Monroe said, "Nash and Tally won't be the only surprise tonight. Brace yourself, because my mother is bringing her new boyfriend. He flew in from New Mexico yesterday."

"What's he like?"

"Completely different from anyone she's ever dated. Short, bald, doting. He really loves her. It's slightly nauseating, but I'm happy for her. His name is Arnold, but she calls him Arnie."

"This is the guy she met in rehab?"

"Yep. Not sure if that's good or bad. I'm hoping they'll keep each other dry. He asked her to move to New Mexico, but she told him he would have to move to Cottonbloom if he wanted to be with her."

"Way to go, Mrs. Kirby."

"I know, right? We'll see. I'm not holding my breath that any of this will work out."

This time Regan put her arm around Monroe and squeezed, no platitudes needed. Monroe's mother had let her down all her life. It would take more than a few months and a new attitude to earn Monroe's trust back. But Monroe would be there for her mother through the successes or disappointments. It was the kind of daughter and friend she was.

Sawyer shook hands and patted shoulders, backing away from the group of men. Cade followed suit. They walked shoulder to shoulder, pacing their steps on their way to Regan and Monroe. The two of them had grown closer with each passing week. Not that they didn't disagree and yell and sometimes wrestle like two kids. But it always ended in laughter.

Cade hauled Monroe close, and Sawyer did the same to Regan. Cade tutted, his smile teasing. "Not much of a showing from Mississippi, Regan."

"Only because you swamp rats cheated. You are not a city employee, Cade Fournette."

Cade made a scoffing sound. "I'm close enough. Since you're taking Sawyer over the line, he's trying to talk me into running for parish commissioner."

"Are you going to do it?" Regan asked. Cade was not exactly the most diplomatic of people. Or friendly. Or compromising. But, he was whip-smart even if he didn't graduate high school. And moving Fournette Designs from Seattle to Cottonbloom had created jobs and tax revenue.

"Not with as much charm as Sawyer, but I have some ideas." He glanced down at Monroe with a smile. "I'm here for good, and I want to make Cottonbloom a better place for us. And our kids."

Regan gasped. "Are you—"

"No, I'm not. Geez, Cade, this is how rumors get started." Monroe leaned back to punch his shoulder, but more tease than force was behind it. "Eventually. Maybe."

"We're going to head to the house. Give us a half hour or so to get organized." Cade checked his watch.

"You're looking mighty fine in that uniform, Cade Fournette." The smile Monroe sent in her husband's direction made Regan bite her bottom lip and look toward Sawyer.

"Strike that. Give us an hour and a half. See you later."

Cade grabbed Monroe's hand and quick-stepped toward the parking lot. Monroe's laughter trailed behind them.

Regan turned and wrapped her arms around Sawyer's neck. "You're looking pretty hot yourself in those pants."

"Not half as good as you're filling out yours, baby." His hand skated over her backside.

"Sawyer," she whispered. "You're still commissioner, and I'm still mayor. We have a certain image of gravitas and dignity to uphold."

"Didn't we prove last summer that both of those are overrated?"

Their smiling lips met with a tenderness and passion rooted in the past, but growing with every day. The future stretched before them, unknown and even a little scary, but they would face whatever came together.